Aamna Qureshi is a Pakistani, N
adores words. She is the award-
fantasy novel, The Lady or the Lion

Aamna grew up on Long Island, New York, in a very loud household, surrounded by English (for school), Urdu (for conversation), and Punjabi (for emotion). Much of her childhood was spent being grounded for reading past her bed-time, writing stories in the backs of her notebooks, and being scolded by teachers for passing chapters under the tables. Through her writing, she wishes to inspire a love for the beautiful country and rich culture that informed much of her identity.

When she's not writing, she loves to travel to new places where she can explore different cultures or to Pakistan where she can revitalize her roots. She also loves baking complicated desserts, drinking fancy teas and coffees, watching sappy rom-coms, and going for walks about the estate (her backyard). She currently lives in New York.

https://www.aamnaqureshi.com/

X x.com/aamnaqureshi_
O instagram.com/aamna_qureshi

Also by Aamna Qureshi

The Lady or the Lion

The Man or the Monster

When a Brown Girl Flees

My Big, Fat, Desi Wedding

IF I LOVED YOU LESS

AAMNA QURESHI

One More Chapter
a division of HarperCollins*Publishers* Ltd
1 London Bridge Street
London SE1 9GF
www.harpercollins.co.uk
HarperCollins*Publishers*
Macken House, 39/40 Mayor Street Upper,
Dublin 1, D01 C9W8, Ireland

This paperback edition 2024
1
First published in Great Britain in ebook format
by HarperCollins*Publishers* 2024
Copyright © Aamna Qureshi 2024
Aamna Qureshi asserts the moral right to be identified
as the author of this work

A catalogue record of this book is available from the British Library

ISBN: 978-0-00-865357-6

Printed and bound in the UK using 100% Renewable Electricity
by CPI Group (UK) Ltd

For Arusa,
my saheli, my very best friend

Chapter One

H andsome, *clever, and rich, Humaira Mirza lived nearly*
twenty-three years with very little to vex or distress
her —

Yet, a pout is plastered on my face.

I am surrounded with the general splendor of a
beautiful walima: glittering chandeliers, melodic Urdu
music, candles and fresh flowers, laughing guests dressed
in smart suits and shining shalwar kameez.

The stage is decorated with white gardenia and pale
pink hydrangea flowers, along with hanging lights and
greenery. At the center of the stage, on an ornate and plush
sofa, sits my Phuppo: radiant and beautiful as ever – and
the reason for my sour mood.

When Mama passed away, Faiza Phuppo, youngest
sister of one Mahmud Mirza, my father, moved in with us.
She was twenty-seven at the time and not yet married – a
sort of self-declared spinster – and she came to the rescue,

even though I was thirteen and my older sister Naadia was fifteen, and thus we didn't exactly *need* someone to take care of us. We had cleaning ladies, and Papa always said we could hire a cook, but Phuppo wouldn't hear it, and I was secretly glad.

Naadia didn't care for the attention – goodness, she was a moody teenager – but Papa says I was more of a delicate sort and needed the extra consideration. Who was I to deny my concerned father?

In the decade since then, Phuppo became my closest confidant and dear friend, and now here she is, being married off! Leaving me, to live her happily ever after! Just like Naadia did the year before. From a technical perspective, you can say it was all my fault, since I was the one to set both of them up with their (now) husbands, but who has time to be technical?

I am too busy pouting and generally feeling sorry for myself. I flit my gaze over to Naadia, hoping for some sisterly support, but she's busy chatting with her best friend, Sadaf Chaudry, who's here with her sister Haya, and her best friend, Zahra Paracha, all friends of mine and Naadia's.

I don't feel like going over and socializing because I'm preoccupied with quietly sulking. (It really requires a lot from me.) Besides, they are discussing Haya's engagement and impending nuptials this spring, and I am only slightly bitter that someone younger than me has found love.

So I stand on the side, looking devastatingly beautiful in a baby pink open-front gown and lehenga that I got designed by Elan in Lahore. It's a very classic walima look, with Swarovski crystals set into hand-sewn embroidery, and weighs about fifteen pounds.

I'm wearing Mama's diamond set, too, the one Papa got her for their tenth anniversary, but you can't tell because it's hidden beneath my hijab. At least you can see the teeka, glistening on my forehead, and a bit of the necklace, peeking out from under my scarf.

Sipping my pina colada (virgin, obviously), I look around, trying not to let my sour mood show. From the outside, I'm sure no one can tell. I stand poised, my chin lifted. My round black eyes are lined with kajal, my cheeks rosy and my cheekbones highlighted.

The wedding was all fun and games until today. I got new outfits made (Zara Shahjahan for the dua, Nomi Ansari for the mehndi, Bunto Kazmi for the rukhsati, all stunning and classic, of course). Phuppo didn't want to have so many events – she felt it was crude of her at the age of thirty-seven – but I told her I simply had to have the outfits made, and unless she wished to have me change every hour, she would oblige me for the functions.

And of course, she did. She always did.

Phuppo had never really believed in love – blasphemous, I know – but she had always waited for companionship, and now she was marrying someone just as reasonable and kind as she was.

Zeeshan Uncle is really sweet. He's sitting up there on the stage now, a massive smile plastered on his dorky face. He's bald and built like a boulder and even at forty-two, he's handsome in a cool-uncle way. He's been a long-time friend of the family and is a pediatrician.

He went through an awful divorce over a decade ago, when some girl from Pakistan only married him for his citizenship, then ran off with her boyfriend the first chance she got (these are the horror stories that keep Papa up at night). He had been a bachelor ever since, until one day I was chatting with him when it hit me – he and Phuppo would be perfect together!

I've been out of college a year and am frequently quite bored, despite my full-time job as a civil engineer, and am always looking for ways to be useful to the ones I love most, so I decided to throw them together, with subtle hints and little suggestions, and it took me some time, but finally he took the bait and proposed!

And the rest is history. Oh, I was so overjoyed. Still am. (Mostly).

But the novelty wore off last night, after the rukhsati, when Phuppo didn't come home with us. It hit Papa pretty badly, too. We stood in the foyer of our dark house, staring at one another, as the realization dawned upon us that Phuppo was really gone.

Her room was empty, and would remain so.

"Don't pout," Naadia says, joining me. My sister is wearing Faraz Manan, part of the outfit she wore to her own walima last year. The champagne and silver getup looks stunning on her. "It's unflattering."

"No, it's not," I reply. I know perfectly well I have a nice set of lips, and with a well-placed pout, I can convince many people to do things for me. She raises her brows and sips her drink, a Shirley Temple.

"And you know it, too," I say, pinching her side. She squeals, and I smile. "What did that loser in college used to say?"

"God, there were too many losers in college," Naadia says. She widens her eyes, recollecting the days.

"My lips were 'a cushion he wished to sink into,'" I continue with air quotes.

"Ew, ew, ew, still so gross," Naadia says. She scrunches her face, and then we both gag. Then, at the same time, our discomfort at the memory fades into laughter.

Everything is always funny with my sister. It doesn't matter how awful or weird or absurd it is, when I tell Naadia, we always have a laugh about it.

Our mannerisms are the only thing that give us away as sisters: otherwise we look nothing alike. Naadia is an inch taller (an inch and a half, as she likes to tell everyone) and thinner, with a dark complexion, and runway-model beauty: thick brows, massive eyes, small face. I'm shorter and more curvy, with a round face and more delicate features: a small nose, pouty lips, and arched brows on a face that never lost its childhood chubbiness.

I look like Mama, at least, that's what everyone says. She passed away when I was thirteen and horribly chubby, but now that I'm twenty-three everyone says I'm her spitting image. That's a compliment; Mama was an absolute babe, regal and stylish as a queen.

"Cheer up," Naadia says, elbowing me. "Look how happy Phuppo is."

I can't argue with that. We both turn to look at the stage. She and Zeeshan Uncle are up there holding hands and giggling as they chat with guests, shoulders touching.

"At least there's that," I say.

"Now give me your lipstick, I need a refresh."

I search through my Judith Leiber silver clutch and hand it to her, holding up a mirror as she applies it.

"Did Darcy not show?" Naadia asks, adjusting her hijab around her face. She hands me back the lipstick and looks around. Tossing the lipstick and mirror back into my clutch, I shake my head.

Darcy is our codename for Rizwan Ali (I'm a massive fan of Jane Austen – personally, I relate to *Emma* quite a bit). Rizwan is Zeeshan Uncle's twenty-six-year-old nephew and his protégé. The whole pediatrician thing is just a side thing for Zeeshan Uncle; he has his own booming business for medical devices.

Rizwan studied biotechnology at Oxford. He's handsome, clever, rich, *and* has a British accent, isn't that just the very best thing you've heard? Ever since Zeeshan Uncle mentioned him, I've decided Rizwan could be a suitable match for me and thus the great love of my life.

He was supposed to come for the wedding, but there's no sign of him. Which only makes my pout reappear.

"I don't see him," I say, trying not to sound as disappointed as I feel. "He must have been busy with work. It's not easy being wildly successful, you know."

"But don't I?" She wiggles her brows at me, then pokes my stomach. I squeal. Unbearably ticklish, always have been.

Because Rizwan isn't there, there's really very little entertainment to be had from the night. There are plenty of boys, some handsome even, but none that particularly draw my interest. I scope the crowd anyways, and there's this guy with a fuckboy haircut who is very clearly checking me out. Gross.

Then, when I go to the DJ to tell him to play "Teri Ore" already, the DJ has the audacity to give me his card. Worse, he winks! Ugh, as *if*.

I'm just recovering from this encounter when I spot an actual cute boy turn his gaze toward me.

He looks decent enough, shareef really. I can see him mustering up the courage to approach. I pretend not to notice until he's right in front of me.

"Asalaamualaikum," he says. "You're—"

But I never find out what I am. In his enthusiasm, his hand convulses, and his drink teeters over the glass he's holding. Accustomed to such behavior, I deftly dodge out of the way, my heels clicking on the ground.

The drink splashes across his shoes, narrowly missing the edge of my lehenga, forcing a little gasp out of me. Oh I would have been very upset if he got his drink on my outfit; this is Elan! It's not a joke!

"Uh, e-excuse me," he says, cheeks turning pink. I sigh, unsurprised and yet still annoyed.

I know I'm cute and that guys think I'm cute, but I want

someone to have the guts to do something about it beyond checking me out, beyond fumbling for words, and beyond being nervous and acting like an idiot. I mean, really, people!

Is it so far-fetched to want someone who completely owns up to being infatuated by me and is confident in his feelings enough to go after me, despite how scary and nerve-wracking it might be?

Beside me, Naadia returns with a refill of her Shirley Temple just in time to catch the drink-spilling encounter, and the sound of her laughter fills my ears alongside Rahat Fateh Ali's melodic voice.

"Damn," she says. "Can you not go anywhere without scaring boys off?"

"I am not frightening at all," I say, brows furrowing. It's true. I'm only 5'2" and have been told I have a very kind face.

"Well, if you would only stop *staring* at them like that, maybe they wouldn't get so nervous and make fools of themselves," my sister says, waving a cherry at me.

"I don't *stare*." I scoff. "It's unladylike to stare."

I know I have an unsettling gaze, I can see it on the receiver's countenance whenever I've fixated on them. But I can't help myself; I love to see how brave the other will be, if they will be brave at all.

It's a trick, of course, because I love to see but hate to be seen.

"God, you're such a grandma," Naadia says, rolling her eyes. "Quit watching so many period dramas. Things aren't 'unladylike' anymore." She air quotes with her free hand. "This is the twenty-first century!"

"I like period dramas," I say. "And there's nothing wrong with propriety."

Mama used to hold propriety in very high regard. Something Naadia hated, but I never minded because it wasn't difficult, it was really very easy. Mama would be so pleased whenever I enunciated my words while Naadia mumbled, or when I sat and walked with my back straight.

She would smile and stroke her hand through my hair, say, "Oh, my lovely girl, you could have been a princess in another life." And I could feel the love in her voice, how proud of me she was.

"Well—" Naadia starts to argue, just like always, but she's cut off as another intrudes into our conversation.

"Looking for Prince Charming?" a deep voice says. I suppress a groan. I don't need to turn to know who it is that stands behind me, and then he's walking to stand right in front of me, a self-satisfied grin on his otherwise beautiful face.

"Fawad! How did you know?" Naadia says, pleased to see him.

"Humaira is terribly predictable," Fawad Sheikh says. This elicits a response from me. I snap my gaze toward him.

"I am *not* predictable!" I reply, realizing too late he's only said it to rile me. His smile spreads, eyes glittering. I go back to ignoring him, though his is quite a presence to ignore.

He's tall, lean, and immaculately dressed in a black suit

tailored to perfection, his white shirt crisp, his tie straight as a ruler. His beard is neatly trimmed and accents the lethal lines of his jaw and cheekbones. His thick black hair is medium length and meticulously combed back, while still maintaining an artful air even as he runs a hand through it.

My eyes snag on the signet ring he always wears on his third finger. He has very nice hands, the fingers long and slender. He's wearing contacts tonight, rather than his thin-rim gold glasses, putting his dark eyes on full display.

Which is all to say that Fawad is handsome (but don't tell him I've said as much, he's insufferable enough) and very rich, and at the ripe age of twenty-nine a very eligible bachelor indeed. I can see more than a handful of girls stealing glances and giggling amongst themselves, but I've been pursued by enough beautiful facades hiding lack of depth to not be swayed.

Besides, he is terribly annoying. Case in point:

"Did Rizwan not show?" he asks, unsurprised. "Don't you get tired of the same disappointments?" His tone is both genuine and mocking. "You're like a child who still believes in magic."

I narrow my eyes at him, unimpressed by his condescension. "There is nothing childish about believing in love."

"Well, if you are such a staunch believer, how do you know that poor guy with the drink wasn't the love of your life?" he asks, eyes gleaming with amusement. "Why brush him off so flippantly? Or the DJ, for that matter?"

I make an irritated sound. He is right, to an extent, and I

do *try* to keep my heart open to everyone – who *knows* who the Great Love of My Life might be hiding beneath! – but a girl must have *some* standards.

I won't admit that to Fawad.

"I just know," I reply lamely, suddenly losing all the wit I can usually be counted on for. Somehow, he is the only one who gets away with making me feel stupid.

He insists on being difficult and is somehow impervious to my charms, so I can't even bat my eyelashes at him to make him shut up. I'm sure it's because he has no emotions at all. Like a robot.

"Anyway," I add crossly, "there is nothing wrong with seeking love."

I bristle upon hearing how much of a child I sound like. I can usually be counted on for my maturity and wisdom and now I just sound naive, which I am decidedly not. Believing in love isn't childish! What is the point of life if there isn't love in it?

"No, there isn't," he replies, voice purposefully patient. I grit my teeth together. "Just as there's nothing wrong with hoping to win the lottery, though you must admit it is unlikely and the ordeal unsavory."

I scowl, opening my mouth with a retort, but stop when Naadia nudges me with her elbow. I turn to see her give me a pointed look, then snap my mouth shut. I remember why I must suffer Fawad's company: Naadia is married to his younger brother, Asif Sheikh.

I am actually the one who set them up, but that's beside the point. If I knew how much of a know-it-all

Fawad was, perhaps I would have reconsidered the match. Though Naadia is absurdly happy with Asif, so I cannot complain.

I give Fawad a dismissive roll of my eyes. He and his opinion are irrelevant, anyway.

Just then, another man passes by, flashing a smile at me as he does. I smile back sweetly in response, batting my eyelashes to let Fawad know he hasn't bothered me at all … and watch as the man passing by crashes into an auntie, who proceeds to curse at him in Punjabi.

"Don't you get tired of making fools out of perfectly reasonable men?" Fawad asks, shaking his head with distaste at the scene before him.

"It is my favorite pastime," I reply haughtily, lifting my chin. "I do so love to be desired."

"It amazes me how you manage to carry around that head of yours," he says, "when it is so clearly full of air."

"I have excellent shoulder strength," I snap. Fawad exchanges a glance with Naadia, and I hit him with my purse. "Now leave me alone, the both of you."

They do, retreating back to socialize with the guests, and I head in the opposite direction to the bathroom. Once there, I repin my scarf, adjust the diamond teeka, and reapply my lipstick, though none of these things were an inch out of place.

I catch my gaze in the mirror and for a moment, the placid expression customarily found on my face melts away into a full-fledged frown. Rizwan really isn't coming, and there goes another chance at love. My eyes quickly well with tears, a habit I've never been able to rid myself of since I was a child. I always cry much too easily.

I know what you're thinking: *poor little rich girl*, she has everything, what else could she possibly need? Well, I'm looking for the great love of my life, thank you very much.

I have had many ups and downs with love over the years, and I know once I've found my love, I'll look back and laugh at all this. But in the meantime, I'm left wondering and yearning and aching.

For me, it's always been about love.

Naadia says I'm way too picky. (We won't even get into Naadia's romantic history because it'll be anything but brief.) But since she's had her heart broken by about a dozen different jerks with nice beards, she thinks she's the Queen of Romance.

She's always telling me that there's no such thing as *the one*, and that it's ungrateful of me to push away so many great guys. But I just know, deep down in my bones, that my soulmate is out there. And when I see him, there'll be a little voice in my head that goes, *it's you*!

Fawad is always telling me that I'm too romantic and real life isn't like that – which precisely proves my previous point regarding the relevance of both him and his opinions.

Blinking rapidly to clear my eyes, I nod to myself in the mirror, then make my way back to the wedding hall, where people are beginning to say their goodbyes and leave. Dread settles deep in my belly, that feeling that comes at the end of a vacation, or on a Sunday night before school. I don't want this to end; I don't want to face what's coming.

Since we're family, we wait till the end to leave, so there's a bit more time, but even then departure is inevitable. I measure my breaths, trying to calm the disquiet in me. I go to stand with Papa, holding onto his arm.

He's a slight man, about a head taller than me, and even at his old age, looks quite dashing in his tuxedo. He's still got a full (almost full) head of hair and a full beard, both of which are a dark grey colour that is entirely natural and not at all thanks to a special shampoo he uses to ensure his whitening hair looks naturally dark.

We watch as Naadia and Asif go to say goodbye to Phuppo and Zeeshan Uncle first, then Naadia comes to say goodbye to Papa while Asif gets her shawl. Papa sighs loudly.

Poor Papa. He is in as low spirits as I am, and Naadia coming to say goodbye only cements his mood.

Naadia was married last summer, and though she and Asif only live an hour and a half drive away, it hurt Papa terribly to let her go. I was happy to see her off for the fact that she was so happy with Asif, and I was glad to have matched them. Of course I missed her a great deal, but back then I still had Phuppo – and now she'll be gone, too.

"Ai, hai, itne drame?" Naadia says, seeing Papa and my sullen expressions. "Don't worry, I'll see you soon."

"You won't go back home with us?" he asks, eyes sad. Losing Mama hit him hard, and most days, there's always this lingering hint of melancholy in his eyes that I hate to see. There are a few too many wrinkles around his eyes too, more pronounced now by his frown. I tighten my grip on his arm, reminding him that I am here, and he pats my hand gently.

"No, Papa," Naadia says, a little edge coming into her voice. "I have class." She's in her last year of medical school.

"But you can study from home, no?" Papa asks, specifically referring to *our* house as her home, not the apartment she shares with her husband.

Naadia sighs. "I could, but Asif has work in the morning."

Papa gives Asif a dirty look from afar. Naadia and I exchange a quick glance, and I bite back a smile. The funny thing is, Papa used to adore Asif. The Sheikh family live down the road from us, and his parents were friends of my Dada's. But then, one day, he asked to marry Naadia, and since then Papa is cross whenever Asif is mentioned.

It's Papa's opinion that there is no need for daughters to marry: they ought to stay with their fathers, in comfort, and live as they please. Nasty business, marriage, he always said. *I agree*, Mama would always say, giving him a pointed look. *But it can't be avoided*, she always added. She always balanced his fussiness out with her own prudence.

"Sir," Asif says, approaching with Naadia's shawl, which is an intricate Kashmiri loom shawl, one of Mama's. As Naadia drapes it across her shoulders, Asif very astutely does not look Papa in the eye.

Asif really is an amiable fellow (unlike his older brother). He's a little bit shorter than Fawad, and more well-built, with floppy hair and a boyish softness around his face. He has deep dimples that always make an appearance.

He is sweet and utterly obsessed with Naadia, which is good because Naadia doesn't have a spine, so it'd be a disaster if she had a strong-willed husband.

Papa makes a displeased noise and dismisses him. Naadia rolls her eyes in irritation and takes her husband's arm.

"Allah Hafiz," Naadia says.

"Allah Hafiz, beta jaani," Papa says, and Naadia is off, holding on tight to Asif's arm, a sight which makes Papa actually gag.

"Oh, Papa," I say, leaning my head on his shoulder. I let go of his arm and he puts it around my shoulder. We go to say goodbye to Phuppo, where Zeeshan Uncle gets a similar treatment of distaste from Papa.

"Sir," Zeeshan Uncle says, despite the fact that Papa is only a few years older than him.

"Allah Hafiz," I say, reaching down to hug Phuppo. Tears flood my eyes, and I daintily brush them away.

"Oh, jaani, I'll miss you so," she says. Her eyes are misty, as well, but she's grinning. I console myself with the fact that I had a hand to play in making her so happy, that even though she is leaving me, she has found her love, her companion, and she will never be alone again.

Even if I will be.

"Never mind that," I reply. "Have the very best time in Europe, and send me a hundred pictures a day! And don't forget to get me—"

"The stationary from Florence, yes, darling, I know," she says, laughing. "Now, give me a kiss, and I'll see you soon, gudiya." I do as I'm told and Phuppo squeezes my hands. My heart threatens to break. I don't want to let go. "And remember," she adds, "when we return, I'm only forty minutes away."

I smile at her, though despair cracks within me. Forty minutes is much too far when I am accustomed to her being just across the hall. Of course, she is a doctor and works long hours, so it isn't as though I saw her all the time, but still. She was always there when I needed a cuddle, and now she would not be.

But I won't make her upset by mentioning it. I give her my brightest smile, though the tears in my eyes betray my true feelings, and then the ordeal is done with.

We must go.

So we do.

"Well, that was dreadful," Papa says, sliding off his dress shoes when we reach home. "No more matchmaking, Humaira, my old soul cannot bear another departure." He frowns, then meets my eyes. "You won't leave me, will you?"

I help Papa out of his coat. "No, Papa, I won't leave you."

This is what we in Urdu call a jhooti tasali, but I don't think there is harm in the false reassurance.

He plants a kiss on my cheek, then retreats to his office, where he spends most of his free time. The big house is empty and quiet and dark, like a museum after-hours, filled with magic but missing it all without the visitors.

I slip off my Manolo Blahniks and release a long breath.

While I don't *want* to leave Papa either, begrudgingly I think about how I will have to fall in love for that to happen first, and at the rate this is going, who knows how long that will take?

My Prince Charming is certainly keeping me waiting.

And how I hate to be kept waiting.

Chapter Two

With the wedding festivities over, it's time to get back to work.

A few days later (after I've recovered from the ordeal that is a week-long Pakistani wedding), I dress in a pair of cute trousers in the most darling shade of lavender and wear a ruffled white blouse with a dark purple chiffon scarf around my head. Not the most usual attire for an engineer, but I refuse to change my sense of style in accordance with my profession.

My wardrobe mainly consists of whimsical and romantic clothes from places like Zimmerman, Selkie, and LoveShackFancy, most of which are feminine, frilly, and absolutely gorgeous (and of course, a bit expensive, but dressing cute is a basic human right!).

After I've spritzed myself with lemon perfume I got from our last trip to Capri (back before Naadia was married,

I recall painfully), I pop over to the bathroom for one last glance in the mirror. As I do, my gaze strays to the door at the opposite end of the bathroom, beside the second sink. It's closed now, but for years it would mainly remain open, as Naadia's room was on the other side of it. We'd spend our morning routine getting dressed, chatting, and listening to our latest favorite songs or reading funny tweets aloud to each other.

Now, I get dressed in silence.

"Chin up," I say to myself. It's much too early to be melancholy. With a nod to myself in the mirror, I grab my Dior book tote (personalized with my name across it), then exit my room. Across the hall, I glance at the master bedroom's door, which is open, as I can already hear Papa downstairs, but the other door is closed. Phuppo's.

I brush away the sadness that follows the sight and instead head down one end of the double winding stairs, hand gliding across the wooden bannister. Downstairs, I set my bag down and pass the family room, which is flooded with light, courtesy of the wall full of windows. Our house has a very classic design, filled with symmetry and sophistication, accented with gilded frames, ornate furniture, heavy drapery, and tasteful chandeliers in every other room.

I go to the kitchen, which has clean cream and beige lines with dark wood accents and quartz countertops. I make avocado toast with eggs for Papa and myself, looking out the windows to the sun washing over our backyard.

The green hedges glisten in the sunshine, the marigolds and azaleas a contrast of yellow and pink. Our backyard is a wide field, with a mini pond and waterfall installed in one corner, and a gorgeous gazebo in the other.

It's the beginning of September, so the weather is neither hot nor cold – it's perfect weather, really – and I open the kitchen window to let in fresh air and the harmony of birdsong. Suburban Long Island is filled with greenery, and I am glad for the wide backyard surrounded by trees that gives our estate the perfect amount of space and privacy.

Despite the pang I felt coming into a clean kitchen – no sign of the little mess Phuppo would make upon assembling her own breakfast – I am resolved to be optimistic. Phuppo is off galivanting in Europe, and I will be happy for her. This is what I wanted after all, when I decided to set her and Zeeshan Uncle up: for her to be content.

I start up the espresso machine, which is cafe-grade and only cost a couple of thousand dollars. Since it is still warm out, I make myself an iced latte, relishing the first sip of coffee, then call out to Papa to come eat. I bite into my avocado toast and finish my breakfast, but Papa doesn't make an appearance. As usual.

I place my plate in the sink. It has an adorable Beatrix Potter print, part of a set from Pottery Barn that always reminds me of Mama, since she would serve our breakfast on these plates when we were kids. I make Papa's cappuccino, making sure it's extra hot (if it is even one degree colder than scalding, he refuses to drink it) then carry his plate and mug out of the kitchen.

"Papa, breakfast," I say, walking over to his office, where he is already dressed and sorting through some old papers in his briefcase. When I appear in the door, he looks up at me from his massive reading glasses. As usual, he is dressed in a smart suit, his hair still a little damp from his shower.

"I'll be there in just a moment," he says. His attention is barely diverted. I place his breakfast plate on the table before him. "Oh." He blinks. "Thank you, jaani."

When he does not give his food attention, I walk over and take the papers from his hand and replace them with his coffee. Papa doesn't drink chai, which is unheard of and, quite honestly, personally offensive to me. However, he does drink coffee, so I don't shun him entirely.

"We are going to the office," I say. "You can look at these there. Now eat."

He eats as I put the papers back into his briefcase. I pick up his phone from beneath a pile of papers and set it in front of him before he can ask.

"Tch, Papa, why don't you get a new screen protector?" I ask, seeing the shattered cover.

"Then how would you buy your new lip gloss?" Papa replies. I shake my head at him in amusement. We clearly have enough money to afford both, but old habits die hard.

Papa is from a small village in Pakistan and immigrated to the US when he was eighteen to go to college. He's never been in the habit of spending. Back when Mama was alive, she would always handle the finances, and I think Papa truly doesn't know how much money he has in his accounts (which is quite a bit).

I shake my head at him, making a mental note to order him one as I leave his office. I slip on my Loro Piana loafers (a bit casual, I know, but divinely comfortable), then wave goodbye to Papa and head to my car, juggling my tote, latte, phone, and jacket.

I set the things into my midnight blue Mercedes and settle in, reciting the traveling dua before putting on some cheerful music. As I am pulling out of the driveway, Papa leaves the house, the door locking automatically behind him, and heads to his own car, a sleek white Tesla.

We are headed to the same place, our office twenty minutes away, but Papa tends to stay longer hours, while I leave once the clock strikes five. (Sometimes earlier, if I am being honest.) Papa is the CEO and chief consultant of his own company, where he designs commercial buildings. I'm one of the engineers there; I studied civil engineering and have been working with Papa since I graduated (with honors) over a year ago last May.

Papa never pushed me to do one thing, he just wished for me to get educated and get a good job, Mama too. She never went to college and was always entirely dependent on her husband. When she was eighteen, she got married and moved to America, where she knew exactly no one. It was good Papa didn't end up being a psychopath because she was entirely reliant on him. Which is exactly why she never wanted us to be dependent on any man.

(Honestly, sometimes a girl wants to be dependent on a man for certain things.)

I am Papa's little heiress, which just sounds right out of a period drama, doesn't it? So I spend a lot of time learning the ropes from him and managing and going to meetings, rather than strictly drafting up blueprints etc.

It's good work, and I enjoy it, but on days like today, I feel restless.

When I get to our office building, I park right in front, then head into the five-story building. Our offices are on the fourth floor, and the other floors are rented out by other businesses. I take the elevator up, then smile and say "good morning" to my coworkers as I head toward my desk. There are about twelve of us on site, which makes Papa feel as though he's running a very quaint Mom-and-Pop store, though our profits are far from it.

I'm not exactly best friends with any of my coworkers; we're cordial, of course, but I think they all keep their distance from "the boss's daughter." So while the work is alright, I can't say I exactly have *fun* every day. And today is especially dreary.

I spend the morning on video conferences that surely could have been emails, and our computer system is running terribly slowly, which is driving everyone nuts.

I tap my nails against the keyboard of my Mac, looking around. My desk is decorated with a vase of fresh flowers, a small stack of books, a vintage teacup and saucer, and a little diffuser which emits a sweet sugary scent.

I reach into my drawer of emergency snacks and pull

out some chocolate (Lindt chocolate from Switzerland really is superior) and nibble on the edge of a bar while I stare at my screen, not wanting to do any work. It's nearly twelve, so I take a deep breath and stand. I'll just go grab some lunch and maybe drive around for a bit.

But even after that is done, I still feel disquieted. Releasing a long breath in my car, I exit and head back into the air-conditioned office building, approaching the elevator. It closes just as I approach, but I make eye-contact with one of the passengers inside as it does. A moment later, the door reopens.

"Thanks," I say, smiling sweetly. The elevator is filled with a few finance-bros from another business in the building, and in the corner, I spot a familiar face.

One of our new workers pushed to the side. From what I recall, she is a graduate student doing her Masters in Architecture and working part-time at our company as an intern. She clutches her purse to her chest, looking like quite the lost lamb.

Clearing my throat, I enter the elevator and stand towards the middle.

"Oh, excuse me," I say. The finance-bros move over when I flash them another smile. They get off on the second floor, and the intern releases an audible sigh of relief, as if she has been holding her breath. From what I remember of her resume, we are nearly the same age, and she is from Pakistan.

"You're Shanzay, right?" I say. It's just us two in the

elevator. She startles, as if not used to being noticed. I wait for her reply, and she nods.

The elevator doors open to the fourth floor, our destination, and she presses the open button.

"After you, Miss Mirza, ma'am," she says.

"Oh, please don't call me that," I say, waving my hand. "I'm Humaira."

She looks at me with wide brown eyes. Something about her makes me want to take her under my wing.

"After you, Humaira," she says, holding her arm out to keep the elevator doors from closing. I cock my head to the side.

"No, I don't think so," I say, pressing the close button. She pulls her arm back and the doors close.

"Wha—"

The elevator takes us back to the ground floor, and I exit.

"Well, come on, then," I say, looking over my shoulder at her.

"Bu—" She has a split second to make a decision, and as the elevator doors go to close once more, she jumps out. "Where are we going?" she asks, falling into step with me.

"I could kill for some cake and tea at the moment," I say.

"Bu—"

I wave a hand. "Oh, don't worry, you won't get in trouble. This is an important errand conducive to our work. How can our brains function without dessert?" I grin wickedly.

Shanzay smiles at that. She has a sweet face. She is of medium height and thickly built, and I think she could be rather pretty, with a few key adjustments made to her appearance. She is wearing her hijab in a rather old-fashioned way, the way many Pakistani women do, with an unflattering undercap and too many pins and layers and folds. We'll need to remedy that.

My scarf is pinned beneath my chin and thrown over my shoulders; it is very easy breezy that way.

"Let's go," I say, opening my car door. She blinks, then gets in. We drive to a bakery nearby. The bakery is small, but it isn't very busy, since it's a weekday and the middle of the day. There's a young mother on one table with a little girl, who looks too young to be school-going. My heart warms at the sight. I love seeing mothers on dates with their children.

It reminds me of going out for afternoon tea in the city with Mama after a shopping spree at Bergdorf's. Naadia and I were too little to have proper tea, but we'd have sweet milk and eat loads of pastries and cakes, Mama sitting across from us and teaching us how to properly apply clotted cream and jam to our scones.

While the memory brings a flood of warmth, it also brings an undercurrent of pain. I miss Mama, always, but now I miss Naadia, too. We used to go out to cafes all the time in high school and college.

But no matter. Nothing a good piece (or three) of cake can't fix.

When our server brings over our orders, I finally get the details from Shanzay.

"So you moved here at the beginning of the summer?" I

ask, biting into my slice of tres leches. "Where did you stay? Was campus open?"

"Yes, I came at the beginning of June," she replies, not touching her slice of carrot cheesecake. She'll need to be quicker about that before I eat it all. "I stayed with a family friend at their house."

"Oh, who?" I ask, sipping my Earl Gray tea (which isn't Fortnum's, but it passes muster). "Perhaps I know them."

"The Rajas?"

It is a common last name, but I feel as though I know who it is she speaks of. "How many children do they have?" I ask.

"Four," Shanzay replies. "Two young boys, a girl in college ... and an older boy."

Her cheeks turn pink at this. Actually pink! *Hmm.*

"Is the girl's name Madiha?" I ask. Shanzay nods.

"Yes!" she replies, seeming to loosen up and talk more freely. "She's at John Hopkins University for biomedical engineering, but she was home for the summer. She's so sweet, I love her."

"Yes, she is," I say, knowing just the family she's referencing. "They're tenants of Fawad – my sister's brother-in-law."

The Sheikh family owns a lot of property, and since Uncle retired a few years ago, and Asif is a lawyer, Fawad handles all that business. He does a lot of investing and reinvesting, making more and more money out of money. Sometimes he even advises Papa on his accounts, his eyes positively alight as he explains multiplication and growth rates.

What a terrible nerd. I mean, who seriously likes math that much? If there was any doubt in my mind regarding his peculiarity, this would eliminate it.

"I've met Fawad Bhai on a few occasions," Shanzay says. I nearly laugh at the term of respect she's used. It's just *Fawad*, for God's sake. "He is very quiet, but kind. He gets along with Huzaifa—"

At this she breaks off, cheeks turning even more pink. Goodness. I have not known such shyness in quite some time, not since I was in high school, maybe.

"Who's Huzaifa?" I ask, and Shanzay gasps a little hearing his name. She looks around as if he will materialize right then. Gracious me.

"Oh, he is the ... eldest," she says, avoiding my gaze. "He and Fawad Bhai get along really well. Sometimes they even played basketball together."

This is positively shocking. I did not think Fawad had an athletic bone in his body. It is also interesting because from what I know, the Rajas are a simple, relatively poor family. I have met the daughter, Madiha, before; we are from the same masjid community, and she's active in the Youth Group for girls there.

"I simply cannot believe you came to New York just as mango season began in Pakistan," I say, changing the subject. Shanzay laughs.

"I know," she replies, "but I was a TA for an undergraduate summer class, so I had to come earlier. The

Rajas were so kind, letting me stay with them for the summer."

"They're family friends of yours?"

She nods. "But now that classes have started, I have my own apartment on campus."

We continue chatting. She tells me about her program, and we discuss things like Pakistani actors' love lives, and the newest fashion collections, and the best places to eat in Islamabad, and trips to the northern areas of Pakistan.

Shanzay is a simple girl: she doesn't go out much and doesn't know about a lot of the restaurants or designers I talk about, but it's still nice talking to her. She's really close with her family, which I can appreciate because I am close with mine.

But while it is just Naadia and I, she has three older brothers who are all married and have kids and are settled in Pakistan. She tells me horror stories about having brothers and I am glad I have none.

"You're so eloquent," she tells me. "You sound like a princess."

I smile. "Courtesy of all the private schools I went to; they insisted upon precision of language." I consider this further. "And Mama always told us to speak properly. Naadia disagrees—she does not hold propriety in much regard, but I like it."

I find it soothing: a semblance of control and order. And it reminds me of Mama, of course. She always had such a way of speaking, always so poised and confident.

"The schools here are really impressive," Shanzay says.

"Baba sent me to America to study, but Mama really sent me here to find a husband." She laughs. "Instead of an MS degree I'm supposed to be getting a MRS. degree. You know how mothers are."

Pain stabs my chest. "I don't, anymore," I say. "But I do remember." Shanzay's eyebrows furrow. "My mother passed away when I was thirteen. Even then, Mama was already telling us about the rishta process and marriage and how one must 'compromise'." This I put in air quotes. Shanzay laughs.

"Ya khudaya, what is it with desi mothers and the word compromise? I swear it's the only concept in their minds when they think of marriage."

"Honestly." We laugh.

"I am sorry about her passing," Shanzay says. "Even though my mother drives me absolutely crazy, I miss her loads, and we talk every day."

"Tell me more about her," I say.

"This one time, we were driving and..."

Shanzay tells me stories about her mother, and I listen. Some people find it uncool to be friends with one's mother, but Shanzay talks about her mother like she is her best friend, which I find very sweet.

Mama was my best friend before she died.

Cancer came and took her too quickly, in just a few months. I barely had time to react to the illness before she was gone. It was hard to lose her, particularly because I was just getting into my teenage angst so I hadn't even properly grown distant from her yet. I was still childishly obsessed with her.

I think if Mama was still alive, she would be my best friend, too.

The rest of the day after that passes with the business of work, and when I finally come home that evening, an empty house awaits me. I sigh, setting my tote down and kicking off my shoes. I put on a pair of plush slippers, the small movements sounding loud in the quiet house.

It's strange because the house would be empty even when Phuppo still lived here, since she got off of work at the hospital later than I did, but it was always nice knowing she would be coming soon, so the loneliness would not be lasting. And before that, even though Naadia would be busy studying at the library, I always knew she'd be home eventually. That we'd have dinner together, or at least, convene over late-night brownies and milk.

Now, the evening spreads ahead of me, long and vacant.

I go up the winding staircase to my room, then wash up and pray. I change into more comfortable clothes before making myself some chai for the evening. Then I sit in the family room and slowly sip it, looking out the windows to watch the sun move across the sky, until the clouds are tinged purple and pink.

The only exciting bit is when there is a knock on the door and food has arrived.

I suppose I could cook myself something, but I'm too tired to do so, which is why I have ordered from my friend, Zahra Paracha. She's in culinary school and does personalized catering as well. She makes the most delicious home-cooked desi food.

"Assalaamualaikum, how are you?" I say, opening the door.

"Walaikumassalaam! Here's your food," Zahra says, handing me an aluminum tray. She's a nice girl, originally from California and definitely has that relaxed look going for her. She's a few inches shorter than me, with dark skin and a full, round face.

"Come in, I'll make you some chai," I say, stepping aside to let her enter. I just finished a cup, but I can always have another. It's always fun to have chai with a friend.

"Oh, no, thank you, I'd love to, but I have more deliveries to make!" Zahra says.

"Aw, boo." I frown. "I feel like we haven't hung out in a while! At least tell me how the others are, Haya and Sadaf?"

Haya was Zahra's best friend, and Sadaf was Haya's sister. Sadaf was also Naadia's best friend – they met in college – but I hadn't seen much of her since Naadia got married, really.

"They're good, too! Haya's busy with wedding planning and her pharmacy program, and Sadaf's being Sadaf!" Zahra replies. I smile.

"Well, we all have to get together soon! Maybe have a movie night or something."

"Yes, definitely!"

I wave goodbye to Zahra, deflating a bit as I shut the door. It isn't that I'm exceptionally close with her or Haya, but they are fun to hang out with. It's nice to meet with friends, to fill the emptiness.

I never really stayed in touch with the friends I made in college. Actually, I'm not close with a lot of people, at least not nearby. I've always had Naadia, a built-in best friend, whenever we went anywhere, and then Phuppo, too. My best friend, Areeba, lives in New Jersey, so I don't see her very often. And my girl cousins are a little older and married, and now even Naadia is married, and Phuppo, too.

Taking a measured breath, I go to the kitchen and set the food down. Then I change again and do a yoga session in the gym in our basement. After I've showered, I make myself a plate of food.

I've ordered a dish of chicken pulao from Zahra, and it's such nice comfort food. Mama used to make the very best chicken pulao, and whenever I go to my Nano's house in Islamabad, she makes it too. I make myself raita to go along with it, and eat the rice with the vegetable yogurt in the quiet kitchen.

After that's all done with, there's still a few hours to kill before sleeping. Papa isn't home yet, so I make him a plate of food, then pack us boxes for lunch tomorrow. Even though of course he can get his own food, as he is a grown man, I don't mind doing little things for him like this. Everything I have is because of him, and with just us two left in the house, it's nice to look after someone, to be useful.

Though sometimes I am afraid he is growing dependent on me.

I put the rest of the food away, then head upstairs, leaving most of the lights on.

I have always adored my house. It's big with lots of wide windows and homey details, and it doesn't feel cold or distant, but when it is empty like this, I feel as though I am not even there, like I am a ghost, haunting the place.

The walls are steeped with memories, echoes of moments past, and I feel like I am just another one of them. So many of Mama, then infinite more with Naadia, who I basically spent every waking moment with when we were home.

Having a sister is so strange because you spend your whole life as extensions of one another – consuming the same shows, books, and songs; sharing clothes; having the exact same sense of humor; cooking and eating food together – and then one of you moves out and everything becomes an obscure reference to what was.

But what can be done? At the very least, she's happy.

I settle into bed with a novel, trying to lose myself in nineteenth century England. I am very much into historical romance, but I have to sneakily read them because of the racy covers. Papa would be positively scandalized if he saw them. Even worse if he read inside.

The settings of these novels feel like a different world yet it's still so familiar. It is amusing how Pakistani culture is so similar to Regency-era England, with all the rules and courting. I also love the way they talk; it is so proper. It reminds me of Mama.

The best part, of course, is the romance. The gentleman is always clever and challenging his heroine while still being fiercely devoted. Plus, they are always so well-dressed!

My cheeks heat as I get to a sex scene, which I flip through (mostly), though I still find it fascinating to see certain parts. Desis are so hush hush about sex education, it is interesting to see how the act is actually done and what is involved.

I have never even been kissed, so there certainly is a lot left to imagine.

Oh, how I dream about being kissed! A lot of Muslim girls are frightened by the concept – even Naadia was so nervous about getting married – because when you spend your whole life not being touched by men, there is a certain terror that comes with someone having complete access to your body in ways you have never experienced.

But I can't wait for it all: to be touched, to be held, to be kissed, to be loved.

The furthest I've ever gone is holding hands with my crush in the fourth grade. He was a white boy with blonde hair and blue eyes (so cliche, I know) and we were on a field trip looking at birds, and his hand brushed against mine.

When a girl's romantic history peaks at the age of ten, there is surely something amiss.

It isn't that no boys have tried since then, it is just that I was not impressed by any of them. I have even gone as far as to try those Muslim dating apps, which I deleted less than a day later because it merely horrified me beyond belief and made me feel even more hopeless.

And I refuse to be hopeless.

I will find true love. I will! If others can have it, so will I.

I am nothing if not determined.

Chapter Three

The week passes just like that.

Papa starts staying at the office later than usual because I don't think he can bear being home either when it is so empty, so it is just me at home. (We still have dinner together most nights, so at least there's that, but it just isn't as fun.)

I don't particularly enjoy coming home to that great big empty house either, so I resolve to become better friends with Shanzay. It will be good to have a new friend to invite over, and anyway, I think it'll be good for her to have me as a friend.

Moments with Shanzay in the office are refreshing and nice, and I find myself seeking her out throughout the day, if only for a little commentary or laughter. She is sweet. I rather like her.

I used to be so content with just Phuppo at the house. She was always ready to watch period dramas with me, which involved more of our own commentary than the movie's dialogues; discuss the latest novel I'd read, in which I would explain the entire plot to her; or bake something together. But now she's gone, too, just like Naadia before her.

I still talk with both of them all the time. Phuppo sends me loads of photos from her honeymoon (the PG version), and Naadia and I basically spend all day sending each other reels on Instagram (cooking videos neither of us will ever try, travel destinations we need to visit, and makeup tutorials). But it isn't the same.

Not even the random mornings Naadia texts me:

my stomach hurts.

almost like having coffee and painkillers on an empty stomach ISN'T healthy

hey i had half a granola bar too

Or when I call her up one evening and explain the shocking plot twist of a new show I'm watching on Netflix and try to harass her to watch it, too. I even send her edits of the main ship on Twitter, but she's not persuaded. If she was still at home, the next room over, I would simply climb into bed with her and force her to watch it with me.

But she isn't. I make commentary to myself, alone.

I am content with my life, but sometimes I'm so lonely, I don't know what to do with myself.

Which is why I invite Shanzay over for chai that Sunday. I busy myself with making chicken bread, keema samosas, egg salad sandwiches, cucumber sandwiches, almond cake, and cream puffs. I know there are only two of us, but it's a good distraction, and it's always better to do more than to do less.

I set the dining table with our Royal Albert set, filling the three-tiered plates with the different foods. I was a little torn between the Old Country Rose set and a Mackenzie Childs tea set we have, but I figure I can't go wrong with the classic red roses decorating the white china of the Royal Albert set.

I am just filling the cream puffs on Sunday morning when someone knocks on the door. Throwing on a scarf to cover my hair, I go to answer.

It's Fawad.

He's dressed in a suit, as usual, and the dark green handkerchief in his pocket matches the precise shade of his tie (and his socks, if I know him at all). Standing in the sunlight, his skin is golden brown, luminous in contrast to his dark eyes. Once again, I am struck by how handsome he is – though thankfully not handsome enough to tempt me.

He holds up a file, a pleasant expression on his face that only causes me irritation. He is always showing up as if this is his chache da ghar and he is free to visit when he pleases!

"You couldn't have just emailed that to Papa?" I ask.

"It's good to see you, too, Humaira," he replies cheerily. "I'm well, thanks for asking."

Releasing an annoyed sound, I hold out my free hand

for the file. He ignores me entirely and steps into the house, walking forward to place it in the office.

"I'm busy," I say petulantly. "I have guests coming over!"

"You aren't dressed," he replies, looking me up and down. I'm wearing an apron over home shalwar-kameez, which I find more comfy than western clothes. "And you have—" He gestures to his cheek. When I wipe my face, powdered sugar streaks across my fingers.

"I'm still cooking."

"Mm, what did you make?"

Without waiting for a reply, he walks into the kitchen, stealing a cucumber sandwich as he surveys the getup. I grab my piping bag and hold it up threateningly at him, but he's unfazed.

"You didn't make those little chicken patties?" he asks, disappointed. I give him a look.

Fawad is often frequenting our house for food. There is usually always home-cooked food at my house (either from Zahra or from me), or at the very least some sweets (I bake whenever I'm feeling Things, which is very often), and he lives alone.

He lives down the street from us, an infuriatingly walkable distance. His parents are retired and have shifted to Islamabad, where the weather is more favorable, but they do come back for a few months in the year.

Surprisingly, Fawad is always in a surly mood during those months – well, more so than usual. I think he prefers being alone.

I've actually known him my entire life, but I'd never really noticed him until Naadia and Asif started talking.

How I miss that ignorance, I think to myself, as Fawad steals a cream puff and devours it in one bite.

"You pig!" I say, swatting him with a towel. "You can't eat it in one bite. You're supposed to savor it."

"Trust me, there wasn't much to be savored."

My eyebrows furrow together in a look that Papa says makes me look like an angry kitten, and I am sure Fawad thinks the same because this only furthers his amusement.

Despite the fact that Asif is twenty-six and younger than Fawad, he is much more reasonable than his older brother. While Fawad is always irritating me, Asif is only ever nice to me. Even when he teases, he has this little smile on his face, so you know to never take him seriously.

But Fawad is – *ugh!*

"Do not insult my baking," I say, trying and failing to keep my tone level. "Everyone loves it. Bashira Aunty asked me to start a catering business the other day!"

"Yes, I know." He laughs, giving me a confused look. "I was just teasing, Humaira."

I release a short breath and resolve to ignore him, instead working on filling my cream puffs with the delicious vanilla custard I have made. I sense Fawad's gaze on me, assessing, analyzing.

"Just because your brother is married to my sister doesn't mean you can waltz over here and eat our food whenever you please," I say, not looking up at him. I don't know why I say it; I don't really mind him coming over.

I don't know what's gotten into me. I should be in a better mood due to all the baking I've done and the fact that Shanzay is coming over. And even if I am in a Mood, I can usually mask it well.

But not in front of Fawad, for some reason.

"You're actually annoyed," he states, regarding me closely. He comes to stand beside me, and I risk a glance over at him. The amusement on his face has been replaced with something resembling concern, his brows furrowed. His lips are parted as if to say something. I bristle.

"I'm fine," I say brightly, but he doesn't believe me. His dark eyes are shockingly perceptive.

"Why are you in such a grumpy mood?" he asks, stepping closer. I feel the heat of his body beside mine. His voice is soft, like a breeze, or a caress. "You don't usually mind when I come over."

The gentle tone unnerves me. I don't look at him, but in a quick moment, I feel placated, like a candle blown out.

To my horror, my eyes grow misty.

"The house is just so empty." I whisper so that he won't hear, but he does anyway.

"But you are not," he replies, voice sure and clear. I startle, suddenly seen. I stop filling in the cream puffs to look up at him. I meet his warm eyes.

He's looking at me, just looking. The breath lodges in my throat. Something sharp stirs in my stomach.

I look away, pressing my fingers against the pulse in my throat to calm myself.

He steps back and clears his throat.

"Have fun with your friend," he says, snagging another cream puff, and is on his way out. I watch him leave, the wide line of his shoulders, his long legs. A moment later, he disappears from sight, and another after, I hear the front door close behind him.

That final shut makes the house seem even emptier, so much so that I nearly wish to call him back.

What did he mean? But that was just it. I knew what he meant, and somehow he knew what I was feeling. Being alone in this great big house made me feel insufferably lonely, but he had disarmed that notion with a few words, telling me that as long as I was content with myself, it did not matter if the house was empty, that I was enough.

How did he know?

I cannot dwell on the matter because there is work to be done. I discard my scarf and go to get ready. I am applying a final layer of mascara just as the doorbell rings.

"Salaam!" I say, opening the door. Shanzay lets out a sigh of relief when she sees me, her wide and frantic eyes relaxing.

"I was afraid I was at the wrong house," she says, coming in. "These are for you."

She hands me a tray of cookies that look to be made from premade cookie dough, then goes to take her shoes off, a pair of leather khussas that go with the shalwar kameez suit she has on.

"Thank you," I reply, taking the tray from her. "You can keep your shoes on."

I'm wearing khussas as well. "Come, this way."

"Oh ... wow."

Shanzay's eyes widen as she takes in the house, cataloging the details. I love our house as well, with its clean scent and classic decor that is the perfect cross of lived-in and decadent.

Mama did all the interior design, and most of the furniture and curtains and rugs are imported from Pakistan. Since her death, we haven't drastically updated anything, but I do try to keep the house spruced up with fresh flowers and new candles.

One of my favorite pieces in the house is a grand jhula, the swing made of intricately hand-carved wood. Mama used to say she wanted to import in an old haveli wooden door as well, but it didn't work with the exterior of the house.

"Come, come," I say, leading her to the family room. The formal living room will only make her feel overwhelmed, I am sure. The family room has high ceilings and one wall consists almost entirely of windows, which lets in lovely sunlight and provides a stunning view of the lush backyard. The waterfall glitters in the sunlight, pouring into the little pond.

"Your house is ... amazing," Shanzay says, still taking in the details.

"Thank you." I smile.

Her attention turns to me.

"And you look beautiful," she adds. "Your hair is so nice!"

While I am used to people fawning over me, it is still

nice to be complimented. I smile, smoothing my hair. It's waist-length, dark brown, and cut into long layers; I blow-dried it for today. I'm wearing a new shalwar kameez suit from Sania Maskatiya, which one of my phuppos sent from Pakistan, with glass chudiyan and gold jhumkas. The gold earrings are pure and were a gift for my thirteenth birthday, one of the last gifts Mama gave me.

Mama loved dressing up; every day she would wear a freshly pressed shalwar kameez three-piece suit with matching gold jewelry. (Her jewelry collection is truly iconic.) Because I always saw Mama so dressed up, I also really like dressing up in traditional Pakistani clothes; they are more comfortable, and I feel they flatter me. People tell me I have a very classic look, like the actress Mahira Khan.

"How was the drive?" I ask, sitting down on a couch.

"Not too bad," she replies, sitting beside me. She sits on the edge of the sofa, as if afraid she'll ruin it. I laugh. "Come, relax," I tell her. She smiles at me, then gets comfortable.

We make a little bit of small talk, then head to the kitchen, where we continue chatting as I cook the chai on the stove.

"Are you making mixed?" she asks. I nod.

"If it isn't mixed, it isn't chai," I say. "Then it's just tea."

She laughs. "I agree entirely. It has to be cooked together."'

I add in some elaichi, as well, to give it a nice aroma, and once the chai is done, I pour it into the teapot and bring it to the dining table in the adjoining room, which is already set up with all the food in pretty dishes and the matching tea set with gold rims and a red rose design. There are vases of fresh red roses on the table as well, along with gold candles and decorative pieces.

Shanzay gasps, taking it all in.

"Oh, this is so nice!" she exclaims. I am quite pleased with the set-up, as well, and am glad she appreciates it. We make ourselves plates of food and chat as we eat.

Despite being the same age, I feel Shanzay is so much younger than I am, like the youth group girls I often interact with. She is so simple. She's from a middle-class background, and most of her world was confined to her family.

I must protect her, I think to myself. I've taken quite a liking to her. I think she'll be a dear friend to me.

"Now, to more important matters," I say. "Do you have any boy drama in your life? If so, you must tell me at once. I'm a slut for a good romance."

"No, not really," she says. Shanzay looks away, fiddling with the ends of her dupatta. I narrow my eyes, staring, and she only grows more shy.

"I knew it!" I say. "You do. Tell me everything!"

"Oh, alright," she says, giggling. "Remember how I mentioned—" she lowers her voice, though the house is empty save for us, "—Huzaifa earlier? The Rajas' eldest?"

I nod, motioning for her to continue.

"Well ... he is very kind." Her eyes fill with light. "He's in graduate school to become an English teacher, and his reading tastes match mine quite well. He lent me some of his books to read over the summer, and we would sit and discuss them together..."

I furrow my brows, instinctively worried.

"Isn't he younger than you?" I say.

"Well ... only a year," she replies.

"Hm."

"Wh-What?"

"Perhaps this is just my experience, but I feel like young guys are immature," I say, tone gentle.

"Oh ... um, maybe." She bites her lip. "I don't have much experience, to be honest with you."

"I unfortunately have *too* much experience." I sigh. "Particularly with immature, stupid boys. It's a horrible waste of time, not to mention a headache."

"Oh."

"Don't you think you might be better off with someone more settled?" I say, after thinking for a moment. "Only because you are an immigrant, and you'll be starting from the ground up, so it might be better to be matched with someone with a more solid foundation."

Her face falls. I'm afraid I've hurt her, but it is the simple reality. People may pretend that money does not matter, but it does. It is best to set yourself up for success rather than failure.

"Yeah, that makes sense," she says slowly, understanding what I mean. Her forehead creases with worry.

"Of course, it is up to you to decide."

"Thank you for your advice," Shanzay says, releasing a breath. "I do think you are right."

But her voice has lost all its earlier excitement. Her lips look suspiciously frown-y. Oh, that won't do! I am determined to help her as much as I can. I'll be useful to her just as I have been with the others.

"Aw, don't be disheartened!" I say, taking her hand. A splendid idea pops into my head. "I can help you find someone more suitable. I am a bit of a matchmaker, you know."

"Are you really?" Shanzay asks, a smile appearing on her face. "You look nothing like the rishta aunties I know."

I laugh. "No, nothing like those aunties, especially since I have a much higher success rate." I flip my hair.

"I trust you, then," Shanzay says, eyes wide and accepting. "I'm a bit new to all this."

"Don't worry," I tell her. "I will find you your perfect match."

Chapter Four

I was thirteen when Mama passed away. The grief of losing a loved one always lingers, always remains, but while most days pass by without any bumps, some days come out of nowhere to rattle you straight to your bones.

While most of the autumn flutters away like the falling leaves, without too much overwhelming pain, when Thanksgiving rolls around at the end of November, I find I cannot get out of bed.

I miss her terribly. It is a physical pain, weighing down on me.

I think perhaps I seek out love so ardently because I saw how it nourished her, even in the end, when she was sick. Her and Papa weren't a perfect couple, but they loved each other, even when they bickered and quarreled. Perhaps they are why I have such high expectations of love, and why I believe in it so fervently.

One sweet anecdote I will share is that Papa used to

exclusively call Mama "begham", and for a long while, we actually thought it was "begum" he was saying, which was the Urdu word for someone's Mrs., their wife.

"How come you call Mama begum?" I asked Papa once, probably when I was eight and Naadia was ten. He shook his head, misunderstood and heartbroken by my question. He poured more chocolate syrup over his ice-cream, our post-dinner treat that warm summer night.

"I am not saying be-*gum*," he replied with a scoff, as if he could not imagine being found saying something so simple when regarding his wife. "I am saying be-*gham*."

It was a slight difference but held a world of meaning. Naadia and I exchanged a glance, drawing out long oooooh's over our bowls of ice-cream, even though we didn't fully understand the Urdu word.

"So what does be*gham* mean?" Naadia asked.

"*Be* – without," he replied, breaking down the word. "*Gham* – grief. The one who keeps me without grief."

"Aww!" I exclaimed. "That's so sweet!"

Clearly proud of himself, Papa cast a glance at Mama, who had been listening silently while she ate her peanut, chocolate-chip ice-cream. In response, she shook her head at the inappropriate nature of such intimate words in front of the children. It was why Mama exclusively called Papa "suno", which meant "listen". There was something too intimate about calling someone directly by their name, particularly in front of the others.

But the face of disgust she made never lasted: I saw her lips pulling into a smile at the last moment.

Some days, like today, I miss her so much I think I won't ever be okay again.

"Can I borrow your black sweater?" Naadia asks, entering my room through the open bathroom door. It's nearly noon, and I am still in bed. Asif dropped her off a little while ago, while he went to the Sheikhs's down the street.

"Which one?" I ask.

"You know, the black one," she says, vaguely waving a hand as she opens my closet and walks in, searching for the sweater in mention. I have about six black sweaters, but I know my sister well enough to know which one she is referring to.

"Don't ruin my closet," I call. "It's on your left, under the Burberry checked one."

"Oh, cute!" she calls back, something catching her eye. "When did you get this? I'm gonna borrow it."

I sink back into my cushions, letting her do her worst. By the time she leaves my closet, her arms are full. I give her a look, and she waves a hand. Or tries to. Her hands are otherwise occupied.

"I'm just gonna try some of this stuff on," she says. "Just to check."

She exits as soon as she came, then returns with empty arms. She approaches my bed, and I squirm away, clutching my blanket close before she can snatch it off.

"Get up," she says, shaking my legs. I groan, trying to kick her from under the blanket. "You have to get ready.

Don't you need to bake your pies? And Phuppo said to get there early."

"I don't want to get up," I whine, pulling my covers over my nose. She cocks her head to the side.

"You don't?"

I shake my head.

"Fine." She plops right on top of me, pressing her weight down.

"Ow!" I scream. "How am I supposed to get up now?"

"Oh, you want to get up now?"

"Get off of me!" I free an arm and grab a pillow to smack her with, but she only spreads out on top of me. "God, did you gain weight? You're so heavy! Get off!"

"What did you just say!" she screams, taking the pillow to smother my face as I shriek. "I've been doing Pilates thank you very much so that is all *muscle* weight!"

We wrestle for a bit, both of us struggling and laughing. Then Naadia gets off of me, dramatically throwing her curly hair over her shoulder.

"Woo, I think I can skip the Pilates for today," she says, catching her breath. "I'm going to go get ready, and you better be up in five minutes or I'm coming back with a bucket of water."

I stick my tongue out at her, knowing she would never dare, but I get out of bed all the same and follow her into the bathroom. She exits to go to her room, which is a mess despite her being there hardly a few hours. I shut both bathroom doors, shaking my head at her sink, which is surrounded with my skincare products that she's no doubt emptied out.

I get washed up, change into some comfortable wool shalwar kameez, then go downstairs to make coffee. Naadia is already in the kitchen with her coffee, and she's left the machine on for me.

"Egg quesadillas?" Naadia asks, taking out the ingredients before I even nod. She tosses her hair up into a high bun, then starts cracking eggs into a bowl. When Papa hears us in the kitchen, he leaves his office to see what we are getting up to.

"Papa, do you want one?" Naadia asks. He makes a face.

"Who eats breakfast at 12:30?" he asks. "This is lunch."

"Do you want one?" I repeat.

"You'll spoil your appetite for all the food your Phuppo is making, and it will go to waste," he replies.

"But do you want one?" we repeat.

He considers it. "If you're insisting."

Naadia and I shake our heads. Papa is so dramatic sometimes.

As Naadia makes the quesadillas, adding in extra spinach because we all have iron deficiency, I make my latte and Papa's cappuccino and set the table.

We eat together, and I text Phuppo a quick photo letting her know we miss her. I send it in the group chat I have with Naadia and Phuppo, which is called MMESG (Mahmud Mirza's Emotional Support Girlies). Phuppo sends back a drooling emoji and a picture of her kitchen, where she is wreaking havoc while preparing Thanksgiving early dinner.

After we eat breakfast, talking about random things, Papa sticks around to leisurely drink his coffee while Naadia and I get to work. We have a brief argument over who will load the dishwasher.

"You do it," Naadia says.

"I always do it," I reply.

"You live here."

"As if you loaded it when you did live here."

But the bickering is good-natured, and I rinse and stick the dishes in. Anything else that needs to be washed can be done by our cleaning lady, who comes every other day.

Then I finish making my pies, which I had started on yesterday, while Naadia makes a potato casserole. All the while, we chat and argue and laugh, Papa ambling around the kitchen, sneaking tastes, keeping us company.

The house is loud and full once more. It's enough to buoy me for now, and my mood brightens, though I still feel the rock of sadness wedged within me, as I suspect I always will. I do not think it will ever leave, but I have learned to grow flowers through the cracks.

"Will Asif pick you up?" I ask, putting my pies in the oven to bake, the pecan one first, then the mixed-berry one. "Or you're coming with us?

"Why would Asif pick her up?" Papa asks, confused.

"I don't know, maybe because he is my *husband*?" Naadia replies.

Papa makes a noise of displeasure.

"Just tell him to meet us there," I say. Naadia opens her mouth as if to say something further, but I make a pleading face with her, and she concedes, though not without dramatically slamming the oven door shut on her casserole.

While the food bakes, we retreat upstairs to get ready. I have my ensemble already ironed and hanging: it's this gorgeous forest green maxi dress with stockings and Chanel slingback heels. I want to look extra cute in case Rizwan comes tonight. Phuppo said he might.

Naadia is wearing leather pants with a nice sweater (my sweater). She also hasn't brought any of her own makeup, so we crowd together over my vanity, handing one another bronzer and brushes and highlighter.

"What do you think you are doing?" I ask, as she slips my lipstick into her pant pocket.

"I'll need a refresh later," she says innocently.

"You always steal my lipsticks."

"I'll put it back! I swear."

I know I will never see that lipstick again.

When we go downstairs to check on the ovens, I make a detour to check on Papa in the office. He's sitting at his desk, massive glasses perched on his nose, drafting floor plans on his computer screen.

"Papa!" I cry. "You aren't ready!"

"What?" he looks up, then sees I am entirely ready, down to my shoes and matching flap-bag. (I considered wearing my Chanel chain, too, but thought it would be overkill, so settled for the Van Cleef necklace.). He furrows his brow. "Where is your sweater? You'll catch a cold!"

I give him a look.

"Papa! Go get ready!"

"Do not worry, do not worry, I am ready, just give me two minutes to shower and change." He gets up and exits the office but is back a moment later to continue inspecting me. "And why such high heels? You'll break your ankles."

"They look good!"

"What are you trying to prove?"

"*Papa!*"

"Okay. Okay." He holds up his hands in surrender. "Now the important question: what should I wear?"

"Hmm, wear the maroon sweater and your tweed blazer."

He frowns. "No suit today?"

Papa loves wearing suits. "No, Papa."

As he goes to get ready, I head over to the kitchen to check on my pies. It smells divine, the air thick with the aroma of cinnamon and sugar. Naadia's put an apple-spiced candle on, too, and the whole house is wrapped in a warm coziness.

I take the pies out of the oven, and they are baked to golden perfection, decorated with perfect lattice-work and pie-crust leaves. The berries bleed through the cracks of the latticework, a gorgeous purple-red, and the pecan pie a perfect golden brown. Naadia is still wrestling with her casserole, so I go to call Shanzay.

"Salaam! You're still coming, right?" I ask. I had Phuppo invite her, since she had nowhere else to go. (She did get invited to the Rajas, but that doesn't count, of course.)

"Yes, yes, I'm leaving right now. The GPS says I should be there by five."

"Yay!" I squeal. "I hope you're wearing something cute! We can get pictures together."

"I'm wearing the corduroy pants and maroon sweater."

"Perfect," I reply. "And the suede purse?"

"Mhm."

We did a shopping spree makeover soon after becoming friends and her appearance has been much improved, especially with a new hijab-tying style. I've taken Shanzay under my wing, and she's all the better for it. I'm quite proud of myself and of her.

"There might be someone at the dinner for you to meet," I tease. Her gasp makes me laugh.

"Ee, okay, I am excited," she squeals.

"I'll see you soon!"

I decided to do some matchmaking for Shanzay; if I couldn't have love, she sure as hell would. After some time, I settled upon the perfect match: my cousin, Emad. He's twenty-five, from a good family (of course) and has a good job working in IT (though not *too* good a job). He is settled, but not too well-off that it would be difficult for Shanzay to adjust.

He and Shanzay will be well-suited.

Even though I am not close with Emad, for the past month and a half, I've been giving him gentle hints that he should look to get married, and he has responded quite ardently, which I am glad about.

I especially texted to make sure he was coming to

Phuppo's house for Thanksgiving dinner, and he sent back an enthusiastic three texts to inform me that he was.

Usually the Mirzas hosted Thanksgiving at my house, but that was back when Naadia, Phuppo, and I were a collective force. Now we're all spread out, and since Phuppo did most of the cooking anyways, she's taken over.

When we arrive in Phuppo's street, the sky is darkening, and it's nearly four o'clock. Zeeshan Uncle used to live in a luxury townhouse, but before getting married to Phuppo, they both chose a new house. It's a bit smaller than ours, but still adequately big enough for hosting, and is quite quaint and lovely.

The outside door is decorated with a wreath. I ring the doorbell, Naadia huddled close to my side to ward off the chill. She's wearing a thin suede jacket over her sweater, while I'm wearing my Loro Piana cape (not the one with the chinchilla fur around the collar and sleeves, I save that for more formal occasions), and the cashmere keeps me toasty as a bun in an oven.

A moment after we ring the bell, Phuppo throws open the door with a massive smile on her face. We squeal, hugging each other tight. I inhale her familiar scent of sweet rosemary, and my heart all but sighs from the comfort.

"Come in, come in!" Phuppo says.

"Phuppo! You look *amazing*!" I scream, taking her in.

"Your hair! And I *love* the suit!" Naadia chimes in.

"Oh, you girls," she says, waving a hand, but I can tell she appreciates it. Her hair is cut short in layers and blown out, and she is a total babe in black shalwar kameez with gold details and red lipstick lining her lips.

"Will I be allowed into the house at some point this evening?" Papa asks from behind us, shaking his head at the commotion.

"Yes, sir, please, come in," Zeeshan Uncle says, appearing at the door. Naadia and I giggle. It is so funny seeing Zeeshan Uncle be so flustered by Papa, who is unimpressed as ever and simply nods in response.

"I'll take those," Zeeshan Uncle says, reaching down to grab the bags of food we brought. We go inside, where the house is warm with the smell of cooking and candles. Zeeshan Uncle closes the door behind us, then holds out a hand to take Papa's blazer, but Papa shakes his head.

"No, no, I'll keep it on," he says. Papa puts a hand on Phuppo's head by greeting, smiling as he says, "Fizzu," and then we all head further into the house.

No one else is here yet, so Naadia and I busy ourselves chatting Phuppo's ear off as we all walk to the kitchen. The lights are on in all of the rooms, showing Phuppo and Zeeshan Uncle's artful decorating of their home; the theme is very elegant and modern country, with botanical touches and wooden furniture, all finished with pale pink and sage green accents.

I'm practically buzzing with the excitement of having us all together again. It's been a few weeks since we last all hung out.

"Ohmygod, everything looks sooo good," Naadia says,

when we enter the kitchen and see all the food set in chafing dishes.

"Truly amazing," I agree.

"Aw, thank you," Phuppo replies. "Now hopefully it tastes good, too. I still haven't lived down that dense banana bread I made two years ago."

Naadia and I laugh. "Papa literally still brings it up," Naadia says.

"Everytime I'm making banana bread, he says, 'And make sure you add baking soda! Not like that time Fizzu made it!'"

"One time!" Phuppo laments. "One time I forget the baking soda, and I have to hear about it forever."

We look at all the food Phuppo has prepared. She's made typical American food like roast chickens (no Pakistani likes turkey), mashed potatoes, steamed vegetables, stuffed shells, mac & cheese, and then also typical Pakistani food like gosht biryani, chicken karahi, and aloo palak. Dessert has the same treatment: pies for American and ras malai for Pakistani.

We're fine eating American food, but since Thanksgiving dinner includes all of our family that lives a drivable distance away, Phuppo made Pakistani food too.

Papa is one of six siblings. Starting from the eldest, it's Papa's one brother, my taya (who lives in Pakistan), then Shahnaz Phuppo (who also lives in Pakistan), Noor Phuppo, Zaineb Phuppo, Mahum Phuppo, then Papa, and lastly Phuppo, who's name is really Faiza.

All my phuppos (except one) live on Long Island or in

the city, so they're pretty close by. They're all grandmothers, their sons married with two to four children a piece, and when we are all together, it quickly becomes a madhouse.

As it does about an hour later, when all the other guests have arrived. (No Rizwan, yet, but I am still holding out hope.) Zeeshan Uncle has invited some of his friends as well, so the house is truly packed.

The little kids run around, screaming, while the uncles (plus Fawad – he really is an honorary uncle) are debating politics and the merits and flaws of Imran Khan (who used to be our neighbor in Islamabad! My Dadi was friends with Jemima). My phuppos are comparing daughters-in-law, while said daughters-in-law are discussing the chaos of their children.

My bhabis are really nice, but I'm not very close with them. Naadia sits and chats with them, now part of the married club, so I amble around, trying to find Emad.

Emad is Mahum Phupo's youngest, and my only cousin left unmarried – which I am hoping to remedy before the year is done. Two birds, one stone!

Some time ago his mother, my father's sister, entertained the notion of him marrying me, but that's a genetic disaster waiting to happen. (I should know – my best friend, Areeba, is a genetic counselor.)

I spot him with a couple of my other cousins, and wave him over. He immediately comes to my side. He has the typical Mirza looks: average height, thick black hair, and a hooked nose. He's dressed nicely in a sweater and dress shirt and is clean-shaven.

"Salaam!" I say. "How are you? I feel like I haven't seen you in so long! How's work going? And the new baby?" His brother just had another kid.

"I'm good! It's nice to see you, too. It has been a while." He smiles. "And that baby is definitely a jinn."

I laugh. "Ohmygod, stop. You can't say that about your nephew!"

"It's true!" He laughs. "Whenever I hold him, he doesn't cry, he just stares at me with these huge eyes. It's freaky."

"Well, I am sure he is puzzled at seeing such a strange specimen as yourself."

We chat a bit, then I get a text from Shanzay, saying she's here, so it's showtime. I bite back a grin. This is going to be lovely. Shanzay is going to fall in love and live happily ever after, and I'll have helped another loved one find their happiness.

"Okay, Emad, I have a mission for you," I say, tone getting serious. He inches closer, listening intently.

"What can I do?"

"My friend, Shanzay, is new in town, and I've invited her over," I explain. "But I must go help Phuppo in the kitchen, so will you be a darling and keep her company?" I bat my eyelashes. "She really is a sweet girl, and I think you'll get along very well! Oh, it would be such a favor to me, as she and I are so close. I would appreciate it so much."

"For you? Of course." He smiles sweetly.

"Yay!" I clap my hands. "Thank you."

I go to open the front door, letting Shanzay in. We squeal, hugging one another.

"You look great!" she tells me.

"So do you!" I say, taking in the sight of her. The pants are very flattering on her pear-shaped body. "Just one last thing." I reach into my pocket and fish out some lipstick. "Put some of this on," I whisper. She does as she is told, and now she's ready. (Lipstick truly is a life-saver. Never leave the house without it.) "Come with me."

I loop my arm through hers and introduce her to Phuppo and Naadia and the rest, then steer her back to the foyer, where Emad is waiting for us.

"That's him," I whisper. Shanzay giggles nervously, squeezing my arm.

"He's so dreamy," she whispers. What can I say? We're a family of good genetics. And it definitely helps that Emad has nice muscles that reveal just how much time (too much) he spends in the gym.

"Humaira," he says, when we grow close, "who's your friend?"

"Emad, this is Shanzay," I say, trying not to giggle. Oh, I am too clever! This is going to go splendidly. "Shan, this is my cousin, Emad."

"It's nice to meet you Shanzay," Emad says, smiling sweetly. "I hear you're new in town?"

"Yes, I'm actually a student..."

And that, dear friends, is the beginning.

Chapter Five

As they start chatting, I quietly retreat, pleased with myself. That business taken care of, I go to check on Papa. He is with the older trio of phuppos rather than sitting with the uncles or his nephews. He sits on the sofa between them, two on one side, one on the other, laughing. I smile.

Papa is in his prime when he is with women. By women, I mean his daughters, wife, nieces, and sisters. For Papa, we are simple and easily pleased. We wanted things like pretty desserts or a new sweater or some hot chocolate. This, Papa can handle. All he had to do was swipe the credit card. In return, we offered fun conversation and listened to his jokes and laughed and teased.

But the boys, i.e. his nephews? They were too difficult to figure out. And they didn't even laugh at his jokes, which was the greatest offense. Papa was too stressed about their futures, even my cousins who were working adults in the real world.

Papa had grown up with five sisters, so it made sense. He didn't even learn how to walk until he was two because there was always someone carrying him places, can you believe that? Plus, he used to cry if anyone ate even a bite of his paratha, then he'd demand a new one.

I mean, what a brat! (It's no wonder his kids are brats, too.)

Next, I go to see if Phuppo needs any help, but when I enter the kitchen, Zeeshan Uncle is there with her. They are both speaking in hushed tones over the roast chicken as he bastes it, their cheeks rosy as they laugh.

What a sight of domestic intimacy. It makes me want to cry. (Out of happiness for them of course. Not at all out of loneliness.)

I feel a little pang in my chest. (Because of how sweet it is.)

Not wanting to intrude, I go back to the family room, resolving to spend time with the babies.

"Humaira Phuppo," my four-year-old niece, Haniya, says approaching me. Her pigtails swing as she walks. "How you sleep?"

"What?" I ask, sitting on the sofa and leaning forward so we are eye level.

"How you sleep?" she asks again. "Like this? Like this?" She demonstrates different positions, then waits for my reply.

"Oh," I laugh. "I sleep like this." I demonstrate, and she nods, cataloging the information.

"Baji sleep like this," she informs me. Then she begins showing me how the rest of her siblings sleep, and Naadia joins in, after spending time with Asif.

"God, Haniya," Naadia says. "Are you spying on everyone while they sleep? What a little weirdo."

We laugh. Haniya asks Naadia how she sleeps, and after gaining the information, she is off again, skipping and pigtails swinging, probably to ask more people.

"Noor Phuppo brought meethe chawal," Naadia tells me. I groan. Noor Phuppo has diabetes, which means she barely adds sugar into the sweet rice dish, but insists we all eat it anyways, which of course we do, or the eldest phuppo would get offended. One never upsets one's phuppos; it's a cardinal rule of survival in a Pakistani family.

"At least we have my pies to push it down, later," I say.

"At least."

Then Naadia is off as well, going to go chat with our bhabis. I could join her, but I'm not really in the mood. She has always been the loquacious one, so I never got into the habit of being so talkative.

There cannot be two talkative sisters; someone must do the listening. I have always been happy to listen. Even as kids. Most nights, after the lights were off and we were told to sleep by Mama, Naadia would last about thirty seconds before sliding through our connecting bathroom to come to my room.

"Move over," she'd whisper, elbowing me. I would shift

over in my bed, making room for her as she slipped under the covers with me and told me every single little thing about all of her friends and classmates. I always loved listening.

After an hour or so, she'd finally slow down, speech slurring from tiredness, and if I had a comment, she'd tap my mouth with her hand, saying, "Shh, let's sleep now, I'm tired."

I didn't mind. She needed me to listen, so I would.

I miss those days. The simplicity of it.

With a sigh, I go to pick up my baby cousin, Aizah. She's eight months old, chubby, and so cute I want to mush her cheeks. She doesn't yet know how to crawl, though, so I resolve to teach her tonight.

"Come on Aizah, we can conquer this together," I say, setting her on the floor in a crawling position. I grab some chocolate and give her a taste, to which her eyes widen with excitement. "Come on!" I sit across from her and goad her with the chocolate, and she reaches for it with her hands but does not move to actually get it. "Come on, don't be lazy!"

"Torturing babies now, are we?" a deep voice asks. I look up from the floor to see Fawad, his dark eyes glittering with amusement. He's wearing a black suit with a crisp white shirt and skinny black tie, as if he's just walked off from an important meeting on Wall Street.

"I am trying to teach her how to crawl," I say, turning back to the baby. "Look she's almost got it!"

Aizah makes as if to move her legs, then falls onto her face. She lets out a cry.

"Dear god, stop tormenting the poor child," Fawad says, crouching down to pick her up. He stands and easily holds her with one arm, using his other hand to bop her nose. I stand up and watch, smiling fondly. I adore babies.

Fawad bops her nose again and she stops crying immediately, instead fascinated by his glasses.

"Oh no you don't." Fawad ducks to avoid her grabby little hands, and she giggles, but after another failed attempt, she gets fussy and starts to cry again, trying to launch herself out of Fawad's arms.

"I know what she needs," I say, holding out my arms for her. Fawad hands her over, and I go to sit on the sofa, Aizah sitting on my lap, her little head resting against my heart. Fawad sits beside me and watches as I massage Aizah's legs. After a few moments, she relaxes, sinking against me.

Fawad laughs. "Well done."

"Thank you, thank you." I bow my head. "I'll be here all night."

I lean back against the pillows, getting comfortable, and Fawad does, too.

"What have you been up to?" Fawad asks. "Have you gotten used to Faiza Baji being gone?"

"I don't think I'll ever get used to that, but it has gotten better," I reply. "I've been trying more baking recipes, but I think the people in my office are getting sick of all the leftovers."

"Hello, I'm down the road for a reason!" he says. "Just tell me next time, and I'll eat them all."

"That will surely be detrimental to your health."

"Don't worry, I work out." Yes, he rather looks like he does. I find it funny how boys always find a way to work their exercise regimes into conversation, but I would not have expected it from Fawad. *Hm.*

"I'll keep that in mind." I smile. "Are Auntie and Uncle coming soon?" I ask. "They usually come in the winter, right?"

Fawad bristles. He always grows a little tense at the mention of his parents, but whenever I mention it to Naadia, she says she hasn't noticed. I think he is so used to being alone, he finds it difficult when they come.

"Yes, they're coming in a few weeks," he says. Before I can inquire further, he changes the subject. "What did you make today?"

"I made two pies."

"Did you make the crust from scratch? Isn't that sort of tricky?"

"It is, but…"

Aizah falls asleep in my arms while Fawad and I chat about random, mundane things. I laugh as he tells me about the new tenants he went to visit, and how the auntie who answered the door thought he was an FBI agent, come to collect her husband because he apparently hasn't paid his taxes for the past few years.

As infuriating as Fawad is sometimes, some days, like today, he is shockingly good company. I am comfortable around him, just the way I am with family members, and I suppose, in a way, he is family, since Asif and Naadia are married.

Not that I think of him as a brother. But on days like today, I do think of him as a friend.

After a little while, Papa approaches us, and the moment he sees Fawad, his face falls. I'm immediately alarmed, until I catch Papa scanning Fawad's outfit, and I instantly know what his gripe is.

Papa shoots me an accusatory glare. "Why didn't you let *me* wear a suit!" He exclaims.

"You can never go wrong with a suit, I always say," Fawad interjects, adding insult to injury.

"Precisely my opinion," Papa agrees, giving me a look. I roll my eyes.

"Was there something you wished to discuss with Fawad, Papa?" I ask, standing with Aizah in my arms. Her head rests against my shoulder; my heart squeezes with warmth. I adore babies so much.

"Yes, about that investment…"

As he and Fawad begin to discuss, I leave to take Aizah back to her mother. As I go back to the family room, another child runs into my legs, nearly knocking me over. Naadia makes eye contact with me during this encounter, and after I've dropped the sleeping baby off, I reconvene with my sister.

"What a nightmare," Naadia says, handing me a glass of apple cider. "Children are absolute menaces."

"They aren't so bad," I protest, grabbing some muenster cheese, raspberry jam, and crackers from the cheese board.

"Asif wants to try soon, but I told him not until I've

finished residency," Naadia says. She is in her last year of medical school and getting matched this March.

"Well, if you have one before then, leave the child to me. I'll be an excellent khala." I've always loved children and cannot wait to have my own. Yet another reason I wish to be married already. If not for the man, then for the babies.

"Don't worry, I will," Naadia says with a snort. "But just give me a few years."

I pout. "I want one sooner." I shake her arms. If there was a baby, the house wouldn't be so empty.

"You work every day, you crazy lady," Naadia reminds me, shaking my arms back.

"I could work from home! I am nothing if not a dedicated khala."

"My unborn child appreciates the enthusiasm. But still no."

"Oh, come on! You know Papa is dying to be a grandfather. I'm sure it'll even make him like Asif again."

We both laugh. "I don't think anything will make him like Asif again."

"A baby might," I sing-song. "Papa always says the best part of his life was when I was a baby and you were a toddler."

"You mean when we would both be up screaming and crying all night long?" Naadia would always respond when Papa said that. Papa would sigh wistfully.

"How I miss those days."

He preferred it to our teenage years, which were quite angsty, particularly on the part of Miss Naadia. I mean, she went as far as to get a nose piercing, despite Papa's express dislike for it. (The piercing is gone now, but it was a wild six-month period.)

"Imagine if the baby looks like Asif, though?" Naadia says, eyes widening. "Papa wouldn't be able to cope."

"You're right about that," I say, grimacing at the thought. "Best to hold off, then."

"The man is crazy."

"That he is," I agree. But we adore him anyway. "I am going to go find some chocolate," I tell Naadia, going toward the pantry, but as I approach, I hear hushed voices.

Perhaps I should not eavesdrop, but then I hear a familiar voice and cannot resist.

"She seems like a perfectly nice girl, but I'm afraid the friendship will only play to Humaira's vanity," Fawad is saying. I inch closer, brows furrowed.

"Surely a few compliments will not corrupt our dear Humaira," Phuppo replies, voice light.

"It's not that," Fawad argues. "Humaira has always been the most clever and most beautiful girl in the room, but her vanity lies elsewhere. Shanzay will play into that vanity, and I'm worried it'll cause harm."

"I disagree," Phuppo replies. "Even if Shanzay feeds her vanity, I think it is good for Humaira to have a companion close by." She pauses. "Humaira is lonely, Fawad, more so than she will ever let on, even to me—lonelier than you could imagine."

There's a quiet pause. Then Fawad's voice, soft and sad, "Trust me, I can imagine."

An emotion I do not wish to identify skims through me, followed by shadowed thoughts I do not wish to see the true shape of.

Not wanting to hear any more, I retreat, back to Naadia.

"No chocolate?" she asks, frowning. I shake my head.

"Tell me about rotations," I say, forcing my face and voice to brighten. "Wasn't someone having an affair with the attending? What happened with that?"

"Ohmygod, I didn't tell you? It's the wildest thing…" She launches into a story I eagerly lose myself to until a little while later, Phuppo's voice carries throughout the house.

"Everyone, please come eat!" Phuppo says, calling us to where the food is arranged. As everyone gathers around the buffet, Phuppo comes over to me and puts an arm around my shoulder, pulling me a little to the side.

"He isn't coming," she whispers.

My heart sinks. I know who she is referring to, and while I had told myself not to get my hopes up, I am still disappointed, more so than I should be.

What a waste of a good outfit.

"Who?" Naadia asks, confused. She was standing right beside me and heard.

"Rizwan," Phuppo whispers. I blink rapidly, swallowing the lump in my throat. I know it is silly, but there's another chance at love struck down.

Perhaps I am being punished for all the hearts I have broken. I never meant it, of course, but I know I have been callous with boys' feelings. In my defense, I didn't lead them on intentionally, I genuinely did think I might grow to like them, and then I never did.

And I am not proud of all the boys' hearts I've broken. I could never be proud of hurting anyone.

Plenty of boys have confessed their feelings for me through the years, plenty of perfectly reasonable boys I am sure Phuppo and Papa would have been content to marry me off to. But I just didn't love them, not as I should.

I did not wish to marry someone merely *tolerable*; I wanted true love. The grand, sweeping, all-consuming love.

Sometimes I feel like my heart is broken, not hurt, but in function, as if I am incapable of love. As if it will never happen.

But I cannot let my thoughts wander down that road, cannot let myself think that, or I will stop believing, and I believe in love with the whole of my heart. I believe in it as surely as I believe in God.

It is an extension, you see. There is love because there is God. So if I cease to believe in love, it means I no longer believe in God, and I will not allow that to happen. What would be the point of living without faith?

And I know plenty of people go through life without love, that it does not work out for most – I am not so naive as to not know this. But I believe there is love written specifically for me, because of the way I am wired.

It might not be written for everyone else, but I know that I have to have it, or I will not survive. Perhaps that is arrogant of me, to assume that I deserve it – but I just know I cannot do without it. I cannot.

I will not.

"Are you alright?" Phuppo asks me. I've lost myself in this train of thought, staring off into the distance. I shake the thoughts away, coming back to the clatter and clamor of the kitchen as people fill their plates with food from the buffet. I smile enthusiastically at Phuppo.

"Yes, of course," I respond. Phuppo kisses my cheek.

"That's my girl. Now, come and eat," she says.

"In a moment. You go on."

Phuppo goes to make sure everyone is properly taking food. I expect Naadia to go with her, but she lingers with me, frowning at the consternation on my countenance.

"You shouldn't be so disappointed," she says. "You don't even know him."

"I'm not," I reply, voice indignant. I don't like her tone. "Really, it's fine."

But Naadia keeps going, voice low as people pass us to grab plates. I don't look at her. Instead, I smile at one of my cousin's kids, waving eagerly.

"You have to stop holding out hope for some magic mystery man who doesn't exist," Naadia says. "Real life and love are not like that. You make the best out of what is around you. Respect and companionship are much more important than whatever ridiculous notions you have of some great romantic love story."

I am once again reminded of the astronomical levels of hatred I can feel for my sister. I turn toward her, eyes sharp.

"Don't condescend," I say, tone biting. "It doesn't suit you."

"Well, I am married and you are not, so I know about these things."

I scoff. "The marriage card is getting old now."

"It will never get old," she says. "Besides, I knew more about these things than you did even before I was married."

Because you were careless with your heart! I want to scream, but I hold my tongue, releasing a long, long breath instead. I have always been careful with my heart, which is why I have avoided such distasteful situations and never been as heartbroken as she had.

"You're so pessimistic," I complain.

"No, Humaira," my sister argues, "I'm just *realistic*."

I'm about to respond when Fawad passes by with a plate of food. Seeing our pinched expressions, he stops.

"Are the sisters in need of a referee?" he asks pleasantly, dark eyes sparkling behind his glasses. I try to keep my eye from twitching. Just what I need!

"No, go away," I say, not wanting to involve him. He steps closer, joining our little conference. "Really, it's—"

"Humaira is upset because Rizwan could not come," Naadia interjects. I whip toward her.

"Naadia!"

"You have to tell her she should lower her expectations of love," Naadia continues, "to save her the disappointment."

"But who can convince her the glasses she sees through are rose-tinted?" he replies, speaking as if I am not there. I do not appreciate his cavalier tone. He says it as if I am a rosy-eyed fool, as if I am nonsensical and cannot be made to see sense.

"I don't mind being a romantic fool," I say, voice icy, "if it means putting my heart on the line. Unlike someone who is resolved to be cold and unfeeling."

He releases a mirthless laugh. My heartbeat quickens violently. I consider upending his plate all over his pristine white shirt and stupid tie.

"Yes," he says, "and how glad I am for it, if it keeps me from making a fool of myself."

He steps back, shaking his head. I curl my hands into fists, nails biting into my palms. I want to yell at him, but he seems to have already dismissed me, about to walk away.

"Just when I was beginning to think you were tolerable," I say. "Thank you for the reminder of what a total ass you are."

Something about Fawad makes me drop all facades and deal simply with truths and raw emotion. I detest being so out of control.

It's as if the remark does not reach him. He does not even turn. He leaves without another word, as if what I said meant nothing.

I hate that! And he knows as much.

"Humaira!" Naadia scolds, grabbing my elbow. "You can't talk to him like that!"

"Leave me alone," I say, throwing her off me. I glare at her. "I'll talk to him however I please."

Naadia always did this, acted like the older sister when

it suited her, not when it really mattered. But I don't let myself think further on that, or I will get really upset.

Instead, I walk away and go to the bathroom, focusing on the sound of my heels clicking on the tiles until I've reached my destination and shut the door. In the silence, I hear the sound of my own heavy breathing and look up in the mirror.

When I do, I am shocked by my appearance. My cheeks are flushed and there is a scowl curling my lips.

I flatten out my expression, doing breathing exercises to calm myself down. Running my hands under cold water, I let the sound of rushing water relax me. I undo my hijab and then my hair, shaking out the strands and massaging my scalp. When the pounding in my head has quieted, I redo my hair, then refasten my hijab.

There, everything is in place once more. I touch up my lipstick, then examine my reflection to find that my cheeks are no longer red, just lightly rosy from my makeup, and my expression is calm.

I am good-natured enough for company once more.

After a reassuring smile in the mirror, I go to check on Shanzay. She and Emad are sitting at the dining table together, eating and talking and laughing. Shanzay giggles often, and she keeps looking away, shy.

Aw. There's something so magical about love: even witnessing others experience it fills me with joy.

"Shanzay," I call. She looks up as if in a daze, then smiles at me.

"Oh, Humaira!" she says, waving.

"Come join us," Emad says.

"Yes, I believe I will," I reply. "I was just going to grab some food first."

"You want me to get you something?" Emad asks, already pushing his chair back.

"No, no, thank you," I say. "But, Shan, will you join me?"

She nods, then comes with me. Emad sends a dazzling smile our way, and Shanzay blushes.

"It's already going so well!" I say to Shanzay, once we are out of Emad's sight. I squeeze her arm, feeling buoyant. "He's being most attentive … and the way he looks at you!"

"No – do you really think so?" Shanzay asks with a little gasp. I nod, and she covers her face with her hands. "He's so smart and nice," Shanzay says. "You're so kind to introduce me to him. Really, Humaira. I don't know what I'd do without you."

"Oh, think nothing of it," I say, putting mashed potatoes onto my plate, then a piece of chicken, and some roasted vegetables. "And a quick note: when you take dinner, it's prudent not to mix cuisines. It looks distasteful."

"I didn't realize," Shanzay says, growing serious. "I've never been to such a fancy dinner before."

"Don't worry, it's hardly a damning mistake, just something to be mindful of," I advise. "It's also best to take small amounts, then replenish your plate later. That way you don't have a gigantic mound of food sitting before you."

"Got it, got it." Shanzay nods, making mental notes.

"Oh! Most important of all: *never* pour raita over your biryani." I shudder. "It is the highest offense in this family. You are lucky none of the elder phuppos saw you or they surely would have blanched."

"God," Shanzay whispers, mortified. "I'm so sorry."

"No, it's alright, don't be embarrassed," I reassure her with a laugh.

"You're a lifesaver," Shanzay says. "Thank you, for everything."

"Of course!" I say happily. We head to the drinks table, where I grab a soda.

"Humaira, I wonder..." Shanzay breaks off, looking away. "It's silly."

"What is it?" I ask, curious. "You must say so now that you have piqued my interest."

"Well, it's only that." She pauses, biting her lip. "I wonder that you're not married yet. You're so accomplished and beautiful and clever; I imagine every eligible bachelor in a hundred mile radius would ask for your hand."

"Oh, that." I laugh, waving a hand. "No one has yet caught my eye," I say, tone nonchalant. I consider it further. "And why should I hurry to marry when I live in the utmost comfort? I believe a marriage should improve one's life, and luckily, I already have a near perfect life. So I won't marry unless it's to the great love of my life, really."

"That makes sense," Shanzay says. "You don't need a husband at all."

"Precisely." Though *need* and *want* were two very different things.

We make it back to the table, where Emad instantly grows animated upon seeing us.

"I tried your pies," Emad tells me. "They're so good. I need, like, a hundred of them in my freezer."

"It's nothing really," I say quickly. "You should try Shanzay's cookies one day! They are simply heavenly."

"I guess I'll just have to," Emad agrees.

We continue talking, and I wait until Emad is in the middle of an animated story to slip away on excuse of getting dessert. Instead, I go to Phuppo, who is sitting with the bhabis, but she is not listening to their conversation.

Rather, her gaze is upon the babies sleeping in their little bundles. There is a wistful expression on her face.

I sit with her on the sofa, and she shifts over to make room for me. I squeeze in beside her and lean my head on her shoulder. She places a hand on my cheek, holding me close. (What did I say earlier? Phuppo can always be counted on for a cuddle.)

"Tell me about work," she says, pulling back to look at me. "What projects are you working on? Mahmud Bhai mentioned something earlier about a new donut shop?"

"Yes! It's a new franchise, and they sent us some donuts to sample. They're so yummy," I say. "Next time, I'll bring you some, there's this one lemon-raspberry one..."

I fall into the easy rhythm of speaking with Phuppo, and a little while later, Naadia joins us as well. Naadia, who went away to college while I commuted, was never as close to Phuppo as I am, but the three of us are still a happy trio when we are together nevertheless.

Any tension between Naadia and I from earlier is gone; it's the way of sisters. I was ready to rip her hair out a little over thirty minutes ago, but with a quick shared glance, we're back to normal. We bounce back with alacrity. Not before long, we are all laughing together, just like old times.

But then, eventually, as the night grows darker, the guests begin to leave. I do not see Fawad before he leaves. He slips away, and something in me hurts when I find he is gone.

I hate to leave things unresolved and unpleasant. Why is he so grouchy when it comes to the matter of Rizwan, anyway? It's one thing for Naadia to be concerned on my behalf, to be upset at seeing me constantly disappointed, but what does he care?

I suppose I'll never know.

Papa and I are the last guests to leave, Papa sitting in front of the fire, Zeeshan Uncle awkwardly trying (and failing) to make conversation with him while Phuppo and I put all the food away.

"Come, now, we should get going," Papa finally says to me and Phuppo. "Fizzu, Humaira, get your coats."

"Papa," I say gently. "This is Phuppo's house, now."

He startles, as if forgetting that Phuppo is in fact married. He frowns once the realization strikes him. "Well, then, you get your coat. It is getting late."

"Mahmud Bhai, let Humaira stay the night," Phuppo says, putting an arm around me. I lean into her, mirroring the act. "You can pick her up in the morning."

I nod. I want to stay. I don't want to go home. Naadia

will be at the Sheikhs's with Asif, since she dislikes leaving him for even one night. (Yes, they are one of *those* couples.)

"I suppose. Alright," Papa says, drawing out the word, hoping I will change my mind. I do feel bad leaving Papa alone, but perhaps the change in scenery for one night will help settle this ache in me.

"I'll see you in the morning," I say, putting his cashmere scarf around his neck. I kiss his cheek. "Goodnight, Papa."

"Goodnight, jaani."

After he's gone, Phuppo and I make qahwa and sit sipping and talking for a while in the living room while Zeeshan Uncle retires upstairs. The house is quiet without all the guests but still warm and cozy.

"I am so happy," Phuppo tells me, smiling into her hand. "I could have never imagined it. He is such a great man."

"That makes me so glad for you," I say, heart warming from her happiness.

"I was so nervous because even though we were compatible and got along well before the wedding, I wasn't sure about the ... chemistry," she says. We both giggle. "It is an important thing and cannot be manufactured."

"You guys have excellent chemistry," I inform her. "I saw you two earlier."

"Yes, we rather do, don't we?" Her eyes have a dreamy quality to them. "I know you don't believe it, but sometimes these things do develop after marriage."

"It isn't that I don't believe it, for I am sure they do," I say, "it's just that I don't believe it will work that way for me."

"Yes, perhaps," Phuppo says. We continue chatting, but a little while later I see Zeeshan Uncle peek his head in, then duck out the moment I notice him. I laugh.

"I think your husband is looking for you," I whisper.

Phuppo giggles. "He can wait."

But I can tell she is keen to go to him, too, so I tell her to go.

"Are you sure?"

I nod. "I'm sleepy, too."

As she exits and meets Zeeshan Uncle in the hall, he reaches out for her hand. She hesitates, glancing at me, all shy, and it makes me smile. I look away, heart pinching.

It reminds me of this one time we were in the city walking around after a fancy dinner out, Naadia and I in the front, Mama and Papa behind us. I turned back to make sure Mama and Papa were still close behind and found them holding hands.

But the instant I registered the sight, Papa quickly retracted his hand from Mama's, not wanting me to see. Mama made an elaborate show of rolling her eyes, and I laughed, knowing she wanted to yell, "Kya hai! We're *married*!"

They were always alternating between who was the affectionate one and who was the abashed one. But there was never any doubt that they both loved each other very dearly.

Releasing a long breath, I head up to the guest room,

where I change into a new set of pajamas Phuppo has kept in the closet for me for impromptu sleepovers such as this. The guest bathroom has my usual La Mer skincare stuff and my favorite papaya hand lotion, too. Oh, how Phuppo spoils me.

I get into bed, but after some time, find that I cannot sleep.

Rain begins to fall outside as I toss and turn, thinking I should have had Papa go back with Naadia and leave the car for me so I could have gone home, but Papa wouldn't have agreed. He does not like me driving so late at night.

Sensing that sleep will not come so easily, I get out of bed and head downstairs to make some chamomile tea. The sound of raindrops against the windows mingles with the sound of the kettle.

When my tea is ready, I sit, pressing my palms against the cold countertops. Then, I warm them against my mug, holding the mug up my cheeks, to my chest.

I close my eyes and listen to the rain, the pitter-patter, the drop ... drop ... drop.

I hear a rattling.

My eyes open. I wonder if I'm hearing things.

Then I hear it again, and it's the front door – not a rattling, but knocking.

I look at the clock in the kitchen. The blue numbers glow to inform me it's nearly two in the morning.

Who could it be? I do not think Zeeshan Uncle will stir; I can hear him snoring.

Grabbing a scarf and wrapping it to cover my hair, I

head to the foyer. I hesitate for a moment; what if it's a burglar or something? But surely a burglar wouldn't knock. With a shrug, I open the door.

And see a gorgeous man completely soaked through with rain. I know immediately who it is.

Rizwan Ali.

Chapter Six

"You're not Shani Chacha," Rizwan says, a slow smile spreading across his face. That *accent*. God, I love the English.

"Is that so?" I reply, raising an amused brow. "I hadn't noticed."

"Well, if you are, you're much more beautiful than I remember," he says, eyes gleaming. He pushes a hand through his wet hair, and my stomach does a little somersault. It's really him! "Can I come in please? I'm afraid I've brought the rain with me from London, and it i getting terribly cold out here."

"I don't think it would be wise of me to let a stran man into the house," I say. Dimples indent into his che which sit between the highest cheekbones and sharpes I have seen on this side of the ocean (rivaling only Fa – wait a second, where the hell did *that* come fro don't have time for intrusive thoughts right now!).

His dark brown skin is smooth and beardless, drawing more attention to his mouth and his perfect teeth when he smiles.

"I'm Rizwan," he says, shocked I do not know who he is. (Of course I know who he is! I'm only pretending. Hehe.) "Surely the man who owns this house has mentioned me before?"

"Zeeshan Uncle mentions plenty of boys," I say cavalierly, "though I do not recall anything memorable about you."

"If you let me in, I assure you I will spend the rest of my time here being memorable." Oh, that accent is like butter melting in the pan of my heart. I try not to grin and shiver instead.

"See!" he says, noticing. "Even you seem to be catching a cold. Let me in now and save us both."

I step aside, granting him entrance, and he drips on the carpet in front of me, dropping down a wet leather duffel bag. His brown hair is darkened from the rain, but his hazel-green eyes are alert and lively as he takes in the quiet house, the darkened rooms.

"Zeeshan Uncle and Phuppo are asleep," I inform him, closing the door.

"Phuppo!" he exclaims, snapping his fingers. "You must be Humaira. Shani Chacha has told me about you."

"All good things, I hope," I say sweetly.

"But of course." He slips off his shoes. "From what I ave heard, there are no bad things to tell."

"All girls have some secrets," I respond, being coy, even though I don't have any interesting secrets at all. But he doesn't need to know that.

I begin walking toward the stairs, and he follows.

"Now I am intrigued," he replies, as I climb the first steps. "You must tell me, for I love a good secret."

"You'll have to earn it," I reply, turning around. We are eye level now. He devours the sight of me, then laughs, shaking his head.

"You are somehow even more charming than Shani Chacha described," he says.

"You do not know the half of it." I continue to climb the stairs, biting back a smile, and he follows. When we have reached the second floor, I lead him to one of the guest rooms and open the door.

"I've already taken the best guest room for myself," I inform him unrepentantly, "so you'll have to settle for second best."

"I never settle," he replies, "but in this case, I will graciously bow out, only for your sake." He enters the room and sets down his duffel bag, then turns around, hand on the doorframe. He leans forward, and my heart rate skyrockets. "I'm going to clean up, but I'm positively famished. Would there be any food left from your silly holiday?"

"Yes, there is, in the kitchen downstairs."

He does not hesitate. "Excellent. Can I expect your company?"

My heart hammers. It is definitely not proper to have a middle-of-the-night meal with this gorgeous, wet man, but who am I to refuse such lucrative opportunities when they arrive? A girl would not want to appear as being ungrateful.

"It would be quite sad to eat alone after a seven-hour flight and numerous delays," he says, sensing my hesitation. He adds in a pout for good measure. Ya Allah.

"Sure," I say. He grins.

"Perfect. See you soon." He disappears into his room, and I walk back to my own, which is shockingly close to his. Quietly, I close the door and rest against it, my heart beating fast, much too fast.

Pressing cold fingers against my cheeks, I try to steady my breathing.

Once I have regained some semblance of cool, I check the mirror. My face is flushed, turning my cheeks rosy, and the pajamas are cute enough. I put on some tinted Chapstick and curl my eyelashes for good measure. I exchange the scarf for another one that falls more nicely, then head downstairs.

In the kitchen, I find my abandoned, half-full teacup and reheat it. Soon after, I hear footsteps coming down the stairs, and I very purposefully do not turn; rather I sit and sip my tea.

"Hello again," he says, rounding the counter until he faces me. I wonder if that accent will ever get old. Certainly not tonight.

His hair is still wet, though this time from a shower, and he wears a t-shirt that shows off well-formed biceps and what Naadia and I like to refer to as a Dorito: broad shoulders, slim waist. (He certainly looks as delicious as the snack.)

"Hello," I say. Setting my teacup down, I get up and open the fridge, taking out the boxes of leftovers and spreading them on the counter. "Would you like American or desi?"

"Hm, so many decisions," he says, coming to stand beside me to inspect the food. He smells clean and fresh and very masculine.

I catch my breath when he leans in close to look over my shoulder. As he does, a bead of water drops from his head onto my collarbone through my scarf. I involuntarily shiver.

If I turned, we would surely be in an embrace. The thought alone makes my stomach twist with excitement.

Lord. I am being tested.

Instead of turning, I step to the side, away from him. I can feel his gaze on me as I walk over to retrieve a plate from the cabinet. His eyes remain on me even after I hand it to him and sit back down at the countertop, slipping a hand around my teacup once more.

"The microwave is just over there," I inform him.

"Ah, thank you." He makes himself a plate of food and sets it to reheat before putting the boxes back in the fridge. The microwave beeps, and he comes to sit beside me, then digs in. "Mm, this is good."

"To be fashionably late is one thing," I say, turning slightly to face him. "But this is another thing entirely."

He laughs, and his eyes crinkle when he does. Cute.

"There were terrible delays," he explains. "Then, when I finally arrived, I found my phone was dead, and I'd forgotten my charger entirely. It was a good thing I knew the address to tell the cabdriver."

"What a story," I say, sipping my tea, which has sadly reached its end. I stand, going to put it in the sink. "As entertaining as this all was, I am rather sleepy. Goodnight."

His face falls as he watches me make to exit the kitchen. "You can't leave," he says, frowning quite adorably. "I haven't even finished eating!"

"My company is not so easily won," I say, without turning around. I wave a hand over my shoulder. "Goodnight."

"I will win you over, yet," he says. I smile to myself, still not turning, despite how much I want to, then head up the stairs towards bed. He does not follow.

When I close the guest room door, I let out a little squeal of excitement.

Oh, he is everything I had imagined he would be! Handsome, clever, funny … and what a spectacular first meeting!

This is the very best part: the initial excitement, the flirting, the wondering. In my experience, the mystery is the most fun. (After you get to know them, men can be quite uninteresting.)

With a dramatic sigh, I fall backwards on my bed, stretching like a contented cat. Perhaps true love is not so far away.

The next morning, I wake up to the sound of knocking on the door. I moan in response as the door opens and Phuppo enters.

"Jaagooooo, hua saveraaa," she sings in Urdu. "Good morning, jaani."

She opens the blinds as I blink away the last vestiges of sleep, recalling where I am, what day it is, and most importantly, what happened before I fell asleep.

"You must wake up," Phuppo says, voice excited. "Guess who is here."

My grogginess immediately vanishes the moment I remember last night's ... adventure. An apt word if anything.

My heart quickens just at the memories. I shiver involuntarily at the phantom touch of a bead of water on my collar.

I bite back a laugh and cover my mouth with my blanket. "I already know!" I squeal. Phuppo gasps and promptly shuts the door. She rushes to the bed.

"Tell me *everything*."

I make room for her, and she climbs in with me, not caring about wrinkling her new shalwar kameez. I giggle as I detail last night's events, highlighting my most clever lines, and Phuppo reacts appropriately, releasing little shrieks and squeezing my arm.

"While as your phuppo and elder, I must say I do not

condone the inherent inappropriate nature of a late-night rendezvous," Phuppo says, tone serious for a moment, "as your dearest friend and self-labeled cool aunt, I absolutely love this for you!" She grins.

With an exhale I fall back onto my pillow, staring at the ceiling with the stupidest grin on my face. Having a crush is so fun! I am overwhelmed with exhilaration.

"Now, come, we must go to breakfast," Phuppo says, pinching my cheek. She gets out of bed and heads for the door.

"I'll be down soon," I assure her, getting up as well. She leaves as I wash up and get ready in my clothes from yesterday sans some of the jewelry. When I arrive downstairs, Zeeshan Uncle, Phuppo, and Rizwan are sitting at the smaller dining table adjoining the kitchen.

"Assalaamualaikum," I say, entering.

"Walaikumassalaam," Zeeshan Uncle replies merrily. "Humaira, this is my nephew, Rizwan. He's here on business from England."

Finally, I turn to look at Rizwan's face, and my breath hitches. He is just as beautiful as I remember, if not more so. A string of exclamation points run through my head.

"Pleased to meet you," he says, smiling benignly, though there is mischief glittering in his eyes. So we are pretending last night did not occur – good plan of action.

Zeeshan Uncle would freak out at the thought of his nephew in a late-night assignation with me because Papa would surely kill (or hire someone to kill) him for allowing such a thing to occur beneath his roof.

"Salaam." I say, going to sit next to Phuppo, in the seat across from Rizwan. "I'm glad to see you're at least punctual for this meal."

He smiles a golden smile that I am sure has gotten him out of scoldings from teachers and law enforcement alike. "Yes, my flight was delayed, so I unfortunately missed dinner." He turns the smile to Phuppo. "Faiza Chachi, I do hope you can forgive me for missing your delicious food."

One thing is for certain: the accent has most definitely not gotten old. I kick Phuppo lightly under the table, and she quickly kicks back.

"No worries at all," Phuppo replies, turning to Rizwan. "I'm just glad you could make it for the weekend." As she butters her toast, she glances at me, then back at him, biting back a smile. I try not to laugh, stirring sugar into my chai.

We busy ourselves with breakfast, while Rizwan delves into further details about his horrific flight, and Phuppo and I tell stories about the babies from yesterday, highlighting my progress in teaching Aizah how to crawl and Haniya's inquiries about various family members' sleeping positions.

Zeeshan Uncle finishes the last of his juice, then puts his napkin on the table.

"When you're done, meet me in the office," he says, standing. "I'd like to get started right away."

"Yes, of course," Rizwan replies. Then he glances at me with widened eyes, "Work, work, work!" I smile, amused.

When Zeeshan Uncle leaves, Phuppo picks up his plate and her own, taking them to the kitchen, but not before wiggling her eyebrows at me in a most indiscreet manner.

Despite being the "cool aunt", she can be tactless at times.

It's just Rizwan and I after she's gone, and of course it isn't inappropriate because she's just in the next room, but even so, I feel my heart quickening nervously. His gaze is on me, and I muster up the courage to look back.

He smiles, hazel eyes warm. While I personally have no gripes with my dark brown eyes, I must admit his eyes are beautiful, all mixed in with gold and green. Pakistani men are usually blessed with nice eyelashes as well, and he's no exception.

I smile back, feeling as though I must think of something clever to say at once. But just as Rizwan opens his mouth to break the silence, Phuppo is back.

"Mahmud Bhai is here to pick you up," she says, giving me a sorry expression before leaving again to get the door.

Drat. Great timing, Papa!

I stand, and Rizwan does too, the sound of chairs scraping back filling the silence.

"You're leaving?" he asks, voice disappointed. "So soon?"

"Yes, my father is here," I reply, voice just as dispirited.

"But I have not yet been given an opportunity to make myself memorable." He pouts, then recovers to say, "I'm here until Sunday. I hope we'll see each other again?"

"Perhaps," I reply casually, as if I couldn't be bothered either way. I flash him a final demure smile before heading towards Phuppo at the front door.

"Allah hafiz," Phuppo says, hugging me tight. We share a giggle, and then I'm out into the cold toward Papa waiting for me in the car.

Chapter Seven

"Where is your scarf?" Papa asks, just as I open the car door. Heat blasts onto my face as I sit down.

"I must have left it," I reply, hand on the door handle. "I'll just go grab it quickly."

"No!" Papa cries, horrified at the prospect. "Do not go out into the cold again. There is an extra one in the glove compartment."

I should have known as much. Papa is perpetually catching cold and is always fussing over us to stay properly warm. Even now, with the heat on full blast, he is sitting in his coat and neck scarf tied tight.

"You girls are so thoughtless, sometimes," Papa huffs, looking at the rearview mirror as we back out of the driveway. "I cannot imagine how a twenty-three-year-old could be so careless. Honestly."

I give Papa a curious glance. He is frowning as he drives, his face scrunched and crinkled. He must be in a mood. Usually when this occurs, it is best to act as if nothing is amiss.

"Why did you come so early?" I ask, ignoring his little comment. "Have you eaten breakfast yet?"

"Early!" he scoffs. "Ten in the morning is hardly *early*. Half the day is gone! Early, she says!"

Most definitely in a *mood*, then. I want to point out the turn he must make, but while he is ordinarily awful at directions, this is one route he has memorized well. Once Phuppo got engaged, he mapped out various ways to reach Zeeshan Uncle's house and even went as far as to practice driving back and forth.

Zeeshan Uncle would always tell Papa to come in for some coffee or fruit, since Papa had driven all the way, to which Papa would give him a bewildered expression and promptly refuse, as if he could not fathom wanting to spend one-on-one time with his dearest sister's fiancé.

"Did you eat, then?" I ask. "We can get bagels on the way home." Bagels always placate him.

"I had a banana," he says, voice softening. "But if you want a bagel, we can stop." Papa never says what *he* wants outright, but I know him enough to understand what I should say next.

"Yes, I desperately want a bagel. We must stop."

"If you insist."

When we get to the bagel shop close to our house, we stop to pick up our usuals, which is an everything bagel with light cream cheese for me, and a toasted cinnamon raisin bagel with butter for Papa. When Papa is out of earshot, I instruct the bagel-boy to put less butter on, for Papa's health.

"Isn't this nice, beta jaani?" Papa says, when we get home. "Now why would Naadia want to miss out on such fun?"

Ah. So this is about Naadia. I could have guessed as much, had my mind not been replaying every interaction and word I had with Rizwan in the past twelve hours.

It must have been something Naadia said or the way she said it. Or both. I'll have to interrogate her once my bagel is done.

It used to be easier when Mama was alive because it appeared as though I was Mama's favorite, and Naadia was Papa's, so things were very neat and even.

Of course, you cannot say as such to Naadia for she will vehemently deny it. She claims I was Mama *and* Papa's favorite, but it's just not true. Sure, they adored me, but I could never get away with even half of what she does. I was loved because I made myself lovable, it was as simple as that. I was adored because I did not screw up.

I don't mean to be cocky, and obviously I screwed up sometimes, such as little mistakes, but nothing major enough for Mama to do her dramatic sigh for three days straight while muttering to herself.

But no matter what Naadia did, no matter how upset Mama was, Mama would always make amends, pulling Naadia out of her sullen mood and relenting until Naadia was smiling and happy again.

Papa was easier because he didn't – and still doesn't –

have any favorites. I mean, truly. Yes, all parents say that, but he is always honest, so I know he is not lying when he says we both have a special place. Naadia because she was the first, and me because I was the last.

"Naadia is coming for lunch, is she not?" I ask gently, as we both eat our bagels in the kitchen. She was to stay over at the Sheikhs's house last night with Asif, then meet us for lunch today.

"No, she is not." Papa scowls. "Something about her and Asif getting a reservation at some fancy restaurant. Now, who would choose a restaurant over her own dear old father? Very strange, if you ask me. I'll be dead soon, dead! And then she'll be sorry."

"Tch, Papa, don't say that," I scold, squeezing his arm. I know he is only being dramatic, as Pakistani parents love to be cavalier about their deaths, but the prospect is something I don't even want to consider, let alone grapple with.

And on the topic of Naadia: *She's going with her husband,* I want to say, but I know it's still a sensitive topic for Papa that Naadia is no longer only his. It does not help that Naadia does not handle Papa with the delicacy required, which is quite a bit, for he is a very sensitive man.

Too sensitive at times, if you ask me, but he is *my* Papa, after all.

Even when Asif's rishta for Naadia came, Papa was in quite a state. After the Sheikh family had left from a lovely dinner, Naadia, Phuppo, and I sat discussing the events of the night with Papa, asking what our next move should be regarding the proposal.

"Proposal?" Papa repeated, confused. "This was merely a social call."

We laughed, thinking he was joking, for the dinner could not in any sense be mistaken for a simple social call. Then we dispersed to pray. Afterwards, Papa was found staring at the wall, a worried expression on his face.

"I feel lightheaded," he said. "Fizzu, get me some water."

Naadia and I exchanged an amused glance.

"Papa, don't be so dramatic," Naadia said, laughing and thinking him silly.

"You think this is a joke?" he snapped. "This could be serious! What if they truly did come with ulterior motives?"

He was upset. He would need to be handled delicately. I turned to Phuppo, but before either of us could interject in a gentle manner, Naadia made an impatient sound.

"Asif explicitly said he wants to court me, Papa!" she said.

"I do not recall him saying such a thing," Papa cried, shocked.

"Well, he did, and I am going to let him," Naadia replied. "I have to get married sometime, so you'll just have to deal with it."

This, of course, only made him more upset. So I had to do damage control then just as I do today.

"Papa, Naadia doesn't mean to be harsh," I say to him. "I remember her telling me about that restaurant, and I think it's really difficult to get a reservation."

He huffs and puffs, upset that I'm taking Naadia's side.

Of course, I'm not pleased she's missing lunch, either, but I wouldn't be very helpful if I exacerbated the situation by saying so.

"She can come over afterwards," I suggest. "Maybe for chai?"

"No, no," Papa says. "It doesn't matter to me. She is a grown woman, of course, and will do as she pleases. Why she would take the feelings of an old man into consideration is beyond me!"

Uffo! Papa is so melodramatic.

"Why don't you and I watch a movie later?" I offer. He softens at this idea. Then shakes his head.

"No, no, I am sure you, too, are busy," he says, self-pitying.

"No, I'm not! I want to."

"Well. If you are insisting."

"I am."

A little while later, after I've changed and freshened up, I have a free moment away from Papa to call Naadia, but right then the doorbell rings. I think it is her for a moment, stopping by before they leave for lunch, but when Papa opens the door, it's someone else entirely.

"Fawad!" Papa says. "What a pleasant surprise!"

"Yes, I heard Naadia could not make it to lunch," he replies. I tie up my hair and slip on a scarf, then head downstairs. Fawad is standing by the door with Papa. "As there is now an empty seat at your table, do you mind if I join you?"

"No, of course not, do join us," Papa replies. "You do

not even have to ask." Papa is already in better spirits as he takes Fawad's coat and neck scarf. Fawad is wearing a sweater, dress-shirt, and slacks—no suit—and I am glad for it, or Papa would be in a fuss once more.

I go to the foyer to greet him, then pause mid-way as I recall the angry comment I had thrown at him last night. Oopsies. I hope it isn't awkward. Fawad is not one to hold a grudge, but I was terribly uncouth with him yesterday, I can admit as much now.

Unsure of what to do, I fiddle with the ends of my scarf. Ultimately, I decide to greet him by the door, or things will escalate further.

"So good of you to come and join us," Papa is saying. "It's so nice to have friends in the neighborhood."

"It's a good walk, and I enjoy it," Fawad replies, just as I join them.

"Papa, I think we're merely a part of Fawad's exercise regime," I say, teasing. "Though I cannot say what walking four houses down will do for your overall health. Especially in this cold."

"One should not venture out in this cold, to be sure, to be sure," Papa says, voice solemn. "But Fawad is a reasonable sort, he did not forget his scarf."

"One should never forget their scarf," Fawad agrees. I seek out his gaze, a bit worried. We usually laugh about Papa's antics, and today I am hoping we can do the same.

He looks at me, and I still. His dark brown eyes are indecipherable for a moment – but then I catch the hesitation in the way he stands. Finally, he raises his brows in Papa's direction.

All is forgiven.

At the same time, we both smile. Tension leaves my body, and I feel lighter. I had not realized it before, but I could not bear it if he was truly angry with me.

"It's good to have you joining us, besides," I add, "because I need a sous chef."

Fawad laughs. "Of course you do. What are you making?"

Papa leaves us to retreat to his office, while Fawad and I walk toward the kitchen. I lower my voice.

"We're making drunken noodles," I whisper, drawing near to him. He smells like rich leather and amber, a deliciously heady scent. I wonder which brand it is. (For scientific purposes, of course.)

I inch toward him and take a deep breath in. God, it smells good. What *is* that?

"Why are you whispering?" he asks, stepping closer as his own voice lowers to match mine. I inhale another deep breath of his cologne, deducing it is probably Tom Ford.

"We can't say 'drunken noodles' in front of Papa," I explain, when I remember he's asked me a question. "He's positively scandalized just by the name."

"I can't say I am surprised," Fawad says. "What should we call it instead? I think the Thai name is pad kee mao."

I laugh at his accent, though I do not think any of us rightly knows how to pronounce the names of Thai food dishes, and we all horribly butcher them.

"Yes, or we will simply say Thai noodles so he is not alarmed," I reply. "Papa is very easily alarmed."

"That he is. Don't you remember when you said you were going for cocktail hour sushi?"

I groan, recalling the instance. "God, I was lectured for a half hour about the perils of such speech, even though I was not going for *cocktails*, merely *sushi*."

"He is a particular man."

We make it to the kitchen, where I take out all the ingredients. Fawad helps with chopping up the vegetables, while I make the noodles' sauce.

"That was not as bad as the time Naadia made naked cake for my birthday," I say, stirring by the stove, while he cuts on the countertop beside me. We fall into an easy rhythm. "We were lectured about it for *days*. Papa's still triggered if we ever mention the incident."

We exchange such stories, and though I'm technically grumbling about Papa's dramatics, I don't feel I need to say I do not mind them. Fawad would not mistake my teasing for complaining, as others might.

While I finish making the food, Fawad sets the table with our Michael Aram dinner set, the porcelain plates decorated with black orchids. Papa joins us, chatting with Fawad while Fawad returns to the kitchen to whip up Thai iced tea for us all.

"What is this exactly?" Papa asks, when everything is done and we sit down to eat at the table. Fawad is sitting across from me with Papa at the head; he and I exchange a glance.

"Dru—" I begin, eyes mischievous.

"Thai noodles," Fawad cuts in.

"Delicious. Well done."

We eat together, and chat about random things. Fawad is over often, since I suppose he rather enjoys Papa's company and probably gets bored being all alone. I can't possibly think of any other reason why he might be over so often.

It's nice when he's here. The house feels more full. Since he's over quite a bit, it doesn't feel like a guest is here, so we can all be casual and comfortable together, and it's enjoyable.

After we finish eating, Papa retreats to his office. I look at Fawad, expecting he'll follow Papa, but he sticks around and helps me clear the table. He brings our empty glasses to the sink as I stack the plates.

I'm just going to take them to the dishwasher when he comes back for them. He holds out a hand to take them from me. I hand them to him, and as I do, his hand brushes against mine under the porcelain, his slender fingers soft yet steady.

It is a small act, lasting just for a moment. It should be something that goes unnoticed – but time slows, and I get this strange feeling, tightening and unspooling all at once in the pit of my stomach.

After having cooked together in the kitchen, eating together at the table, now cleaning together … it is as if I glimpse into the future.

I withdraw my hand quickly, alarmed by the thought.

Fawad is unperturbed and turns to carry the dirty dishes to the sink. My pulse quickens.

How strange. Perhaps I was really thinking of Rizwan and our future together, and my mind got confused because Fawad is here.

Fawad is always here, so it is an easy mix-up to occur.

Later, after he's gone, I lie down on the couch and call Naadia. She's back from her lunch and details how spectacular it was, and I listen before going into Lecture Mode. As the younger sister, you would assume I am usually on the receiving end of such lectures, but Naadia and I love to subvert cliches in such a manner.

"I'm glad your lunch was amazing," I say, "but please be gentle with Papa. You know he takes things personally."

"I didn't even do anything," she says, automatically defensive. I make a face she can't see, but know from the pause I take before replying that she'll understand.

"Miss Ma'am," I reply in a warning tone. She groans.

"Papa is just dramatic," she says. "I just said I couldn't come for lunch, that was it! You know Asif and I have been trying to get a reservation there for weeks! Besides, I spent all day with you guys yesterday."

"I knoooow," I respond. In a way, what she is saying is right, too. "But you know Papa misses you, and he was looking forward to Thanksgiving break, and all that. Come over for dinner at least."

"Ugh, whatever, fine, I'll come for dinner," she says.

"He'll be fine."

Of course he would. I would manage him, as I always did. But she still ought to be considerate.

I don't say any of that because I'm tired of the subject, and when I'm right all the time, Naadia gets irritated with me.

Instead, my voice brightens and I gear up to tell her something much, much better.

"*Anyways*, do you want to hear a saucy story?"

"Always," she says. "But what could have happened in the past twenty-four hours?"

"You will not believe this." I giggle. "Guess who showed up to Zeeshan Uncle's house last night, soaking wet and beautiful?"

"*No*," she gasps. "No. Way."

"Yes!" I give her a brief rundown of last night's events, ending with breakfast this morning, and when I am finished, Naadia screams.

"WHAT?"

"I KNOW!"

"*What is it, what's wrong?*" I hear Asif ask in the background, concerned. Naadia squeals. I hear her shaking him and his responding groans.

"Can I tell him?" she asks me, returning to the phone.

"Yes."

"Basically, Rizwan, AKA Zeeshan Uncle's nephew, AKA London's most eligible bachelor, AKA the man Humaira thinks is her match, AKA—"

"Naadia, you suck at telling stories," I say. She draws

things out so much, and not in a good way.

"Hey! Asif loves the way I tell stories, don't you, Asif?"

"Yes, angel, of course," he replies in the background.

"Tell him the abbreviated version!" I say. "The one in which I seem least like a hoe."

"I gotchu, sis," Naadia says to me, then turns back to Asif. "Basically Rizwan is here, and spoiler alert he is a major hottie, whose accent is, and I quote, 'like butter melting in the pan of Humaira's heart,' whatever the hell that means? You know how poetic she can get."

Asif says something in response to this, but I don't catch it.

"I can't hear him!" I cry into the phone.

"One sec." Naadia puts her phone on speaker.

"I said, is he as charming and *dreamy* as you thought he would be?" Asif asks in a dramatic tone. I giggle. Asif is such a great team player.

"Yes!" I squeal. "He is! Also very amiable and clever."

"Who is?" I hear Fawad ask.

"Rizwan," Asif replies. I can almost see Fawad roll his eyes.

"God help us," Fawad mutters.

I make an indignant sound at his scornful tone and am about to say something when Naadia says, "Don't bother, he left."

"Whatever," I reply. "Anyway…"

I continue telling her and Asif more, feeling excited. Even Fawad cannot ruin my good mood.

Rizwan is here!

Chapter Eight

The next day, on Saturday, Naadia has gone back to her place, which is literally perfect for me.

I could never invite Rizwan over to my own house for various reasons (beginning with Papa, then going on to I don't want to seem too interested, then going on to it would not be proper, then ending once more with Papa) but because Naadia is a *married* woman, she can do such things. In desi society, married women can get away with quite a lot.

"You have to throw a brunch party tomorrow," I tell Naadia on FaceTime, while I sit on a patch of sunlight in the family room, painting my nails (halal nail polish for the win!). "I've already worked out who to invite: me, of course, then Shanzay and Emad, and Rizwan. And whoever else you want to invite, I guess."

"Why don't you just throw it?" she asks.

"I can't!" I reply. "I need to be *aloof*."

Naadia snorts. "Fine, but I'm just going to order food because I don't feel like cooking."

"Um, lame, but okay," I reply. "I would come early to help, but I would rather show up late and have him wonder where I am. Ooh, and you could say you don't know if I am coming or not! That would be a great touch. Have him wonder, you know? Give me a mysterious air."

"Excuse me?" she replies. "You want me to *lie*?"

"Don't be dramatic," I say. "Remember all the trouble I went through to set you and Asif up! Need I remind you of a certain beach excursion?"

"Okay, okay, I get it." She laughs. "You're a crazy lady, but I will pretend to wonder where you are, or if you are coming at all."

"Yay!" I clap.

"But you'll have to make me chocolate croissants as payment."

"Ooh, fantastic idea! I can woo him with my divine baking."

"Um, no, because I'm going to eat them all. He can't have any."

"You're delusional if you think you're eating all of them."

"You mean *you're* delusional if you think I'm not."

"Hello, I'm trying to bribe the prospective great love of my life! You can't have all of them!"

"Fine, but you're making me a batch just for me next time."

"Deal."

After laboring for hours over the very sensitive croissant dough, I am gratified to find they have baked to flaky perfection the next morning. I hand one to Papa as I am heading out the door hoping it will distract him, but he makes me stop in his office for an interrogation.

"Where are you going?" he asks, even though I have told him half a dozen times I am going to Naadia and Asif's apartment in downtown Brooklyn. Her medical school is in Manhattan, a quick subway ride away, and Asif's law offices are in Brooklyn, walking distance from their place.

"To Naadia's for brunch, remember?" I say patiently.

"You're driving all the way to Brooklyn? For brunch?"

"Yes, Papa."

"Doesn't seem like a good idea." He says this every time I go to Naadia's, which is about an hour and a half away (without traffic it could go down to an hour and ten, but there's always traffic). To be fair to Papa, driving in Brooklyn *is* a headache, but they live in a very fancy building and there's a parking garage right next door, so at least I never have to worry about parking.

"Well." I tap my feet impatiently. He won't stop me, of course; he'll let me go, he just needs to be fussy about it first.

"Hm." He chews his croissant, analyzing me. "Why so much makeup? Who are you trying to impress?"

"Maybe I'm trying to impress a boy," I tease. Papa's reaction is visceral and immediate.

"Impress? A boy? Why would you ... why would you

even do that?" he sputters. "Or think that? None of these boys are worthy!"

"Papa, I was joking, please," I reply. Obviously not the moment for some humor. Noted. "You know I wouldn't do such a thing." Though I did take extra care with my appearance today.

It's as if he doesn't hear me. He begins a lecture about "aaj kal ke larke" and how useless boys are these days. Surely he must know I will eventually have to marry one of them.

"Besides," Papa adds, at the end, as if sensing my thoughts, "you cannot get married and leave me."

"I know, Papa," I reply, smiling sweetly to placate his frown. "But can I go for brunch now? I'm running late. I'll be back by the evening."

He nods. I move to exit, and his voice calls out. "Where is your coat?" I hold it up to him. "Gloves?"

"It isn't so cold," I reply.

"If your car breaks down and you are stranded on the side of the road and it starts to snow, then what?" I release a measured breath, clenching my jaw. Papa is of the attitude that catastrophe can come at any moment, so you must prepare for the worst. "Perhaps I should go with you."

"I'll be fine, I'm leaving, Allah hafiz," I say, kissing his cheek and scurrying out the door before he can follow.

It is cold out, but my car warms quickly, and I'm on my way. It is a bit of a hassle to get there, and I don't understand why they choose to pay so much in rent when they could stay at the Sheikhs's, which is such a large house. Fawad lives there alone, but Naadia and Asif wanted a place of their own – even if it is only a modest two-bedroom – to save them the commute.

By the time I reach my destination, everyone has already arrived. While I hate to be late, I do love making an entrance.

It has the desired effect. I walk in through the front door, which is unlocked, and loudly say salaam.

Everyone immediately looks my way as I saunter in: Shanzay, Emad, Rizwan, Fawad, Asif, Naadia, Sadaf, Haya, and Zahra. Everyone is squeezed together on the dark green sofas in the living room. Naadia's apartment is small and feels even more so with how much she's decorated it.

Every surface is covered with interesting lamps, photo frames, trinkets from various travels, or ceramic pieces from her college days. The walls are filled with art prints, and the sofas have various throws and pillows messily arranged on them. Tassel curtains hang in front of the windows, and a huge, fluffy rug covers most of the hardwood floors. Still, the boho interior has a warm ambience to it, especially with all the people crowded inside.

"Oh, you made it!" Naadia says, tone loudly surprised. She gets up to greet me in the entryway, and Rizwan does as well, trailing behind her.

"It's good to see you again," Rizwan says. He takes one of the plates of chocolate croissants from me, and I hand the other to Naadia, who slips away to the kitchen, leaving me and Rizwan alone. Good job, Naadia.

"I couldn't let you go without giving you a chance to

make yourself memorable," I reply, taking off my coat. "I am quite generous like that."

Rizwan smiles, taking my coat with his other hand, but a moment later, he scrunches his face with puzzlement, remembering he does not know where the coats go.

"I'll take that," I laugh, going to hang my coat on a hook. "We can put that in the kitchen."

Rizwan follows me to the kitchen with the chocolate croissants where Naadia is brewing coffee. There is a nice spread of bagels and eggs and lox on the countertop with orange juice and milk.

Fawad is in the kitchen, as well. He is standing in front of the counter, his shirtsleeves rolled up as he cuts up some strawberries. I watch his slender hands move, the deft fingers, his signet ring glinting.

Fawad looks up as I enter, and our eyes meet. Then he looks behind me, to Rizwan holding what I've baked, and his eyes narrow.

"Fantastic," Fawad mutters to himself. I furrow my brows at his comment, wondering why he is in such a surly mood so early on in the day.

"These smell *amazing*," Rizwan says, distracting me. "I love chocolate croissants, and even if I didn't, I'm sure after today I would have been converted."

I smile up at him, butterflies fluttering in my stomach. He is so *sweet*. Naadia exchanges a glance with me, wiggling her eyebrows as he sets the croissants down. I go to stand beside Naadia, elbowing her while I pretend to help her with the coffee.

"Do you need any help?" Rizwan asks Naadia and I.

"No, she's alright," Fawad cuts in before Naadia can answer. I give him a strange look, which he ignores.

"I'm fine, thank you," Naadia says to Rizwan. "You can go sit with the others."

Rizwan nods, taking his leave, and I huddle close to Naadia so we can giggle together. She pinches my arm.

"What a *cutie*," Naadia affirms. "That accent!"

"I know right," I respond in a hushed tone.

"And you'll be pleased to know he came in a gray trench coat," Naadia adds. We love a man in a good Burberry trench coat. I gifted Asif one for his birthday when he was courting Naadia, and it definitely played a hand in her falling in love with him.

"How long has everyone been here?" I ask.

"Not too long."

I glance at Fawad, who is clearly trying to listen to our whispers without seeming like he is.

The warmth and comfort of two days ago has gone. There is a cold expression on his face. I want to make a childish comment at him about how Rizwan is here and just as handsome and spectacular as I had always thought, and how the waiting was worth it, but before I can, Sadaf comes to the kitchen to grab some water.

"Humaira!" she cries, enveloping me in a hug. "I haven't seen you in forever, where have you been?"

"I knooow," I say, leaning into her tall frame. We pull back and smile at each other. Sadaf is almost half a foot taller than me, wearing a pair of dark jeans over her long legs and a black sweater with a black hijab. Her gold nose ring is the only jewelry she has on, and it gives her a very striking look.

"I'm glad Naadia threw this little brunch together and I got to see you," Sadaf says.

"Yes, so good of Naadia," I say, giving her a conspiratorial smile.

"What?" Sadaf asks, confused when she catches the look on my face. She has a sister, too, so she knows all about the silent communication. "Fill me in."

Naadia gives her the rundown about Rizwan, only sidetracking a few times.

"Oh! This is *him*?" Sadaf says. Naadia and I have of course mentioned Zeeshan Uncle's enigmatic nephew before. "He's a total hottie. I love this for you, Humaira. Ten out of ten."

"Right!"

"Even though all men are trash," she reminds me. Sadaf is tough with a capital T and takes no nonsense from men. "When they look that good, a girl can make an exception."

"Amen to that," Naadia agrees.

"And what an entrance, Humaira! Love the new skirt," Sadaf says.

"We are just so *glad* you could make it," Naadia says in mock gratitude, fawning over me. I laugh, shrugging her off.

"I decided to grace you with my presence, after all," I reply, flipping my hijab end. This, at last, prompts a comment from Fawad, who is putting the tray of fruit beside the rest of the food.

Oh. I forgot he was in the kitchen with us.

"You didn't know if you could come, yet you had time to bake croissants?" Fawad asks, tone unpleasant. I cut my glance his way, but before I can say anything, he walks out.

Um. Okay. Whatever.

"Everyone come eat," Naadia says to the others. Everyone comes in to get food, and Rizwan goes straight for the croissants, piling three onto his plate and smiling at me as he does. I giggle, then go to grab Shanzay, who looks great in a black jumpsuit and cardigan.

I had already called her about Rizwan, so she knows. It's *him*.

"He's so handsome," Shanzay whispers to me.

"Isn't he!" I squeal. "How is it going with Emad?" I ask, voice low.

"Well, I think!" she replies. "He's a great listener, and asks me all about working at the office with you, and what types of projects you and I work on, and what we do for fun."

We both grin, then join the others to get food. I properly greet and hug Haya and Zahra, who are engrossed in their own conversation. I'm glad to see them, too.

"I'm sure everyone's been asking, so I won't ask how wedding planning is going and will instead ask something much more fun," I tell Haya. "How's *honeymoon* planning going?"

Haya blushes, her cheeks turning the same pink as her

glasses. She's wearing a pastel blue sweater with a matching hijab and a pair of cream pants. She has a heart-shaped face with big brown eyes and is just the sweetest thing. Zahra elbows her, giggling.

"I bought her the cutest sets of lingerie," Zahra informs me. She's wearing boyfriend jeans and a blouse with an oversized cardigan on top, her scarf a dark green.

"Stop," Haya says, covering her face with her hands for a second. Then she turns back to me. "Carlos is booking everything, it's going to be a surprise."

I gasp. "A surprise? That's so stressful."

"Don't worry, we're guiding him," Zahra says. "He texts me and Sadaf like every other day asking for our opinions. At this point, *I'm* planning her honeymoon."

Haya giggles. "Perfect."

"And not to toot my own horn, but it's going to be amazing. I will be living vicariously through you."

"It could be you soon," I say to Zahra. "Any romance in your life?" (If you couldn't tell already, I love a good gossip.)

Zahra laughs. "No, nothing interesting going on in my life."

"What about that guy who works at the restaurant with you?" I ask. "I feel like you always have funny stories about him to tell."

"Yaseen? What? No, no, no, he's just my coworker! Friend, if anything."

"She *is* always talking about him!" Haya says, voice vindicated. She turns to Zahra. "See, I told you so."

Zahra's jaw drops. "I am not! And even if I am, it's because I see him, like, every day."

"She's always giggling," Haya tells me.

"That's because he's objectively funny!"

Zahra is giggling even now. Interesting.

We chat a little more, then I leave the best friends to go attend to Shanzay, though Emad and Rizwan have been very attentive toward her. Emad makes room for me on the couch, and I squeeze in beside Shanzay, bumping her shoulder with mine. We share smiles.

Fawad must truly be in a mood, for he sits on the side, a sullen expression across his face. I wonder if his parents called; he is usually in a mood after that...

"Humaira, you're such an excellent baker," Rizwan says. "I am sorry to have missed your pies from Thanksgiving."

"Ugh, those were so good," Emad agrees. "You should open a catering company, Humaira, you would literally make a fortune."

"Aw, thanks," I reply. "You know, Shanzay is my protege, and I have been teaching her some of my recipes."

"I am not half as good as you are," Shanzay says, voice high.

"No you are!" I respond. "She is," I tell the boys. "She loves baking. She's so good at it, too!"

Shanzay gives me a funny look. "I don't really *love* baking..." But her voice is low, so I do not quite hear her.

Besides, the effect on the boys is immediate: they look impressed.

"With Humaira as a teacher, I'm sure your desserts are

just as good," Emad says to Shanzay, eyes warm. She smiles.

We continue chatting, Emad and Rizwan both talking about their work in very grand terms, clearly trying to impress us and outdo one another. I loop my arm through Shanzay's and lean against her. She leans back, the both of us pleased with our crushes' notice.

After a little while, I take out my mini polaroid camera and hand it to Rizwan. "Will you take a picture of me and Shan?" I ask sweetly.

"Of course," he replies. We angle together, and I see Emad looking at us intently, just as I hoped he would.

"Emad, why don't you join in, as well?" I say.

"Sure!" he replies, too enthusiastic to hide it. He comes to sit beside me, but I shift so there isn't much room, and point to Shanzay's side. She elbows me as he comes to sit beside her.

"Ready?" Rizwan asks.

"How do we look?" I ask, adjusting my hijab.

"Perfect," he replies, but he's looking at me.

"Three ... two..."

As he snaps the picture, I shift to be half out of frame, and when it prints, I see I have been mostly successful. You can only see the corner of my smile; the main focus is all on Shanzay and Emad.

"We look amazing," Emad says. "I will be keeping this, thank you."

Shanzay and I exchange a glance. Ah!

When everyone disperses to pray, I pull Shanzay aside for a private moment in the corner.

"Emad is most definitely interested in you," I say. She gasps.

"Really?" she asks, excited, then nervous. "How can you tell?"

"From the way he is so attentive, of course! And his gaze was on you constantly," I say. "Plus, did you not see how excited he was about the polaroid? It's your first picture together! No wonder he wants to save it. So sweet!"

"But what should I do? How do I behave?" She nibbles her bottom lip. "I've never done this before."

"Do not worry, dear Shanzay," I say. "I will teach you, of course."

"Humaira, you're so kind," Shanzay says. "I don't know what I would do without you."

I give her a hug. "Happy to help."

We go to pray, then join the others back in the main room, where everyone is spread out on the sofas and floor, broken off into little pairs. Naadia is sitting on the edge of a chair with Asif, the pair talking with Sadaf, while Haya and Zahra are in their own little world. Emad and Shanzay have their own conversation, while Rizwan asks me about my job and where I studied, then I ask about him.

"How was Oxford?" I ask. "I've always wanted to go. When we went to England last, I didn't even get to visit!"

"I did enjoy my time there," he replied.

"I love all those old libraries," I say. "Even though the

books must be terribly boring, the architecture and design is so beautiful and enchanting."

I hear a little noise behind me and turn to see Fawad over my shoulder. He's been listening in, expression sour.

"Only you would forsake such a wealth of knowledge and history for aesthetics," Fawad says, dark eyes stormy.

I bristle at his tone. That was an unfair thing to say, and he knows it is. I open my mouth to set him straight, blood drumming through my veins, but before I can, Rizwan speaks.

"Aesthetics are important, too, and cannot be entirely ignored," he says as I face him. "We are a shallow sort of people, drawn to what is beautiful."

And as he says *beautiful*, he smiles just at me. My cheeks warm and I smile back, mood placated.

I turn around to give Fawad a superior glance, to which he makes an exasperated face and rolls his eyes. Without another word, he stalks away.

No one else really makes anything of it, for he moves quietly and quickly, but it does not escape my notice when he disappears from the main area entirely and goes to Asif and Naadia's bedroom.

I know I should let it go, but after a moment, I follow him. When I enter, he's loosening his tie in front of the mirror atop the dresser and releasing a long breath. I close the door behind me and walk further into the room.

He sees me in the reflection and turns, face stunned.

"Humaira—"

"What is your problem?" I ask, irritated. "Why are you

being rude to Rizwan, when he has come from so far, and after so long?"

Whatever he was going to say evaporates on his lips. He shuts his mouth, clenching his jaw. He turns back to the mirror and tightens his tie. Then he faces me, taking two long steps toward me.

He stands so close I have to lift my chin to look up at him, and he must angle his face downwards to look at me.

"I am being perfectly civil," he replies evenly.

I scoff. "You should revisit the meaning of the word."

I don't understand it. Why is Fawad in such a bad mood regarding Rizwan? Fawad is probably just upset that I was right once again and that Rizwan is just as handsome and charming as I thought he would be.

"What are you doing with Shanzay and Emad?" he asks, changing the subject. He succeeds in surprising me. "You keep pushing them together."

"I'm not doing anything." Now it is my turn to look away. I take a step back. "If they are interested in one another, that is their own business."

"Interested?" He scoffs. "You must be mistaken, as you usually are."

I give him a dirty look, taking another step backwards. My shoulders hit the door, and I rest my hands against the wooden panes.

When I do not respond, Fawad gives me a puzzled expression, stepping forward so he is right in front of me again. The space between us is treacherously thin. "From what I know, Shanzay is interested in someone else."

"Where did you hear that?"

"From a ... credible source." He must mean Huzaifa.

"Your tenant should not go around spreading horrible rumors!" I snap. His eyes blaze.

"It's not a rumor," he snaps back, "but something told to me in confidence."

"Well, it's not true." I pause. "Shanzay feels nothing for him."

A muscle in his jaw tics as he looks at me with both awe and horror. "You're a real piece of work, you know that?"

"Thank you."

"It wasn't a compliment."

"Of course it was. All the best things in life require a bit of work."

He shakes his head. "Last I heard, she was very much interested in Huzaifa, and from what I saw this summer, I would confirm it." He frowns. "I hope you haven't persuaded her out of this."

"Even if I had persuaded her, which I haven't, she must not have had deep feelings for him to begin with, to be so easily swayed," I reply, breathless.

"You know she looks up to you and is easily impressionable!" Fawad exclaims. "Your *dear* friend." This he says with sarcasm, as if Shanzay and I are nothing but surface level friends and I merely project a closeness unto us. "Of course she would be swayed, and it would be no mark on her feelings if she was. Humaira, you must behave."

"Make me!" I snap.

His eyes flash. "I might just have to."

My pulse quickens.

"Please, stop this nonsense," I say, holding up a hand. His gaze galls down to it, and then so does mine. I see how close we are standing. If I shift my hand even a few inches forward, it would be resting over his heart.

I bring my hand back down to my side. "She is older than me and has her own mind," I say, trying to sound more confident than I feel.

Fawad runs an agitated hand through his hair. "You don't understand just how easily you get into peoples' heads."

"Pity I could never get into yours!" I say. "Or I would make you less infuriating!"

"I thank God I still have my senses about me," he says, voice hard. We are both breathing heavily, glaring at the other.

Despite how furious I am with him, something sharp turns in my stomach at our proximity, the scent of his cologne invading my senses. This close, I can see the curve of eyelashes, my own reflection in his dark eyes.

I turn around so I don't have to face him.

"I've had enough of this."

I pull open the door and leave. Behind me, he lets out an audible groan of frustration.

I join the others, hoping Fawad will get over his surly mood and join us as well, but he never does.

He leaves early, slipping away when no one is looking, but I notice.

And I do not want to notice.

He was being weird, weirder than usual, and I did not appreciate it one bit. I focus instead on Rizwan, how well he and I get along. (Naadia even takes a discreet picture of us to send in our MMESG chat for Phuppo to see.)

I focus as well on Shanzay and Emad, who look to be enjoying themselves, as well. Emad does keep trying to pull me into the conversation, but that must be because he is shy speaking to Shanzay alone.

Eventually, it is time for the rest of us to go as well. When Emad leaves, he says goodbye to Shanzay, then shares a private smile with me, and I give him a wide smile in return, understanding his excitement.

Then, it is time to say goodbye to Rizwan, indefinitely, for his flight back to London is tonight. My stomach drops with disappointment, and I can see he is dispirited, as well, as we say goodbye.

"I do hope you will remember me when I return," he says, giving me a slow, sweet smile. "For I will not so easily forget you."

My heart skips a beat.

"Come again, and we shall see," I reply, feeling excited already.

Chapter Nine

Most of December came and went quickly in anticipation of the next holiday break. I went to work and schemed to set Shanzay up with Emad, and I missed Mama, and Papa was mercurial, and Naadia was away, and I was sad, and I thought of Rizwan.

Then, the real fun began.

Winter in New York. It's romanticized in holiday movies and in novels, but for me, it has always simply been home. The sprinkling snow like stars and the frozen wind howling against our house were the backdrop while I sat by the fire, a steaming cup of hot chocolate in my hands, my toes wrapped in fuzzy socks.

Naadia came home on Christmas Eve. She had the week off and was spending it with us, so Papa was in high spirits, not even protesting as we went out for a girls' brunch.

"You're sure Rizwan is coming to dinner?" Naadia asks me, taking a bite of lemon ricotta pancakes. Rizwan is coming to Zeeshan Uncle's tonight, to stay for a week, and we're hosting a fancy dinner in a few days, on the weekend.

"Yes," I say, cutting into my eggs benedict. "Zeeshan Uncle is picking him up tonight, and he's staying until New Year's."

Phuppo called to confirm as much, and I'm jittery with excitement to see him again. Oh, to be in love! Just the idea warms me.

The taste of old dreams is at once bitter and sweet: like too strong coffee with too much sugar. First, you recoil from the flavor, but then it settles, and you remember just how much you love the taste.

"How exciting," Naadia agrees, waving a waitress over. "Hi, yes, can we have virgin mimosas please?"

The waitress is clearly confused by this request. "So ... orange juice?"

"Yes," Naadia says. "But in champagne flutes."

"The champagne flutes are imperative," I affirm.

"Okaaay." The waitress gives us strange looks but goes off to get them. Naadia and I giggle.

I miss having her around for stupid little things like this. We have such a specific sense of humor, compiled of random references to movies or things Papa has said or old Tumblr posts, and no one else understands but the other.

Which is why we are laughing at the most insane things throughout the day. Later that day, while I bake peppermint brownie cookies, we're chatting and laughing and being obnoxious. We only grow more and more delirious as the evening advances, and then we lounge out in front of the fire.

"You know someone was telling me to buy you pepper spray, like he got for his daughter," Papa tells us in a somber tone, as he listens to us cackle over an Urdu Tweet. He is sitting on the couch in his NYU Medicine sweatshirt. Whenever Naadia visits, he wears it. "But I told him there is no need, for if my daughters are ever robbed, they would surely annoy the poor robbers so much, they would leave of their own accord."

This, of course, only makes us laugh more.

"Papa!" I scream. Naadia laughs so hard she snorts, which is such an indelicate sound, I reach over to smack her. "Naadia! Stop snorting! Be a lady!" She hits me back.

"As if I can help it!"

"Oh, you girls," Papa says, smiling to himself.

He enjoys it when we are so hyper. It makes the house feel full again, and our laughter is constant background music. He also dearly loves the attention as he tells us stories from his childhood. Today's story is from when he was about eight or so.

"I used to visit the village during the summers, when I was off from school," he tells us. "And I had this little goat I would play with. A baby goat, very cute and fluffy."

"How sweet!" I comment.

"Aw!" Naadia adds.

"Then, one day, this boy from a neighboring village came and said he wanted my goat!"

"No!" we exclaim.

"Yes!" He shakes his head. "My Ammi said he could have it, but I was very sad. It was my goat! So I told the boy no."

"As you should have."

"But one day, I went, and the goat was gone!"

"What!"

"So I had to get my friend's older brother, and we went to the village, and stole the goat back."

These are the little stories from rural Pakistan Papa likes to keep us entertained with.

That night, Asif comes for dinner. Fawad does not join us because he is allegedly meeting a friend. I didn't even think he had friends. I am sure it is one of his tenants, and he just wants to seem social.

I do hope he isn't avoiding me. I have seen him a handful of times since Thanksgiving, and he was a bit awkward but otherwise his normal, unsavory self.

At dinner, Papa is surly to Asif, more so than usual, which puts Naadia in a bad mood. Papa used to like Asif, until he married Naadia, and she moved out. Now if there is anything going wrong, it is Asif's fault.

Asif is blamed for everything from the cleaning lady being late (It's that wretched Asif's fault. If he hadn't gone and married Naadia, she would have been here to let the cleaning lady in.); to Papa's coffee getting cold (Awful Asif. Marrying my dear daughter! Naadia always made my coffee just right – this is also a personal affront to me, because Naadia rarely made him coffee and I make excellent coffee!); to the bathroom sink getting clogged (I am sure this is Asif's fault! He must have shaved that big, awful beard of his!).

I can go on but you get the point.

Asif is a dear though and tolerates it very well.

Sometimes Naadia gets upset and tries to call Papa out, saying that the blame isn't Asif's really, but mine, seeing as I was the one to suggest the match.

To this, of course, Papa blames Asif once again. (Turning you against your own sister! The audacity of the man!) Naadia should have seen that one coming because I am positive that, even at gunpoint, Papa could not find a fault in me.

It helps that I have no faults, but even if I had them, he would deny them. Of course, sometimes I do make little mistakes, as all people do, but even then Papa doesn't think the blame is mine, not really.

———————

When Rizwan arrives in New York, I plan to visit "Phuppo" (as I tell Papa). The day of the planned social call, it begins snowing in the morning, and I find this divine intervention excellent. I pack an overnight bag in case I get stranded at Zeeshan Uncle's house (just like Jane Bennet at Mr. Bingley's!), but at the last minute, the plans are derailed by Papa, who panics very easily when it comes to the snow.

"Either I drive you there and back," he says, "or you go tomorrow, when the roads are clear."

I elect to go the next day because a girl simply cannot

romance a handsome man when her father is just in the next room.

When I drive over, everything is covered in white, a perfect snowglobe. The bare branches of the trees sparkle in the sunlight, the evergreens covered in snow like powdered sugar. Everything is pure and clean and perfect. I love it! The magic of snow never ceases to amaze me.

"Humaira, how lovely to see you again," Rizwan says, opening the door. He lets me into the house and takes my coat from me, smiling brightly all the way. He is happy to see me, and I am excited as well, which is a relief.

"It is good to see you, too," I respond. "Look at all this snow! Isn't it wonderful!"

"Yes, it is." He smiles. "Though I cannot enjoy it much, Shani Chacha has me working like a dog."

We walk over to the living room and sit down, where he explains that the company Zeeshan Uncle runs was founded by Rizwan's grandfather. When Rizwan's father, Zeeshan Uncle's older brother, moved to England, Zeeshan Uncle took over, and now he is teaching Rizwan the ropes to take over one day.

Another heir, just like me! Fateful.

"I am here for business, but of course, I have some time for fun, as well." He wiggles his eyebrows at me, and I giggle.

"There must always be time for fun," I agree. "Can you see yourself living in America, then?" I ask.

"It is a possibility. The more time I spend here, the more I like it," he says. "Certain people could surely persuade me to stay." He gives me a warm smile. "I certainly would not be the first to move continents because of love, either."

I bite back a smile of my own, not responding.

"My mother, of course, has been badgering me to get married," he continues. "Do you feel the same pressure? I know a lot of desi girls do."

Excellent steering of conversation. It's always a good thing to let girls know one has marriage on their mind.

"Not at all," I say. "Papa is quite the opposite where he doesn't want me to marry. And I have a pretty good life, alhamdulillah, so I understand his perspective that I should be in no hurry to leave it. I suppose I will only marry for love."

"Reasonable," he agrees.

"I do not think someone should marry simply because 'it's the right time' or whatever else people say," I continue. "Look at Phuppo and Zeeshan Uncle. They waited for their right person, and now they are so happy."

He listens attentively as I speak. "It is good to believe," he says.

I sigh-laugh. "It is not always easy, but yes having faith is good."

I wait a moment to see if he will deepen the conversation.

If people have the courage to ask, I'd like to think I have the courage to answer.

But he does not ask. I wish he would, though I must say a part of me is secretly relieved when he does not. Perhaps I enjoy being the martyr. Naadia would say so, at least.

We continue conversing, and I find that we get along well. It must mean *something*.

This is the part where my best friend, Areeba, would say I am making leaps and bounds, and I should take it slow, but I just can't. I am so sure of my heart, and I am rarely wrong, so I trust this feeling.

"Let's go out and see the snow," I say, after we have drunk coffee. Phuppo and Zeeshan Uncle have been nowhere to be seen; as my designated cool aunt, she does make an excellent wing-woman.

"Let's," he agrees, grabbing our coats.

We head outside, and I take in a deep breath of the brisk air, shivering. Rizwan watches me as I do, an amused expression on his face.

"What?" I ask, when his staring continues.

"Your nose is red," he says. "Like Rudolph. Very endearing." He teases.

I let out a mock gasp of insult. While his back is turned, I pick up some snow and pack it tight into a little ball.

"Rizwan!" I say. The instant he turns, he receives a face full of snow to the face. "Hah!"

I laugh, triumphant.

"How rude! And here I thought you a delicate lady!" he exclaims, stooping down to pack snow into his own hands. When he rises with a sizable snowball, I give him a warning glance.

"You wouldn't," I dare. He comes closer, eyes gleaming, and I squeal, making a run for it.

"Oh no you don't!" He reaches out and grabs me. It's

really not inappropriate, given the approximate seventeen layers of clothing and gloves between us, but my stomach lurches all the same. I swat his arm away, but I know I cannot outrun him. I stop.

"No, no," I say, covering my face with my hands. I peek out to see Rizwan grinning.

"I'll be very gentle," he says, the snowball hovering over my face. There's no escaping it. I nod slightly, and he mushes the snowball against my nose. It spreads across my cheeks, my lips, melting instantly upon contact, and I giggle as the icy water enters my mouth.

"The debt is settled," he says dramatically. I slip off my glove to brush the snow aside from my face, my skin frozen. He does too and our fingers brush, ice-cold but warming quickly.

When I finally go inside, I press my fingers to my cheeks, catching my breath.

"Oh, you're flushed!" Phuppo exclaims when she sees me. "Is it windy outside? Your cheeks are positively red."

"Oh, yes, it is," I say, heart beating fast. "Excuse me."

I rush to the guest room and close the door, leaning against it. Across the room, I catch sight of myself in the mirror: my cheeks are rosy.

I meet my eyes and grin.

Chapter Ten

When I arrive home, Naadia is not there.

"She is down the road," Papa responds when I ask. He is holed up in his office and does not look up from his papers.

"Have you eaten?" I ask.

"I'm not hungry," he grumbles, nibbling on a bowl of nuts. I sigh. So he is in a mood again. I wonder who could possibly be the cause.

Though we are in our twenties, Papa is still recovering from us no longer needing him. Which is why he handles everything car-related, tax-related, shoveling-snow-related. Even if he hires someone to fix it, he still deals with it. It makes him feel useful, like he still has a purpose.

I allow it, but Naadia does not. She wishes to be Independent and Self-Sufficient.

I call Naadia to ask what has happened, but she does not let me get a word in.

"If you're going to lecture me, I'd prefer you do it with Asif present so he can defend my honor and duel you to the death," she says. "Come over for dinner. I'm making mac. And brownies."

Before I respond, she hangs up. She and Papa are both ridiculous. It's a good thing she's making brownies to soften my mood; her brownies are to die for.

I change into comfortable shalwar kameez and a cardigan, then drive over, since it is a bit chilly out, and I do not want to put Papa in a further state by walking.

When I get to the Sheikhs's, Fawad lets me in, taking my coat.

"Humaira," he says, and his voice is ordinary. Any awkwardness I might have imagined between us is gone. "How are you?"

"I suppose we're about to find out," I say, raising my brows. I share a smile with him and head into the house.

The Sheikhs's house is of similar size and layout to ours and is decorated with a classic interior that mirrors ours, though it isn't as ornate or thorough. I believe it used to be more so, before Fawad's parents shifted to Islamabad; I think Fawad prefers minimalism.

I walk to the kitchen, where Naadia is making sauce, and Asif is watching over her shoulder, his arms wrapped around her waist.

I say salaam, and she turns to respond. Her face falls when I give her an unamused look.

"Don't look at me like that," Naadia says, waving her spoon at me. Asif looks between us.

"I think I'll go," Asif says, moving away from her.

Naadia's jaw drops. "Asif, you traitor!" She throws a cube of cheese at him, which he catches and promptly eats. Naadia makes a disgusted sound, shaking her head at him.

"I get enough lectures from Fawad!" he calls, exiting swiftly.

"Yes, but he is your *older* brother," Naadia grumbles to herself.

"Since when do I lecture you?" I ask, offended. "All I was going to say was stop fighting with Papa. I am the one who has to live with him. You can say whatever you please and retreat here or back to your own apartment, but I'm the one who has to see him upset."

"That doesn't sound like a lecture to you?" she asks, though she is chagrined. "There is something seriously wrong with him, he is only getting more unpleasant and it doesn't help that you coddle him like a child."

"I don't coddle him!" I protest. "I'm simply trying to be nice to him. After all, we do owe him *everything*," I remind her in a pointed tone.

Naadia groans, avoiding my gaze as she strains the boiled pasta. "Anyways, if you weren't such a kiss up, I wouldn't look so bad. So really, it's all your fault."

I stiffen. She and Papa must really be getting on each other's nerves for her to say such a thing. It's the gripe she used to have with me years ago, when she was more rebellious and constantly staying out late with friends, or sneaking around driving when she didn't yet have a license, or the one time she went to a hookah bar.

"What are we, in high school?" I ask, tone unpleasant. "This is an old argument, one I thought we were past."

I am used to being the beloved, but it isn't as though it's entirely unearned. I've worked hard for years for the regard Papa has for me. I am loved because I work for it. Not like Naadia, who is allowed to be prickly and is still adored.

We can't *both* worry Papa and Phuppo; they wouldn't be able to handle it. *Someone* had to be good, and if it wasn't going to be her, it *had* to be me.

Did that affect my adolescence? Of course it did! Was it enjoyable? Not always! But what choice did I have?

I release a measured breath. I do not allow myself to go any further down that line of thought because I do not want to get into a proper fight. I do not want to dwell on what has passed.

"Let's move on," I say, resigned. "Just come home tomorrow and Papa will be fine."

She opens her mouth as if to respond, then decides to drop it, too. "Okay. Now go sit, and tell Asif to come help me," she says instead. "I can't get this stupid pot out of the drawer. I don't know why Fawad insists on using cast iron skillets."

"I wonder how he lifts them," I say.

"Fawad looks lean, but he's pretty strong," Naadia replies. "I've seen him and Asif wrestling."

This is not at all interesting to me.

I wave a hand, then go to deliver the news to Asif that he is needed. When I enter the family room, he and Fawad are playing chess.

"I'd offer to take over for you, but Fawad is unbearable when he wins," I tell Asif, sitting down next to him.

"We'll continue this later," Asif tells his brother, before getting up to help his wife in the kitchen. That leaves Fawad and I.

"Try your hand, you might win," Fawad says, but I won't be fooled. I only play chess with Naadia because we are evenly matched in that we play once or twice a year. Fawad plays much more often than that and even reads those boring books about strategy.

"I don't think I will," I reply. "Let's play ping-pong instead."

"I thought you didn't want to lose?" he says cockily.

"And I am in no danger of it," I reply just as arrogantly.

We go down to the basement, where there's a ping-pong table set up next to a billiards board. We play, and while we are neither of us particularly skilled, something about playing games loosens something inside of me. I get very competitive and high-spirited.

Which makes me lose my good senses and fall prey to delirium.

Fawad dives for a few shots and misses them, or gets struck right in the face by the ball (which is worth losing the point), or slips and nearly falls in his enthusiasm to stretch to the shot, and I cannot stop laughing.

And the more I laugh, the more I laugh.

I try to cover it up, not wanting Fawad to think I am enjoying his company, but I cannot help it. Suddenly, everything is funny, and I am sure Fawad is exaggerating his motions to make me laugh further because it is making me lose.

"No fair!" I say, trying to stomp my feet as I miss another point. "Stop making me laugh!"

But he doesn't. He only becomes more ridiculous, until I lose. And then he looks at me, just looks, an amused expression on his face as he watches me giggle and giggle. I clutch my stomach, trying to stop, my cheeks aching.

Good God. I must be terribly tired or some other reasonable explanation for such strange behavior.

"E-Excuse me," I say, disappearing to the bathroom. Once there, I flatten my cheeks, pulling my mouth down to stop the smiling.

When I return, Fawad is sitting on the couch reading some dreadful looking novel. Even the cover is all black and white, and the font is very severe. I sit beside him and turn the book so I can read the synopsis on the back.

"This looks like it does not have a hint of romance in it!" I exclaim, appalled. He closes the book to pay attention to me.

"None whatsoever," Fawad confirms. I scrunch my face with revulsion, and he laughs, tapping my nose with the book. "Some people enjoy reading realistic fiction, rather than fanciful stories."

"I don't see why," I say. "Is life not bleak enough for you? These books are so gray."

"Yes, but therein lies the allure," he replies, eyes animated. "Reading about others' misery puts things into perspective." He pauses. "And of course, it is comforting to have company in one's loneliness."

"I suppose." I do understand that. "But I find life distressing enough and believe literature and other forms of amusement should be an escape. I prefer to live life in vibrancy."

He smiles. "Yes, you would say that," he says, more to himself than me. But before I can comment on that, he says something else, voice more clear. "Now that we have discussed our tastes, I think we should recommend something to one another."

"Oh, yes!" I exclaim, sitting up with excitement. "Discussing books is so fun."

I love recommending books to people. It feels like a game of how well you know that person and their tastes. Actually, it is quite an intimate act, though I do not think of it in such a manner when considering what to recommend Fawad.

With him, I will simply enjoy being right. I am also interested to see what he will recommend to me, and by extension, see how well he knows me. For all that I go on about loving romance, I really am particular in my tastes for novels.

"I recommend *The Secret History* by Donna Tartt," he says, after thinking for a moment. I have heard of it but haven't read it because of the mention of murder. I am very easily spooked by such things. "It is not scary at all," he adds, as if reading my mind.

"Is there—" I begin.

"Yes, there is a bit of that," he says. "Not in the way you are used to, but in a manner I think you will appreciate all the same." His eyes turn mischievous. "I am talking about romance, of course, not sex."

I balk, cheeks heating. "I knew what you meant!" is all I can manage to say. He gives me a knowing smile, and I look away.

"I will recommend…" I have to think about this for a moment. For a second, I consider recommending a lurid novel, filled with sex scenes, just to unnerve him, but that would surely be crossing dangerous territory, and I want to give him a serious recommendation, like he's given me.

I need something without too much romance, for I know he will not like it, and I need something sad and lonely but filled with hope and love all the same.

I've got it. Oh, this will be perfect for him!

"*The Piper's Son* by Melina Marchetta," I say. "It's one of my absolute favorites. I read it every year."

"Is it—" he begins, but I cut him off. He'll ask if it's realistic, not fanciful.

"Yes, it is very raw," I respond. This time, it's my turn to be mischievous. "I mean the story, of course, not sex."

He is shocked by my assertion and assessing glance. I know he does not read romance, but surely I must be allowed to get back at him.

"I do not read those types of books!" he sputters.

"Mmhm," I drawl. "Sure you don't." But I cannot hold the face for long and let out a laugh. He laughs too, realizing I am joking.

A slow smile spreads across his face. I feel a potent flurry of excitement in my chest. I wonder if he will like it! I love discussing books with friends.

"Shall we—" he begins, but my focus is diverted when my phone rings.

It's Shanzay.

"Sorry, I should take this," I say. He nods.

"I'll meet you back upstairs." He exits, and after he's gone, I pick up the phone.

"Shan, what is it?" I ask.

"Humaira!" Her voice is an octave higher than usual. "Thank goodness you picked up. There's been an *emergency*! I'm at your house, and Uncle says you're not home. I hate to pull you away from your plans, but can you please come? I need to speak with you urgently!"

"Woah, slow down," I say, alarmed. "What's happened? Are you okay?"

"I'm okay. Please, can you just come?" she pleads.

I'm already heading up the stairs. "Yes, I'm coming. Give me five minutes."

I say goodbye to Naadia, Asif, and Fawad, who are all disappointed I'm going, then head home, where Shanzay is being interrogated in the foyer by Papa about her lack of a scarf when it is so cold out.

"Thank God you're here," Shanzay says, breathless. Her eyes are wide with excitement and nerves.

"Come," I say, leading her up the stairs to my room. I have her sit on the chaise, then sit beside her. "What happened?"

"Huzaifa called me!" she squeals. I blink.

"Huzaifa?" I repeat. How dreadful. I thought that entire ordeal was done with.

She nods, standing up. "He called to say that he wanted to grab coffee together, so we did, and it was really nice, and then at the end, he said that he has very strong feelings for me, and if I could ever feel the same, he would like to begin courting me! Get our parents involved, send a formal rishta, and everything." She lets out a long breath, then collapses backwards onto my bed. "Isn't that so straightforward and honest? I find it commendable."

"Almost too commendable," I say, unimpressed. "I'm sure his sister told him exactly what to say."

"Oh, yes ... well..." She swallows. "I don't know what to do."

"What did you say?" I ask. "In response to him."

"I said I would give him a response soon." She clutches a pillow to her chest.

I hate to see my dear friend so unnerved, it is very unbecoming. Especially when she can do so much better than Huzaifa, and I do not see why she should tie herself down to the first boy who has paid her any interest.

Besides, what about Emad, my choice for her? I am sure he's the right fit for Shanzay, and I'm never wrong.

"You should not keep him waiting," I say, voice calm and sure. "You must give him an answer straight away."

She sits up, the pillow in her lap. "Yes, I knew you would know what to do. That's why I came to discuss it with you first."

"That is what friends are for." I smile reassuringly. "Now, in your response, you must be sure to be conscious of the pain you will inflict on him."

Shanzay hesitates. "Pain?" She fiddles with the tassels on the pillow. "So you think I should say no?"

Now it is my turn to hesitate. "Oh, I'm sorry. I did not realize ... you wish to accept? I thought you liked Emad."

"I do! But..." Her voice wavers. "I don't ... I – I don't know!" She lets out an exasperated sigh. "I did not know Huzaifa liked me so much." She looks at me with desperation. "Please, tell me what to do."

"I can't do that," I say. "You must decide this for yourself."

She bites her lip, looking here and there, confused and clearly distressed. Perhaps a nudge is in order.

"As a general rule," I say, tone gentle, "if someone is so filled with doubt, I think they ought not to accept. It is best to trust your doubt, rather than ignore it, and live to regret it."

Shanzay nods, understanding this.

"It is up to you, of course," I say. "But is he not still studying? How would that work?" I pause. "I don't think a man should be thinking of marriage until he can provide for his wife. Unless, of course, he has the financial support of his family."

"Yes, he is still studying," she replies, voice low.

"Shan, you seem so disheveled," I say. "So not like yourself. Are you quite sure this is the type of relationship you want? Something that makes you feel erratic?" I pause, letting the words soak in. "In the end, of course, it is up to you to accept or reject. I do not wish to influence you, for it is your decision to make, but as your friend, I do want whatever is best for you."

"Yes," she says, finally looking at me. "I think I have ... I have almost made up my mind ... I decide, well – I have decided to…" She takes in a big breath, looking at me from the corner of her eye. "Reject him?"

She waits for my reaction. I hesitate a moment, then sigh with relief.

"Thank God," I say, taking her hand. "I was hoping you would say that, and I am so glad you came to the conclusion on your own." I smile. "I agree with your decision entirely."

Shanzay releases a sigh of relief as well. "Alright, good." She nods. "Okay." She bites her lip. "So I will call to refuse."

"Do so now," I say. "There's no use in delaying."

She nods, dialing his number, setting things right once more.

Really, this is what's best for her. I only want her to be happy, and I believe she will be happiest with Emad. Besides, I have such a good track record with these things. Just look at Naadia, and Phuppo. Shanzay will not be led astray so long as I am her friend.

Chapter Eleven

On Saturday night, we're hosting a nice fancy dinner. It'll be a good chance to push Shanzay and Emad together, and a good chance to see Rizwan again.

Naadia comes over to help, and we cook desi food and a pasta dish. Phuppo is bringing kheer (I'm not that skilled at Pakistani desserts yet) and I make flan. The last thing to do is make magic bars today, which are always a hit.

I shuffle through the cupboards but find we've run out of vanilla extract.

This cannot be happening.

"Naadia!" I scream.

"What!" she screams back from upstairs.

"Did you finish the vanilla extract?"

"Uhhhhh…" Her prolonged pause is enough answer. I groan.

"I am going to sue you!"

"My husband is a lawyer!" she shoots back.

I do not have time for this ridiculous conversation.

Luckily, Fawad is good for something, and that is his house being closer than a grocery store. I grab my coat and dash out. It isn't so cold that I can't walk, though it looks like it will rain soon. The sky is filled with stormy gray clouds, the sun nowhere in sight.

With a brisk pace, I am at the Sheikhs's house in a few minutes. I knock on the door and as I do, find that it is already partially open.

"Hellooo," I call, pushing the door open. Asif must have just stepped out. "Anyone hooome?" I sing-song, entering. Just as I do, Fawad comes down the stairs to meet me.

"Coming!"

His hair is wet from a shower, tufts of hair falling to his forehead like curved blades of grass weighted down by dew in the soft sheen of early morning. Droplets of water fall from his hair and land across his collar, which is open at the neck.

My eyes snag on the long line of his throat, the bare skin of his exposed collarbone.

I am so used to seeing him with a tie and blazer that he looks practically undressed to me. My stomach twists violently. A bead of water drips down his neck and I watch its slow descent as it disappears into his shirt.

My lips part open. I am momentarily stunned.

As Fawad comes closer, I get my wits about me and clear my throat.

"Should I close the door?" I say.

"I got it," he says, going to close the door, but my hand

is already there, and his hand covers mine as we push it closed together.

His hand lingers for a moment, just a moment, his palm warm against my cold fingers. Something skitters across my chest. I fidget, restless.

Before I can think anything of it, he withdraws his hand. I find I rather miss the point of contact.

"Would you like some coffee?" he asks, heading to the kitchen. I shake my head slowly, as if in a daze. *For fuck's sake.* I must be losing it!

"No, I actually came to see if you have any vanilla extract," I say, following him in.

"Yes, I do," he says, taking it out and putting it on the countertop. I slip it into my coat pocket as he pours coffee into two mugs, carrying one to the fridge. "Caramel creamer?"

I nod. "Thank you."

He puts in just the right amount, then hands me the mug. I look at him warily. He seems to be in a wonderful mood as he takes a sip of his own coffee, which he takes black.

"I'm glad you came. I wanted to talk to you anyways," Fawad says, leaning against the countertop across from me. He crosses his arms over his chest, the muscles flexing as he does so. I take a pointed sip of my coffee for fortification.

"What's up?" I ask, sitting down on one of the seats in front of the island.

"You know my tenant, Huzaifa Malik?" he asks. Oh God. Maybe I shouldn't be sitting. "I have always gotten along with him, and he often comes to me with advice regarding investments and other such things. Recently, he asked me for advice on a new opportunity and told me that he was looking to take care of his family and a wife sometime in the near future." He pauses, clearly enjoying the expression on my face before continuing. "I would say that your friend Shanzay can expect to hear from him soon."

"Why would you say that?" I say, sipping my coffee. He has made it just the way I like, which unnerves me further.

"Because I know he has an attachment toward her," he replies. "I've seen it myself."

"Hm?"

Fawad grins. "Have I surprised you? I must say, when Huzaifa was telling me, I was only thinking of you. Are you not pleased?"

"I am not surprised," I say casually, putting my coffee mug down on the island and stepping away. "Shanzay already told me." I pause. "And she has refused."

Fawad blinks, taking this information in. The joy from a moment before vanishes. Then something dawns on him.

"Please do not tell me this is another one of your matchmaking ploys." Something must show on my face because an irritated sound escapes him. He pinches the bridge of his nose before taking a deep breath and fixing me with a fierce look. "Humaira, you must stop meddling!"

"I am not meddling!" I reply, appalled at the accusation. "And I detest that you think I am."

"Why else would she refuse?" he asks, voice harsh. "Is she brainless?"

My anger stirs. "You would say that! Men think any woman is brainless to refuse an offer of marriage." I scoff. "You think so highly of yourselves."

"You must be mistaken, as you usually are," Fawad says, shaking his head. "I am sure she wouldn't do such a thing."

"I am not mistaken, as I usually am not," I reply, indignant. "Shanzay called him right in front of me."

"In front of you?" he repeats, tone livid. "You mean to say you persuaded her!" I roll my eyes, walking away. He follows close behind me. "I'm sure you did! You never could lie to me."

"Huzaifa is not her match," I reply, tone clipped as I turn back to him. We stand in the foyer, our loud voices echoing through the empty house. "I know it because she is my close friend. She can do much better than Huzaifa."

"No, I don't think she can," Fawad replies. "They are well-suited, both from simple families, both building their lives from the ground up. Huzaifa at least has the love and support of his family here with him, while Shanzay's family will probably never come to America." I make a face, not listening to him as I head toward the door to leave. "Moreover, *moreover*, Shanzay is pretty and good-natured, but unrefined. Thus, she will do well with Huzaifa, who does not care for frivolity or high society."

I whirl on him. "I don't see why she should settle for Huzaifa when apparently any man will want her! She is just the wife a man wants: pretty and good-natured, like you said." I make a small sound of derision. "If you ever marry, I am sure your wife will be the same!"

"What?" he asks, lethally close. His mouth is a hard line. He stands so close, I must look up to meet his eyes with mine, which I do with a furious glare.

"Men do not like women who argue!" I cry. "Who quarrel and have thoughts of their own!"

His eyes gleam murder. He opens his mouth as if to say something, the perfect rebuttal to my claim, but he snaps his mouth shut, releasing a long breath through his nose. With an indignant sound, I approach the door.

"My God, it's better not to have a mind than to use it the way you do!" he shouts at my back.

I laugh. "Are you not proving my point?" I open the door, then turn back. "And why should Shanzay accept the first proposal she's offered? She's at the beginning of her life. I am sure she will receive better options."

Fawad shakes his head. "I used to think your friendship with her was a detriment to you, but now I see it is a detriment to her. How can you say she is your *dear* friend yet behave in such a manner? Do you even know what Shanzay wants? Or it doesn't matter so long as she nods and agrees with everything you say? So long as you're right?"

My jaw drops. He has no idea what he's talking about. I won't give him the satisfaction of a response. With one final dirty look, I leave.

The second I step outside, the wind blasts against my

cheeks, freezing and wet. It has begun raining. Thunder rumbles above me, the sky a marbled gray and white.

Raindrops pitter-patter onto my shoulders, increasing in intensity until the drizzle has turned into a downpour. The steady fall beats in tandem with my heart. I cross my arms, pulling my coat close as I stalk away down the driveway.

A moment later, I hear him follow, the door slamming shut behind him.

"Men of sense do not want stupid wives!" he shouts above the rain.

"Well, she has made her choice now and must stick with it!" I shout over my shoulder. "I don't have that much influence, really, so stop blaming me!"

"Your love of matchmaking blinds you," he cries. He has not reached me.

I turn around and walk down the street toward him this time. His coat is open at the front, his white shirt translucent from rain to show the brown skin beneath. I shiver.

"So that is what this is about," I say, voice calm. He stands so near that I can see the mist wetting his eyelashes. I lift my chin to meet his eyes.

Rain wets my face. I blink the water from my eyes angrily, breathing fast.

Droplets of rain fall down my lips and onto my tongue. His gaze moves to my mouth. He is standing very, very still, scarcely moving at all, as I step closer. "You gave your advice and I gave mine, and you are upset because you were wrong and I was right."

He starts back. This wounded him, more than I intended. His dark eyes flash with hurt.

His voice is low when he speaks next. "If you truly think so little of me, there is nothing left to be said."

He turns, walking away from me, the stiff line of his shoulders a slash of black coat that rain falls against.

Ugh! I hear the crunch of gravel as he recedes back into his home and I start the walk back to mine.

Then, the sound of footsteps reverses and becomes louder rather than lighter, and he is there when I turn around once more. He is breathless, cheeks red from the icy wind, dark hair drenched. His eyes are blazing.

"You would not dissuade her unless you had someone else in mind," he says, "and if it is who I think it is, you should know Emad will never marry her. He thinks too highly of himself."

I open my mouth to respond, but he holds up a hand.

"Shanzay and Huzaifa are not dolls, your little playthings, to set up and discard – they are people," he says, his words barely a whisper, but he is close enough for me to hear the severe tone imbued in each word. "You will bitterly regret this."

In his dark eyes, I see disappointment beyond anything I have seen before. He has never scolded me like this.

Without waiting for a response, he dismisses me, evenly walking home. Heart hammering fast, I watch him go, his hands tight fists at his sides.

A gust of wind pushes against me, and I turn to go home. Suddenly, my eyes flood with tears and they spill out, mixing with the rain. I hastily wipe them away, pressing my palms against my cheeks and eyes before entering the house.

"Are you coming from outside? It's raining!" Papa immediately asks, mortified. His office is just by the front door, so one cannot enter or leave without his notice. "Why are you not wearing a neck scarf? Where did you go?"

"Papa, *please*," I say, kicking off my shoes. I pull off my wet headscarf and throw it on the floor. Even my hair is damp. I am in no mood.

"It is no wonder your face is all red and your eyes are tearing," he replies. "You really ought—"

I walk away before I say something I regret, pushing my anger down. When I walk to the kitchen, Naadia is there making herself a latte with the vanilla syrup she made using the last of my vanilla extract. I set the vanilla extract down harshly and she cringes, making an *oopsies* face.

I do not want to speak to her; I do not want to speak to anyone.

My throat is closing, so I rush upstairs and go to take a long, scalding shower, and I cry.

I do not know why I do, but I just cry and cry, Fawad's scolding voice ringing in my ears over the rushing water, his hurt face before me even as I clench my eyes shut.

Why must he ruin everything?

I cannot even properly focus on Rizwan for all the irritation Fawad is causing me. It is unkind and unfair. This is the beginning of what could be Rizwan and I's love story, and Fawad keeps meddling his way into my mind! It is insufferable! Unbearable!

He is the bane of my existence.

I stay in the shower until my heart calms.

Then, afterwards, I lounge in my bathrobe, doing a face mask to lessen the puffiness.

As I paint my nails, I reassure myself that Fawad is overreacting. I am right, as I always am, and there is nothing to worry about.

My mood has long since cooled off: the anger never lasts, it quickly fades, but gives way to something worse, to acute melancholy.

But no matter. We have guests arriving soon. I go to get ready.

Naadia and I are wearing velvet outfits from Farah Talib today: her suit is a deep green kurta and trousers, while mine is a deep red patiala shalwar and kameez.

We used to hate matching when we were younger (her more than me) but since we've reached adulthood, we wear complimentary outfits. We are each other's best accessories (until she got married, but I still think I'm a better partner for her than Asif).

"Humaira, check on the oven will you?" Naadia says, sliding jhumkas into her ears in the bathroom. "I'm almost ready."

"Okie," I say. Nothing like dressing up to put me in a better mood. Something about it makes me feel closer to Mama, who was always dressed up in the best three-piece shalwar kameez suits and gold jewelry and pretty khussas to match.

Of course, with my hijab on, I am not as pretty as I am with my hair done, and the scarf does cover my earrings, but that is sort of the point: to privatize a woman's beauty so they are sought after for something other than their physical looks, like their intellect and heart.

It is all I want: for a man to *see* me, to see my soul. To truly know me. And then it will be all the more fun for him when I turn out to be stunningly gorgeous without my hijab (and without clothes on for that matter).

I head downstairs, and everything looks good. The rain has slowed to a soft drizzle outside. I am just lighting some more candles when the doorbell rings.

Checking my appearance in the mirror to assure I look just as good as I did a moment ago, I go to greet whoever has arrived.

The guest list includes our phuppos and whichever of their children and grandchildren can make it, plus Shanzay, plus Rizwan.

"Salaam, ao, ao," Papa says to Mahum Phuppo and her husband. Behind them is Emad.

"Salaam!" I say cheerily, kissing my elderly phuppo's cheeks, then greeting Emad. Before Papa closes the door, Asif arrives as well, and Papa lets him in with a curt nod of his head.

"Sir," Asif says.

Papa takes the elders to the other room, while I am with

Emad and Asif. I expect to see Fawad behind Asif, but he is not there.

He would not refuse to come, would he?

My heart sinks at the thought, but before I can think of it further, I realize Emad has been talking to me.

"Emad," I say, tone warm, "Shanzay has had a bit of a tough week. Would you be a darling and spend time with her to make her feel better while I host?"

"I'm sorry to hear that," Emad says, frowning.

"She's such a dear friend; I cannot bear to see her upset. You will help me, won't you?" I bat my lashes.

"Of course! Of course," he replies, then lowers his voice. "Anything for you."

"Thank you, I do appreciate it," I say, smiling one of my winning smiles.

"I'm so glad we're seeing more of each other lately," Emad says.

"As am I," I reply. "Funny is it not, that we were never very close before the past few months? And I have a feeling we will only get closer."

Emad is pleased by this comment, and I am sure he is mostly in love with Shanzay already. I knew I was not wrong to push him and Shanzay together.

"Something to drink?" Emad asks me.

"A Coke please," I reply, and off he goes to get them. I rub my temples. All that crying has given me a headache, and now Fawad is not even here for me to scold him for it.

"Humaira, bestie," Asif says, voice hesitant. I startle. Goodness, I had forgotten he was there.

"Yes, dear Asif," I reply, confused by the strange look he is giving me.

"Why are you being so encouraging to Emad?"

I blink. "What do you mean?"

"Your manner with him is very ... spirited." He bites back a smile. "He might get the wrong idea."

"What?" I balk. What a preposterous notion. "Asif, really you are so silly sometimes." I wave him off. What has gotten into these brothers today with their ridiculous ideas? "Where is Fawad, by the way?" I ask, changing the subject.

"No idea." He shrugs. "He's been in a wretched mood all day." My heart stills at that, but I ignore it. "Our parents are coming mid-January," Asif says. "Naadia is stressed, but you have to tell her not to worry."

"Yes, but in-laws can be quite frightening to manage, especially when they are only around for a month or two in the year."

"She knows my parents adore her, just like I do," he says. I smile. Asif really is such a dear.

"Don't worry," I say. "I will console her. And remind her not to be crazy."

"Thank you, Humaira," he says. "What would we do without you?"

Yes, what would they?

Shanzay arrives shortly after. I spend time with her and Emad, watching their interactions. Emad is quite animated and very attentive. The best part of the evening occurs when he takes out his phone and is holding it up very blatantly so we can see his phone case.

And in the phone case is the polaroid of him and Shanzay.

Shanzay and I exchange a glance, eyes wide with excitement. I feel vindicated. A confession is surely forthcoming, it is only a matter of time.

Fawad really was wrong.

Speaking of, he does end up coming (quite late might I add) after dinner has already been served, and then proceeds to ignore me! I would feel more terrible about it if I was not annoyed with him. Every time I seek him out, he deftly avoids me.

Not that I am so preoccupied with him. I have Rizwan to entertain me, and entertain me he does. He is quite attentive and pleasant to talk to.

I am sure the only reason I cannot be as vigilant in my company to him is because I have a headache.

Then, finally, as most people are leaving, I find Fawad sitting alone by the fire in the living room, which is still blazing. I intend to give him a piece of my mind.

When I enter the room, he looks up, firelight dancing across his features, shadows drawing attention to the sharp lines of his cheekbones. He says nothing. His attention is averted to baby Aizah, who sits on his lap, most comfortable since no one is trying to teach her how to crawl.

His silence sobers me. Any anger I felt dissipates.

"Please, let's not fight," I say, coming to sit beside him on the couch. Heat from the fire warms my skin. "For some reason I find I cannot bear it."

"What, you cannot handle anyone being upset with

you?" he asks, tone cold. He does not look at me when he speaks, instead focuses on baby Aizah's hands wrapped around his slender fingers.

"No, it isn't that." I have always been well-liked and think it is the fault of others if they do not like me. But that is different – that is with people who scarcely know me.

I cannot bear for Fawad, who truly knows me, to dislike me.

I inch closer to him on the couch, looking at him until he finally turns his gaze upon me. "As irritating as you are, you are a ... friend. And Naadia's brother-in-law. We will know each other for the rest of our lives. It will not do to be fighting." I smile sweetly, batting my eyelashes for full effect. "Please?"

He releases a resigned breath, rubbing a hand across his beard. "Well, there is nothing to be done now anyways," he concedes. "Huzaifa called to tell me of Shanzay's response."

Despite myself, I still. "I hope he was not too disappointed?" I ask, voice quiet.

"I have never known a man to be more so," he replies, looking down.

I do feel bad, but there is nothing to be done. I swallow the lump in my throat and brush a finger against baby Aizah's cheek.

"You must do better than your Humaira Phuppo," I instruct her.

This gets a smile out of Fawad. He shakes his head, looking at me. His dark eyes are warm, flickering with firelight and some emotion I cannot decipher. I feel my heart rate quicken.

Fawad lifts baby Aizah's little hand up and presses it to my cheek.

"Your face is flushed red from the fire," he says, voice low.

I press the backs of my cold hands to my cheeks. They are unbelievably hot.

And it is not just from the fire.

Chapter Twelve

There's a New Year's dinner at Rameela Auntie's, one of our family friends.

Papa is excited about it, for some reason, but I am not particularly enthused about going, since Shanzay is sick, so I cannot bring her along, and Rizwan has left to go back to London. I stopped by Phuppo's yesterday to say goodbye to him under the excuse of wanting to see Phuppo.

It was a strange encounter. I did not feel very sad to see him go; I did not feel much of anything, really.

I do not want to analyze it too deeply, however; not yet at least.

I arrive to the dinner party with Papa, just as Naadia arrives with Asif and Fawad. Emad is already there, having arrived just before us, without either of his parents. I believe he is friends with Rameela Auntie's son, or something. One can never draw conclusions as to why certain people get invited and why certain people don't at dawats.

"Here, let me take your coat," Emad says, while we all crowd in the foyer of Auntie's large house. She lives a few towns over on the north shore and also has a well-decorated, tasteful home.

"Thank you," I reply, handing my Loro Piana cape (yes, the one with the fur! These aunties are always dressed to the absolute nines with their gold and designer shoes and purses) to Emad, just as Asif gives me a pointed glance, trying not to laugh. I give him a dirty look, remembering his comment about being encouraging towards Emad.

"Behave yourself," I warn. He sobers for a moment.

"What's going on?" Fawad asks, glancing between the two of us. He's dressed quite smartly in a black suit, though instead of his usual crisp white shirt, he's wearing a black dress shirt, and no tie, the top button undone and exposing a triangle of skin at the base of his throat that momentarily makes me forget my name.

"Nothing," I say quickly. I do not want to get Asif's ridiculous notion into Fawad's head as well. It will only aggravate things, and I do not want to fight with him (beyond our standard bickering, of course).

"It might snow tonight," Asif says, looking out the window. Naadia and I gasp at the same time, whipping our heads to Papa to see if he's heard. Thankfully, he hasn't. Naadia hits Asif with her gloves.

"Don't say that," Naadia warns, glancing at Papa. "You'll send him into a panic."

"And when he was so looking forward to this dinner, too," I add, tsking at Asif.

"You heard the Mirza sisters," Fawad says, clapping his brother on the back. "We best behave." He offers me a half-smile.

Emad returns and asks if I would like anything to drink.

"No, I'm alright, thank you," I respond, distracted as Asif whispers something to Naadia. She glances at Emad and I with a puzzled look. "Emad, I'm afraid to say Shanzay is down with a cold, which is why she couldn't come tonight."

"I am sorry to hear that," he says, not looking it one bit. I furrow my brows. "But I'm sure she'll be fine. Shall we go get some appetizers?"

Surely he should be more concerned. I resist the urge to frown, especially as Asif raises his eyebrows at me.

"Actually, I think I will sit with Rameela Auntie," I say, grabbing Naadia's arm. "Let's go sit with the ladies. Goodbye, boys!"

I wave at them, then drag Naadia with me to the room full of aunties, all dressed to impress, with their fancy three-thousand dollar shawls and decades old jewels.

"Your husband needs to see a psychiatrist," I whisper to Naadia, before she can say anything. "He is positively delusional."

She bites back a laugh. "If you say so," she sing-songs.

I pinch her side. "Behave. Or I'm telling Phuppo."

(Phuppo was always playing judge between us, even when we were girls.)

We sit with the aunties, who fawn over us, the young blood. Unfortunately, this is not much better company, for as the only unmarried woman there, I get bombarded by questions. It is a full-on interrogation.

"Has your papa begun looking for a husband for you?" one auntie asks. "It must be so difficult without your mama here to do it herself."

"But do not fret! We will help you," another auntie adds. "I have a handful of eligible nephews."

The eligible nephews in question all have secret girlfriends, drink, or smoke copious amounts of weed, so I'm not particularly interested. Naadia and I exchange a knowing glance.

"Thank you, but I am alright, at the present," I reply.

"Yes, but it does take quite some time to find a good rishta," the auntie replies. "You must start looking early. You are not getting any younger."

I suppress a sigh. Some aunties can be simple-minded about age, believing women should be married off once they strike eighteen, and that they will expire by the age of twenty-four. Most of our social circle is more refined than that, but some are still of the old, backwards thinking.

"Did you not find anyone in college?" someone asks. "There must have been plenty of boys there."

"Unfortunately, I did not realize I was there to husband-hunt," I respond pleasantly. "Sadly, I was instead focusing on my education."

I throw in an enthused smile so no one gets offended, and the aunties laugh at my mischief, though I am deadly serious.

Besides, boys in college were so *stupid*, for lack of a

better word. Which was precisely why I was steering Shanzay away from Huzaifa.

All college boys are immature, with no idea of the future, or they are simply there to have fun with no intention of commitment. I knew plenty of boys with girlfriends who were actually engaged to their cousins back home, or boys who dated girls, then broke up with them just to date their best friends.

Overall, a terrible mess. Zero out of ten would recommend.

"Are you sure you do not have a secret boy hidden away you are not telling us about?" one auntie teases. "A pretty girl like you, I am sure there must be someone."

"I wish, Auntie," I reply. "Would that not make things simpler?"

We laugh, though I am positively mortified by the thought of having a secret boyfriend. Who has the emotional stamina for that? I love to read about forbidden romance, but in real life, the angst would surely kill me.

Besides, I agree with the Islamic ideals of no-dating. It is the most sensible course of action. People should only get involved with one another if they are serious and have intentions of marriage in mind. Of course, I do not judge others, I just know for myself, dating would not work, for I do not have the heart for it.

I am glad for the structure Islam gives my life. It is not just a religion, but a way of life – a mindset, an entire way of being.

When the aunties move on to interrogating Naadia as to

when she'll get pregnant (even married, you can never win with the aunties), I flee, but just as I do, Emad finds me.

He begins conversing with me over the pani puri bar, telling me random stories as I fill the little puffs with chickpeas, boiled potatoes, onions, yogurt, and tamarind chutney. And he does not mention Shanzay once! I bring her up a few times, but he is not interested in speaking about her.

Perhaps he is being shy.

From the amused look Asif gives me as he places another samosa onto his plate, I would say he disagrees.

"Excuse me for a moment," I say to Emad, approaching my brother-in-law instead. I kick his leg with my heels.

"Ow," he says, though I've only just tapped him. "You could kill a man with those."

"They're Aquazzura. I wouldn't dirty them with a man's blood."

"Are you having fun with your new bosom buddy?" Asif asks. I make a face.

"Ew, Asif. Don't say bosom buddy."

"I regretted it once I said it." He hangs his head for a moment, then is back to his foolishness. "The sentiment still remains. Are you having fun with your *friend*? You have been awfully close all night."

"Don't be preposterous," I say, frowning. "If he is seeking out my company, it is probably to ask news of Shanzay."

Though even I must admit that Emad has not been very diligent in his duty to ask after Shanzay.

As if sensing my self-doubt, Asif raises his brows. "I do not think so…"

"Where's Papa?" I ask, looking around. "I'm tired."

"He already left," Asif replies.

"He just *abandoned* me!" I exclaim.

"Don't worry," Emad says, joining us just then. "I can drive you home."

I bite back a groan as Asif bites back a smile.

"No, that's alright," I say quickly. "Asif and Naadia can take me, they are going back to the Sheikhs's, and we live on the same street, after all."

"No, no, you go with Emad," Asif replies, giving Emad a wide smile. "I think we'll stay a little longer, and weren't you saying you were tired?"

"I am not too tired," I respond. He is enjoying this entirely too much. I glare at him.

"I'll take you," Emad says, looking positively enthused. "Really, it's not a problem at all."

"Well, where is Fawad?" I ask, looking around. "He can take me. I really wouldn't want to inconvenience you, Emad." I bat my eyelashes at him, succeeding in shutting him up.

"Fawad offered to drive Mahmud Uncle back, since he was so panicked due to the snow," Asif replies. Traitors, all of them! "Really, I don't think it'll be an inconvenience, would it, Emad?"

"None at all," Emad says, stepping closer to me. "I'd love to drive you home."

So I am left with no choice.

"Okay," I concede. Emad dashes off to grab our coats before I can change my mind, and I glare at Asif and Naadia, who's joined us to snicker with her husband like a child.

"You will pay for this, dear Asif. You will pay." I tsk at him. "I take cash or check or a week-long vacation to the Maldives."

Unfortunately, Emad comes back, and I must go with him. With a final pout directed at Asif and Naadia, who simply wave cheerfully, I go with Emad to his car. The air is frigid, and the snow is really coming down, thick white clumps swirling around the air. I quickly get into the car, and Emad puts the heat on blast.

We ride mostly in silence, Emad plays some weird music I do not listen to the lyrics of, and I focus on looking out my window, hoping to get home soon. At least Auntie's house isn't too far away.

"Should we stop for dessert?" Emad asks, pulling into a McDonald's parking lot. Ooh, I *could* go for a cookie. But this is certainly not the time.

"No, that's alright," I say. "I'd rather not. I'm very tired."

But he pulls into the drive-through anyway, ordering me cookies and himself apple pie. I know I should probably ignore him and not eat, but who am I to resist warm cookies? I do not have that much willpower. Of course, I eat them.

As I do, I focus on the snow falling outside, the flurry of white against the dark sky.

Instead of driving away from the eating establishment,

Emad puts the car in park, then shifts to face me in his seat. I prickle, alarmed.

"I'm glad to have a moment alone with you," he says, voice nervous. "I wanted to talk to you about something – about strong feelings I have for someone."

I turn to look at him, heart beating fast.

I knew Asif was wrong! Ha!

"I am so glad to hear that!" I exclaim, smiling warmly at him. Perhaps I shouldn't spoil the surprise, but oh, I cannot hold it in. "And I think you will be pleased to learn that she feels the same way."

He grins, excited. "Really?"

I nod, squealing.

"Humaira, you have no idea how glad I am to hear that," he says. "I have been looking for a way to tell you that I love you and—"

I still, not hearing the rest. "Wait, *what?*" I shake my head, thinking I heard him wrong. "You mean you love *Shanzay*, right?"

I laugh nervously.

"Shanzay?" he repeats, confused. He shakes his head. "*Her?* And me?" He laughs as if I have said the funniest thing. "You must be joking."

Oh GOD no.

"But you've been spending all this time with her," I say, still hoping he has made a mistake, rather than me. My voice comes out high. "You have a picture of her on your phone case!"

"No, it's a picture of *you* and me." Shaking his head, he

pulls out his phone and shows me the polaroid. I am half in it. I make a whimpering sound. *Oh no, oh no. No, no, no.* "I only spent time with her because *you* asked me to," he continues. Ya Allah, this is not good.

"She and I wouldn't work," he says, "but *you and I* would be happy together. I love you."

"You *don't* love me," I say, shaking my head. "You merely *think* you do."

"I know what I feel," he replies, voice patient as if I am being silly. He reaches for my hand, and I snatch it back, appalled.

"Don't touch me," I warn.

"Yes, yes, I understand, you wish to wait until we're married," he says. My god, he is full-on delusional!

"Let me say this slowly, so you understand," I say, voice even. I harden my face. "We will never be married. I do not like you. At all."

He blinks, confused. "You're only saying that to play hard to get, and if that is the case, I will say it is working—"

"Ew! I am not!" I cry. *Ugh, as if!* "I am desirable enough without such games! I really do not like you and do not know why you would ever think we could be married."

"Because you encouraged me," he says, patience thinning. "You constantly sought me out. You called me, and at parties, you would always come over to talk and spend time with me."

"For Shanzay!" I cry, exasperated. I can't believe this is happening.

"I could never be interested in *her*," he snaps. "She's a

FOB. We aren't suited at all. Doesn't her father work in a textile factory?" He shakes his head. "No, I was always interested in *you*. You and I would be well suited. We are both from good families, well-educated, well-off individuals."

"You are a snob and a half." I make a disgusted face. "I see now that even Shanzay is way too good for you, so how you could even consider me to be in your league proves just how little your brain really is."

I say this with as much derision and contempt and cruelty as I can, which is a great deal. His eyes flash with anger.

"Now drive me home," I snap, "and I won't mention your egregious behavior to Papa. But if you insist on being a total dickhead, I'll tell Papa a number of things, and he will surely ruin your life."

I'm not sure how true this threat really is, but it is enough to have Emad take the car out of park and begin driving me home in absolute silence. People always assume rich people can do anything if they set their minds to it, so I'm sure with ample incentive, Papa really could ruin Emad's life.

Though he would never do such a thing to his sister's son. God, this will be a mess with Mahum Phuppo later. But for now, all I think about is getting out of this car and to the safety of home.

We make it to my neighborhood shortly, and Emad stops at the end of the street.

He cannot be serious. I fix him with a glare, waiting for

him to drop me off in my driveway, all the way down the street, but he avoids my gaze, staring out the window, where snow is falling even heavier than before.

How rude! Men and their pettiness know no bounds.

This only serves to confirm the fact I already know: he doesn't love me, despite his declaration. If he truly loved me, he would never behave in such a manner.

No, he simply loved the *idea* of me, as so many others did. He did not see me, not really. All he saw was what I could offer him.

I don't even care. I get out of the car and slam the door. His car pulls away with record speed. I cannot believe he actually left me here, at the end of the street, at night, while it is snowing! In my heels and cashmere cape! (The cape really is cozy, but my shoes will be utterly ruined! And I love this pair.)

As I trudge through the snow, I walk past the Sheikhs's. I have half a mind to go up and yell at Asif for not giving me a ride back, but think better of it.

I just want to go home and sleep, and that is exactly what I do.

The next morning, I am in my pajamas, making myself coffee, when Fawad arrives.

"It's me," he calls from the foyer. He's let himself in with the keycode. "I knocked but I don't think you heard, so I let myself in."

"Yeah, that's fine. One sec!" I call back, grabbing a scarf. "Okay, you can come now."

I pour foamed milk into my latte, then turn to say salaam to him. He gives me a look, eyes narrowed behind his glasses, and my stomach drops.

Oh, he is going to scold me. He must have heard about the Emad debacle from Asif.

Damn Naadia. I texted her the rundown of events last night, to which she sent a slew of laughing emojis, and I replied with copious knife emojis. I want to yell at them both.

Actually I don't care about Asif knowing, but I know Fawad is going to be patronizing about it.

"I only know because I asked Asif why on earth you were walking home last night in the snow and he told me," Fawad prefaces, coming round the counter to face me.

I pout, putting my coffee down. He is angry. He has that scrunched look on his severe face, his lips flat in a frown.

A lecture is forthcoming. I know he will say I deserve this for all my meddling, and he will be right, which is worse.

"I know it's a mess," I start, "but will you at least hear my piece before you start scolding?"

He shakes his head. "No."

"Well I'm going to say it anyway." I throw my hands up. "I didn't know he liked me!"

"You pride yourself on how well you perceive people, yet you scarcely see things!" he says, tone condescending and cruel. I frown.

"Why are you yelling at me?" I whine. "I didn't even do anything!"

I abandon my coffee and exit to the family room, which is much brighter and open. Outside the windows, the backyard is covered in a blanket of white snow. I want to dive in and hide away, but there's no hiding from Fawad as he follows me, long legs stalking purposefully.

"Humaira," he says, voice exasperated. "You have no idea just how many boys are obsessed with you! And you callously make fools of them all!"

"What do you care, anyways?" I snap, whirling around. He's right behind me and the motion puts me eye-level with his throat. I lift my chin to glare at him. "Don't tell me you are one of those fools."

Emotion floods his eyes – anger, and something else. He stares down at me, breathing hard, his chest rising and falling. My heart ricochets against my chest, erratic and unsure.

"No." He sets his jaw. "I thank God every day that I am not."

He steps closer, but I do not back down. We are hardly a few inches away now. If I took a deep inhale, we might be touching. A chaotic little voice dares me to do it.

I hold my breath. Even so, I can feel the heat of his skin seeping in the thin gap of space between us. I want to lean into it.

His gaze flicks to my mouth, so quick I think I have imagined it – then with a final glance, he exits the room.

The instant he does, cold air washes over me. I shiver.

He slams the front door shut, and I hear his groan of frustration just outside it.

I grab a cushion and bury my face in it, letting out a scream of my own.

I do not *want* to break boys' hearts. I do not pride myself on causing others pain! Why did he have to be so stern?

But the anger dissipates quickly, bubbles full of air popping, and I collapse backward onto the sofa.

With a great sigh, I go to the kitchen to get my coffee and phone, where I see I've received a text from Naadia.

sorry about unleashing fawad on you

am making lasagna and will bring some over when done

you owe me brownies and a movie. i get to choose.

done

I am not angry with her, really, nor am I angry with Fawad. I am just sad.

I was wrong, and I hurt Emad, and I'll hurt Shanzay, and I was wrong. I only wanted to help, to be useful and good, to make others happy, and I've made a royal mess of things, just as Fawad said I would.

I hate that everything funnels down to this: sadness.

I get up and go to the kitchen. I take out lemons and a zester and a double boiler. I make lemon curd, and after twenty minutes of whisking, I feel calmer. I stare out the windows at the all white, how fresh and clean it is. Another ten minutes, and I am almost right as rain once more.

The lemon curd is just setting in the fridge when Papa arrives home. He sees the kitchen in the aftermath of baking.

"What did you make?" he asks, looking around in search of a treat.

"Lemon streusel bars," I reply, as he opens the fridge and spots the lemon curd. "But—"

The curd is a little tart and the streusel mix will balance it, I am about to say, but he dips a finger in to taste before I can.

He makes a face, lips puckered. "It's so sour!" he exclaims.

Something in me snaps.

"Sometimes things don't come out perfect!" I say, raising my voice. Papa is startled. He blinks, then clears his throat.

"One time, when I was in college," he says, beginning a story, "I was trying to make…"

Usually, I love to listen to his stories, but today, even Papa can't make me smile – that's when I know I'm in a really wretched mood. I zone him out until he is done, then muster up a polite smile, but it is of course not what he is used to: Naadia and I making commentary and oohing and aahing at the appropriate moments.

"Do you miss Naadia, is that it?" he asks. I always miss Naadia.

I always miss someone or something.

"No, that isn't it," I reply quietly, blinking rapidly at the tears that well in my eyes.

"I knew she should not have gone so soon," he says, starting up again. He isn't looking at me. "I told her to stay here – she has no need to stay at the Sheikhs's when she has her own perfectly good room here – but does she listen to me? No!"

"Papa." I pinch the bridge of my nose. "She is coming here in a little while." But my voice is a whisper, I am so exhausted, and he does not hear.

"You won't leave me, will you?" he asks, focus shifting back to me. I resist the urge to pinch the bridge of my nose again and instead settle for a prolonged blink. Sometimes, it feels as though he is the child and I am the parent.

"No, I won't," I say, smiling enthusiastically. I love him to pieces but he drives me absolutely mad sometimes.

I just want to be alone.

But after Papa has gone back to his office, and I am alone, I do not feel at peace. I wish there was a way to be away from myself, to truly be *alone*, but I take my bleeding heart with me wherever I go.

Chapter Thirteen

After work that Monday, I invite Shanzay over. She has recovered from her cold, and I must tell her the dreadful news. How I wish I did not have to tell her about Emad, but I know I must.

I wait until we've had a delicious meal of tomato soup and grilled cheese and are sitting cozy in front of the roaring fire before I do.

"Shanzay, at the party..." I begin.

After it is done, she is in a state of shock.

"O-Of course," Shanzay says, swallowing hard. "It was silly of me to imagine... Of course he loves you." Her lower lip trembles like a child's. "You are so much prettier and refined and cleverer—"

"No, no," I say, taking her hands. I want to cry, but hold off. This isn't about me; it's about her. "Shanzay, he will regret this, he *will*. There is no one better than you! I'm so sorry."

"Thank you for saying that," she says, eyes welling with tears. "I just feel so foolish."

My chest tightens. "I am so sorry for the pain I have caused you," I say. "I want you to be happy, and I was so sure of his feelings for you..."

"No, it isn't *your* fault," Shanzay says, shaking her head. "You were only trying to help, and I appreciate it so very much."

But she is heartbroken all the same. She is crying and trying very hard not to.

"God, this is all my fault," I say, feeling wretched. "Shanzay, I'm so sorry. Come, let's make you feel better." I think for a moment about what's to be done. "I can call the spa!" I offer. "We can get facials and massages and pedicures, then go to the mall .... or out for afternoon tea! That always cheers me up. Then—"

"No, there is no need for all that," she says. I think she is just saying that for takaluf's sake, and I want to say I'll pay for it all, of course, but I can see she means it.

I am reminded of something someone in college said to me once: *You can't use money to solve all your problems!* To which I replied, *Why ever not?*

Perhaps this is one of those situations.

"What can we do then?" I ask. I realize I do not know what to do to cheer her up.

I miss Mama fiercely at that moment. She would know what to do. And despite not being the one rejected, I feel awfully sad as well. I wish Mama was here, even if not to give me advice, but just to lay my head in her lap, the way I used to.

I would set the pillow down on Mama's lap and cuddle against her. Once, she went to lay a hand down to my hair but missed and ended up smacking my face.

"Ah, Ama!" I whined, but it made me laugh.

"Oops, sorry, gudiya," she replied, pinching my cheek. She moved to stroke my hair, tucking it behind my ears. "Teek?"

I nodded. "Hmm."

I miss moments like that: simple and filled with love.

"We don't have to do anything," Shanzay says, voice trailing. She nibbles on her bottom lip.

"No, no, we must," I say firmly. I reach for her hands and squeeze them.

"Well ... we could stay in?" Shanzay suggests. "Maybe eat junk food and watch movies?"

"Excellent idea," I say. Thank God. Something I can *do*. "Consider it done."

I instruct Shanzay to pick the movie while I grab all the unhealthy food I can find. Unfortunately, when I return with cookies, chips, popcorn, and chocolate, I see Shanzay has picked a horror film.

"Is this alright?" she asks, cocooned in blankets and pillows. I do not have the heart to tell her I hate horror films and never watch them.

I simply nod, smiling brightly, and suffer through it.

And she does not stop with one. Apparently they are her favorite type of film, which I did not know because previously whenever we had movie nights we would watch *my* favorite type of movies: period dramas.

But Shanzay is positively obsessed with horror movies. We marathon three in a row, breaking for prayer and pizza.

Despite closing my eyes and ears through most of them, the few moments I am watching, I end up screaming from jump-scare moments and even upend an entire bowl of popcorn. At the very least, Shanzay seems to be enjoying them, her eyes wide, enthralled. She's made of stiffer stuff than I realized; she does not scream once.

It is a good distraction.

"Thank you for tonight," says Shanzay, after the movies are done and it is quite late. She actually looks relaxed, whereas I'm too frightened to even get up from my position on the sofa in case there's some monster hiding beneath the rug.

Why do we have so many windows in my house? To let all the murderers and rapists know just where in the house I am?

The entire house is dark. It creaks from the wind, and I startle. Does the house always sound like this? And why is it so *big*? A dozen robbers could be hiding in various closets, waiting to attack, and I would be none the wiser!

"Shan, please turn on the lights," I say, peeking out from beneath my blanket. "All of them, thanks." She does, and I dash up quickly out of sight of the windows to walk her to the door.

"I better get going now," she says, grabbing her purse. Oh God, she's going to leave me alone!

"Why don't you sleep over?" I ask, tone casual. "You can leave early in the morning to make it in time for class."

"That's sweet, but I don't have any of my things."

"You can borrow mine!"

She laughs. "You're not afraid, are you?"

"No, no ... no," I say, waving a hand. She raises a brow.

"Okay..." She makes a quick motion towards me. I shriek and jump back. "You *are* afraid!"

I scowl at her. "Okay, fine, I am afraid! What type of sadist enjoys those movies?!"

Shanzay laughs. "I really can't stay, but you'll be fine," she says. "Just go to bed. I'm sure your dad will be here soon."

I pout, but she really must be off. She gives me a hug, then leaves, and I lock the door behind her, watching from the side window to make sure she makes it to her car without being abducted. Then I am well and truly alone.

I know I should go clean up the mess in the family room where we were sitting, but there are too many windows there. I don't even go to turn the lights off. I feel like going into hiding so I head to the safest place, my room.

I settle into bed, leaving my side lamp on as I am too afraid of the dark. I lie flat on my back, too afraid to turn to one side.

I close my eyes, trying to sleep, my thoughts slowly drifting towards unconsciousness...

The house creaks. My eyes fly open.

Did I lock the door?

Oh God.

It does lock automatically, but did I *hear* it lock? What if the automatic lock is broken? Anyone could come in! My heart hammers against my chest. I reach for my phone and quickly dial Papa's number.

It's nearly midnight, why isn't he home yet?

"Papa, when are you coming home?"

"I'll be home in an hour or so, the Hoffman plans are all wrong, and there's no one around to fix them, so I must do it myself—wait a minute." He pauses. "Why are you whispering?"

"Oh, no reason," I say, increasing my voice only a little and staring warily at my bedroom door.

"Is everything alright?" His tone is worried. "I can come home now…"

"No, no, the Hoffman plans are due tomorrow," I say, trying to sound calm. "I was just wondering—"

The house creaks again. I gasp, a little scream escaping my lips.

"What is it?" Papa asks, alarmed. "Is everything okay?"

"Yes, yes, everything is fine," I say quickly. "I watched a scary movie with Shanzay so I am just a little jumpy and can't sleep, that's all."

"Beta, you know you shouldn't watch those movies," Papa tsks. "You have no stomach for them."

"I know, I know, I'll be more careful next time."

"Go drink some warm milk with honey," Papa instructs. "You'll fall asleep in no time."

But that would require going downstairs. After hanging up the phone, I contemplate what to do, and after about fifteen minutes of debating, I decide some action is better than none.

I get out of bed and edge towards my door, opening it slowly. I know it's silly, and of course the house is just as safe as it is every other night, but I am thoroughly spooked and must take my precautions.

The coast clear, I run down the stairs and dash to the kitchen, where the lights are thankfully still on. I am just pouring honey into a mug of milk when I hear something.

At first, I imagine it is the house settling, but then the noise grows louder.

It's the front door. Opening.

I hold my breath, waiting for Papa to call out salaam like he always does, but his voice never comes. I still.

I wonder if I should call out, then think better of it. Heart beating fast, I tip-toe to the knife drawer and pull out the biggest knife we have.

This is ridiculous, I tell myself. Who would be stupid enough to attempt robbing us!

"If you're a robber, I kindly suggest you leave right this instant," I call out, trying to keep my tone level and confident. "We have a very proficient security system installed with cameras recording your every move, and the police have already been notified. If you leave now, you might be able to escape." I swallow the lump in my throat, knees shaky. "Besides, most of the valuables are in the bank." A horrible thought strikes me. "And I am very ugly!"

I hold my breath, ready to throw up.

Then, the most befuddling thing happens: I hear laughter. Laughter!

"I must agree with the last bit," a voice says.

You have got to be joking me.

All the fear vanishes. Within me brews a deadly concoction of relief and anger, and my eyes well with tears.

"Don't come over here!" I yell, when I hear him growing closer. "I'm indecent."

Letting him marinate with that image for a moment, I go to find a scarf hanging in the pantry and throw it on to cover my hair. When I go to meet Fawad in the foyer, his cheeks are suspiciously pink, and he is staring intently at his shoes.

I look for something to throw at him but can find nothing.

"Just a second," I say, heading to my shoe closet. I take out a pair of loafers and throw one at his back.

"Ow!" he cries, turning around just in time to get hit in the chest with the other. "Hey!"

(I don't feel bad because they're Gucci and thus very soft leather.)

"I cannot believe you would frighten me like that," I say, giving him my deadliest glare, though the effect is rather lost as he takes in the sight of my matching flannel pajamas, decorated with candy-canes. "What are you doing here? How did you even get in?" I demand, then remember he knows our keycode. Drat.

"Uncle called and told me to check on you," Fawad says, rubbing his chest where I hit him. Hm, he has a rather solid chest. Noted. "And I know the keycode, in case of emergencies. Such as this."

"Papa called you?" I repeat, fingers pressing into my throat. My pulse races against my palm. He nods.

Papa must really trust him, or he would never have asked Fawad to check on me at such an hour. I am still a girl, and he is still a boy, and we are both alone in this great big house. I'm not even wearing a bra, for God's sake! Remembering such a detail, I surreptitiously cross my arms across my chest.

Why such a potential-ripe opportunity must be wasted on Fawad is beyond me. Though even I must admit, I feel a little breathless.

But I am sure it is due to the intense emotions of the last few minutes rather than this alarmingly handsome off-duty look with ruffled hair and sleepy eyes behind his glasses. He's wearing a black hoodie and black sweatpants. Damn my weakness for a good black-on-black combo.

"Well, sorry to have wasted your time, but I am perfectly fine," I say.

"Yes, you had the situation well under control," Fawad agrees. "You provided a very compelling argument as to why I should not attempt to rob or harm you."

His eyes are amused. I scowl, but the anger is gone in a flash, and I pout.

"Don't make fun," I say, voice small. "I was actually scared."

"I'm sorry," he says, voice softening. He comes closer, face tender. "I should have called out. I just didn't know if you were asleep or not." He pauses, staring intently at my face. "Are you okay?"

"Yes," I say, trying to keep my tone petulant, but I am tired.

"What made you so spooked?" he asks, heading towards the kitchen to pour a glass of water. I follow him. He hands the water to me, and I drink it, releasing a long breath.

"Shanzay was upset, so I watched some horror movies with her," I explain.

"You hate horror movies," he states, then hesitates before asking: "Why was she upset?"

"Emad."

"Ah."

"I had to tell her what happened, of course." I pinch the bridge of my nose. "Please don't be insufferable."

I give him a pleading look, and he holds his hands up. There is not a trace of wretchedness on his face as he leans against the countertop.

"I am sorry she was hurt," is all he says.

"Me too," I reply miserably. It hurts twice-fold because I do hate to be wrong.

"Don't worry," he reassures me, "she'll recover, and no one will think any less of you."

I nod, his words placating me. Now all that is left is exhaustion.

I should apologize to him, seeing as he might have been sleeping, and he came all the way over just to check on me after I became frightened by something so silly, but it's just Fawad. I don't mind being an inconvenience to him.

"You can go now," I finally say. "Seeing as I am perfectly fine."

"No, I'd rather stay," he replies, heading towards the family room. "You know, in case a real robber comes."

I follow behind him and watch as he settles onto the sofa. A small smile plays on my lips.

"Will you protect me, then?" I tease.

"Always," he says, but there is no mirth in his voice. His eyes burn into mine, steady and sure. My breath catches, and I look away.

"Stay if you'd like," I say, clearing my throat. "I'm off to bed."

"Sleep tight."

But as I retreat upstairs, I do feel rather bad about leaving him. After fixing my scarf, I return back downstairs with two books in my hands. I go to the family room, where he's sitting on the couch.

Fawad's eyes are closed. I observe him unabashedly for a moment. The fan of his dark eyelashes, the cut of his cheekbones, his rather full, cushiony lips. The column of his throat.

Then further down, his wide chest, tapering to his thin waist, his hands folded in his lap, the silver signet ring, the long, slender fingers. To be touched by those hands...

Something stirs low in my stomach.

I shake my head, cheeks flaming. *Goodness*. It must be the late hour.

I throw a book onto his lap, and he opens his eyes.

"What are you doing?" he asks, looking at me curiously as I sit on the other end of the sofa.

"Giving you backup," I say breezily. "You know, in case a real robber comes."

Leaning against the corner so I am facing him, I pull my legs up and set my own book on my knees. I do not look at him, I simply begin reading, and from the corner of my eyes, I can tell when he has picked up his book and begun reading as well.

I've given him my copy of *The Piper's Son* by Melina Marchetta, the book I recommended to him at dinner a few days ago. In my own hands, I have my copy of *The Secret History* by Donna Tartt, the book he recommended to me. I haven't started it yet, but even now as I try to read, I find I cannot focus at all.

My gaze sneaks away from the page to linger on his face: the dark shadow of his beard, the glint of his glasses, his warm eyes half-lidded and enraptured as he reads his own book.

His hair is disheveled, sticking out in all directions, and I want to bridge the gap between us, to tip his head up and smooth his hair with my hands. I focus back on my book, but reread the same passage a dozen times, sneaking a glance at the end of each, imagining his soft hair between my fingers.

Good Lord. *What* has gotten into me?

He is doing nothing to warrant such attention. We sit in comfortable silence, and yet...

It must be the hour, muddling my senses. He is a man, and I am a woman, after all, and with him sitting so close, smelling of rich leather and amber, it is easy to be distracted.

Too easy. He does smell lovely, and the couch is so comforting and warm, and after all the fear of the past hour, the exhaustion and sadness of the entire day, it is easy to nestle deep into the pillows, my eyes dropping languidly with each blink, dropping ... dropping…

I wake to Papa shaking me gently.

"Humaira, wake up now, jaani," he says. I blink away the confusion, looking around. I am in the living room, my book on the table.

There is a blanket across my lap, tucked around my legs; when did that get there? The room has been cleaned as well, all the stray popcorn and chocolate picked up and disposed of.

"Go to bed, jaani," Papa says.

"Did Fawad leave?" I ask, voice scratchy with sleep.

"Yes, just now when I got in."

My heart squeezes. I press a hand to my chest to push back the strange sensation. It hurts.

I feel as though I've missed something vital while I was asleep, and I have no way of recovering it.

Chapter Fourteen

With Rizwan back in London and no Emad for Shanzay, we are sadly back to square one in the romance department. I decide to give up my matchmaking, due to the catastrophic result it's most recently yielded. We begin the new year in low spirits, even after another movie night (period dramas this time, thank God).

January is sullen and filled with snow which is usually magical, but with Shanzay's anguished mood, it appears more as sleet, and I cannot be happy either.

Fawad and Asif's parents also come in mid-January which means Naadia is busy with her in-laws. I go over a few times, when Auntie invites me, but it isn't much fun. Fawad is quiet, suspiciously so, and is always in a rush for the lunch or dinner to end. He looks exhausted, not his usual self, but when I mention it to Naadia, she says she hasn't noticed anything amiss.

By mid-February, after lots of hot chocolate and baked

goods, I believe Shanzay is recovering, and the snow has regained some of its magic again, though tinged with something I cannot place.

It is a strange sensation. Do you ever see something so beautiful it makes you sad? Most days, I sit watching the snow fall and there is an ache in my chest.

I think love and grief come from neighboring chambers in the heart, and sometimes they overlap, so you cannot tell which feeling it is that you feel. A mix of both, to become something else entirely, red and blue mingling to create purple.

Though Shanzay is on the mend, she mentions Emad whenever she can, and constantly seeks news of him. He had the common sense not to complain to his mother, so no argument has erupted between Mahum Phuppo and Papa. I have not seen him since that dreadful night, but I know Shanzay secretly hopes her path and his will cross again.

She is very prone to crying, which I do not appreciate, for it is so messy and fussy. It isn't that I am averse to the *act* of crying, for I find it very healthy, it is just that I think it should be done in private.

I cry all the time, nearly every day, but *I* have the good graces not to subject others to awkwardness by doing it in front of them. But she needs me to be a shoulder for her to cry on, so I will be that for her.

Then the very worst thing happens.

We are sitting at home, drinking the very best of my Fortnum and Mason tea. I've even ordered a shipment of Pierre Herme macarons from Paris (Laduree can be a bit overdone) to chew on while we play cards. Papa is in his office going over investment stuff with Fawad when he gets a phone call. I think nothing of it until I hear him exclaim.

"What great news!"

Curious, I go to investigate.

"What is it?" I ask. Fawad is as intrigued as I am, as Papa looks very happy indeed. He sets down the phone and grins at us.

"Emad is engaged! To a girl named Yasmine!" he exclaims. My heart drops straight to the floor. I glance over my shoulder to make sure Shanzay is not there, and thankfully, she isn't.

Fawad and I exchange a worried glance.

"How wonderful," I respond quickly. "Papa, would you—"

But it is too late. I hear crying from the other room. Stifled, but still crying. Papa hears it too.

"You girls are too emotional," he says. Sliding his reading glasses on, his focus is once again on his papers. I feel like crying myself when I go to see Shanzay.

"I-I'm sorry," she sobs, covering her face. "I'll just be a moment."

"It's alright to cry," I say, sitting beside her. I put an arm around her shoulders. "There, there."

I look for the nearest box of tissues and instead see Fawad entering with one in his hands. Wordlessly, he hands it to Shanzay, who sniffles before taking it.

"Th-Thank you," she sputters gratefully. He nods, then exits just as quickly as he came.

I meet the dreadful woman in mention a few weeks later, when Papa, Naadia, and I go to say congratulations to Mahum Phuppo, who greets me without her usual affection and instead pushes her new daughter-in-law forward like a prize.

"This is Yasmeen," Mahum Phuppo says.

"*Jasmine*," the girl in question says. Jasmine smiles at us, then looks us up and down, raising her brows as she takes in our shalwar kameez and hijabs, her gaze amused. Before we can help it, Naadia and I exchange a quick glance.

Jasmine is wearing garish pink lipstick in a shade I know my phuppos would call "loud," and worse than that, she is wearing tight skinny jeans and a sleeveless blouse. She is most definitely one of those "modern" types.

It's all well and good to wear what one pleases outside of the house, but *inside* of the house, there is a certain dress code. My phuppos are from Pakistan and still uphold a certain level of conservatism, which the rest of the family then upholds out of respect for my phuppos.

There are family-wide rules the other daughters-in-law – and Naadia and I – must abide by, and there is no way Jasmine would not be made aware of them. (One time, my shirt was tucked into my trousers, and my Zaineb Phuppo casually came over and just untucked it!)

I do not know why Yasmine – sorry, *Jasmine* – would purposefully ignore such mandates unless she simply thinks she is above them.

"It's nice to meet you, how are you?" I ask, in Urdu, because that is how we always speak to relatives.

"I am doing very well, thanks for asking," she replies in mangled Urdu. I physically cringe, then stop myself midway. I can see Naadia doing the same. Her Urdu is *atrocious* in a very purposeful manner I have heard only in Islamabad, from rich girls at Nabila's Salon in E-7, who think the language is beneath them, and thus make no attempts at speaking it properly.

Jasmine confirms as much herself, when it is just Naadia and I sitting with her.

"English is so much better," she says. "I don't get why we even bother with Urdu anymore when we're in America? But you know the aunties, some of them are too old to learn anything new."

Naadia and I, versed well in the language of sisters, merely exchange a glance that communicates everything we need to say to one another.

Oh, but it gets better! Just a little while later, she pulls a little tube out of her bra – her bra! – and drinks the clear liquid inside.

Naadia and I cannot stop our jaws from dropping.

"Sorry, I should have asked," she says, covering her mouth with an acrylic-nailed hand. "I have another one in here somewhere. Do you want?"

First of all, I would rather die of thirst than drink a liquid procured from this woman's bra. Second of all—

"Is that ... alcohol?" I ask, still overcoming my shock. She nods, then takes in our expressions. She laughs.

"Don't tell me," she says, looking at us as if we are aliens. "You don't drink?"

I slowly shake my head. I mean, to each their own, of course, but again – stashing location aside – maybe don't bring alcohol into a house that has never seen it before? Terrible form.

"How sad," she says, tone pitying.

Things do not improve much with Jasmine, nor do they improve anywhere else, for the rest of the month.

In fact, things seem to get worse. Shanzay's eyes are constantly puffy, and it pains me to see her so distressed. I try my best to cheer her up, taking her out shopping and for cute lunches, but she is in a terrible funk.

On top of that, Papa seems to be getting clingier. Emad was the last unmarried cousin before me, and I think he's starting to receive pressure from my phuppos and the aunties to get me married.

Sometimes, I will be sitting in my room, trying to enjoy a book, or in the kitchen, trying to bake, and he will just call my name, as if on instinct, and he will call and call until I come, and then it will be something silly, like handing him the television remote, or getting him a glass of water.

It's as if he is checking I am still here and needs constant reassurance of it. While ordinarily I would not mind, recently it has begun grating on my nerves. He used to do the same to Mama, from what I recall, and she used to get annoyed, too.

"Your father," Mama said once with a heavy sigh,

pausing dramatically. "Kuch garbar hai; there's something wrong. I think he's getting old."

"Kyun?" I asked in response, genuinely concerned. "What happened?"

Mama sighed again, shaking her head.

"The other day," she said. "He got upset with me. Because I said I would watch a movie with him, but I fell asleep. He's getting so ... clingy."

Me and Naadia exchanged an amused glance.

"Mama," I said calmly. "You need to see a psychiatrist if you think your husband wanting to spend time with you is a sign of old age."

Mama was genuinely insulted by this.

"It's strange!" she said. "He wasn't like this before!"

"Mama!" Naadia cried, laughing.

"I don't like it!"

But she was his wife, so she could keep him in check. I cannot scold Papa or it will break his heart.

At least tax season keeps him relatively busy. I have him deal with mine as well. I know I am twenty-three and a verifiable adult and should do my own taxes, but who am I to decline when Papa says he will have the accountant handle it?

It is give and take, after all. If I had to, I am sure I could handle it, just like Papa could make his own coffee, if he had to, but as long as there is mutual respect and care, there is nothing wrong with doing certain tasks for one another, just as long as you are capable of being independent should the need arise.

Unfortunately, it seems Naadia is getting too independent.

"I'm sure you'll hear it from Papa soon enough, since he just lectured me about it," Naadia says on the phone one day, "but here it is: I've been interviewing at residencies outside of New York."

"*What*? Why? Papa won't be able to cope." I don't mention that I won't be able to cope. Even having her in Brooklyn is too far away. Another state would be awful.

"Because there are some great hospitals and opportunities," she replies, defensive already.

"And there aren't any in New York?"

"I've been in New York my entire life. Maybe I want to spend time elsewhere!"

"What about Asif's job?"

"He can ... transfer."

"But ... why? I don't understand."

"I want to have options!" she cries into the phone. "I want to feel like I can make choices! It's suffocating to just be *stuck* here."

"You're not stuck," I say, defensive now. "Stop feeling sorry for yourself. You have a great life, filled with great things, and it's all because of Papa."

"I know," she groans. "I just – I don't know. Papa will have to deal with it if I go away for a few years."

"Well, yeah, obviously he'll have to deal with it," I say. "You are an adult. But he'll be upset about it."

It isn't fair because the more careless she is, the more caring I must be.

"You can't live your whole life for Papa and coddle him," she says, and the words seem harsher because I can't see her face. "It's been ten years, and I miss Mama too, but he cannot be dependent on us, or Phuppo either, which is why I'm glad she is married off and happy in her own life. You should live your own life too."

But what she does not understand is that it makes me happy to care for others, to be needed, to be loved. It costs me nothing to do so. It is difficult, at times, but overall, I would prefer to do more than less.

If I cannot be needed, I cannot be loved.

People love me because I am useful to them, and if I am no longer useful, no one will care for me. It isn't hatred or dislike, but something far more insidious: indifference.

They won't notice I am around. And I need all these people in my life to fill it with color or everything will fall to gray, and I'm afraid I won't be able to get out of it if it does. When Mama died, I was severely depressed for months, and it nearly killed me.

Naadia will not understand, for she is not the same. I am quiet on the line, unsure of how to respond, and Naadia sighs.

"I don't want to put you in the middle," she says. "Let's drop it. Did I tell you about the new pediatrician? She's so Type A. The other day…"

She launches into a story, but I am hardly listening. She doesn't want to put me in the middle, but I am in the middle anyways, perpetually caught between them. Papa does not help by being surly, so unlike himself as of late. He used to be so happy when Mama was alive.

"Do you want me to bring anything?" he would ask Mama.

"Mmm." She'd pretend to think. "Just you," she'd say.

"Vo toh hai-e tumhara." He'd smile. "That's already yours."

It was always teasing and sweet. They were always laughing. I feel Papa has not laughed in quite some time now, and that makes me sad.

I wish I could bring that grin back to Papa.

In the evening, Fawad comes over. Since his parents have been home, he hasn't popped by as much, and I find I've missed his presence. When it is just the three of us occupying the homes of our street, he visits us nearly every other day, if only for a little while.

Today, he seems tired. Discarding his blazer, he collapses on the sofa beside me, loosening his tie. His hair is messy, like he's been running his hands through it. It rather suits him.

"How are your parents?" I ask.

"As they always are," he replies.

With a sigh, he takes off his glasses and closes his eyes. As he leans his head back, I get a lovely glimpse at his collarbone.

He looks just like I feel. With a sigh of my own, I nestle deeper into the sofa, pulling my legs up.

"They're leaving in a few days," he adds. He does not open his eyes.

"Oh," I say, thinking that is the reason for his mood. "Will you miss them?"

He shakes his head slightly. I frown.

"Are you okay?" I ask, voice soft.

He shakes his head again. I frown. His chest rises and falls as he breathes, and for a moment, it looks as though he is asleep save for the furrow between his brows.

I want to reach out and smooth the crease away, and the impulse startles me. I blink, confused. My fingers go to the pulse in my throat; I press in, steadying my heartbeat.

Before I do something foolish, he opens his eyes and slips his glasses on to look at me, dark eyes perceptive. When he sees my expression, he turns his body toward me, coming a little closer.

"Are *you* okay?" he asks, voice low. Something about him asking disarms me. A lump rises in my throat. We must change the topic before I begin to cry. I nod.

"How is work?" I ask. He isn't fooled.

"Good," he replies. "How is yours?" I am not fooled either, but it looks like he doesn't want to talk.

"Boring, I want to quit," I say, being dramatic.

"Go on a sabbatical," he offers. "Uncle will surely allow it. Perks of being a nepotism baby."

I do like my work, and it is good to have something to do, but it is not my *life*'s work. I have always imagined I'd

215

quit my job when I marry and have kids. I want to be home for them the way Mama was for us: juggling swimming lessons and tutoring and karate class and tennis lessons and everything in between, making us home-cooked food every day and waking up early to give us breakfast before school.

She was such a *presence* in our lives. Then, gone.

The memories hurt and heal me both. I am often struck by the duality that exists: the very things that pain me, nourish me. The very people who hurt me, bring me great joy. The things that make me cry, make me laugh and smile.

Why is it so? What can be done? I grow tired of it, which is what makes me afraid.

One day, I will grow too tired of it all, and that will be the end. I will fall asleep, and I won't wake up.

Shaking my head to clear the thoughts from it, I focus on Fawad.

"How has it been with your parents?" I ask. He lifts and drops a shoulder, not speaking, which is strange behavior from him. He is usually so sure and has an answer ready. I suppose to this question he does not wish to offer empty pleasantries. He never could lie to me. "You don't want to say?"

He shakes his head. "No, not really."

"Whatever it is," I say, voice sure, "you'll handle it. You can handle anything."

He smiles, nodding to himself. Some of the dismay on his face fades away, replaced with something else, something I can't decipher.

"I *can* handle it," he says, "but you're wrong. I can't handle everything."

I raise a quizzical brow. He looks at me, just at me, his expression both amused and perplexed that I do not understand what he means. A warm sensation spreads through me. His voice is soft when he speaks.

"I cannot handle *you*."

Chapter Fifteen

Time passes into spring.

The snow recedes, the ice thaws, and things grow pleasant once more. Naadia gets matched for her residency, and it is in New York after all, and all that fuss was for nothing. We are all relieved, even her, I think.

"I just wanted to have options," she tells me on FaceTime one day. "So I can *choose* this, so I can choose you all. It makes me feel like things are in my control."

I can understand that.

Ramadan comes and goes. It's our first Ramadan without Phuppo and her daily pakoras, which is a sad sight indeed, but we text each other our daily iftar spreads in our group chat and send each other food videos on Instagram. (We also, of course, do spiritual things, like check in with how much Quran we've read, or exchange dua lists.)

On the second day of Eid, Rizwan returns for another visit. It's the beginning of April, and while the weather is still chilly, the days are longer and the sun is gracing us more and more often with her presence. The birds have returned and the sound of their singing fills me with hope.

Phuppo and Rizwan stop by for chai, and she expressly tells me not to go overboard, so I only make shami kebabs, egg-salad sandwiches, chicken bread, spiced bundt cake, and raspberry jam thumbprint cookies with the chai and spread it out on the Tiffany and Co. tea set, which is decorated with delicate illustrations of birds, butterflies, and flowers.

"Yes, I can see you did very little," Phuppo laughs, when she sees the spread.

"Only the best for you, dear Phuppo," I respond, hugging her side. She kisses my cheek, holding me closer.

Papa seems to be confused as to why Phuppo has brought Rizwan along, particularly when Rizwan keeps trying to talk to me.

Papa has unfortunately noticed Rizwan's interest in me and does not like it one bit.

"Do you find such a haircut makes you appealing?" Papa asks. Rizwan laughs, running a hand through his long hair.

"Yes, I rather do," he says. "We'll have to ask Humaira to confirm, however."

My heart just about stops. He cannot flirt with me in front of my father! Papa is sorely unimpressed.

"Papa, this is how young men style their hair these days," I tell him. Papa rolls his eyes.

"Do not try so hard to be a CD," Papa tells Rizwan. I groan.

"Papa," I whine.

"CD?" Rizwan repeats.

"Cool dude," Phuppo translates. We exchange a long-suffering glance.

"Ah," he replies, as if this is a normal thing. I shake my head at Papa.

"Why are you in the US again?" Papa asks.

"I am working with Shani—Zeeshan Chacha on business," Rizwan replies easily.

"What business?" Papa asks, launching into a full-fledged interrogation. I smile at Rizwan, heading to the kitchen to check on the chai, which is nearly done.

After it is poured and served, I come back to the kitchen, busying myself with this and that. I rearrange the oranges in the fruit bowl, throwing away one that looks to be getting old. I cannot trust Rizwan not to say anything else untoward in front of Papa, who is especially sensitive in such matters.

"Can I have some water please?" Rizwan asks, coming up behind me. I startle, upending the fruit bowl in my hands. Oranges scatter across the floor, bouncing and rolling out of place.

I drop to pick them up, and he does as well.

"Let me help you with that," he says. I avoid looking at him, nervous.

His fingers brush against mine, sending a jolt through me.

What is he thinking?! Phuppo and Papa are right there, sipping chai!

Clearing my throat, I stand. He sets the bowl of oranges on the table, then notices the trash bag is full.

"I'm gonna go take this out," he says, oh so casually, but with a glance towards me that says I should follow.

His eyes are full of mischief. My neck heats. I am filled with exclamations and question marks. What on earth is going on?

Without looking at me again, he walks away, heading out. I wait a few seconds, make sure Papa isn't looking, then head in the direction he's gone.

I don't need to make an excuse – I know Papa wouldn't suspect me of anything. It is my house, anyway. I could be doing anything.

Halfway there, when I'm out of sight, I freeze, my whole body tingling. *Bad idea*, I decide.

Swearing under my breath, I head back to the living room, picking up the discarded tea time snacks. I bring the tray to the kitchen, shuffling the items, trying not to think of him waiting for me. I feel lightheaded. Too hot.

I open the fridge and take a deep breath of cold air. I press my cold fingers against my hot cheeks.

Wordlessly, he comes up behind me. My heart is beating so fast I can't hear anything else. We don't touch, but he stands so close to me, I can feel him; if I shift back even an inch, I'll be leaning against his chest.

What are you doing? I want to scream. Papa! I can hear him chatting away in the room adjacent to the kitchen, from where they have a clear view of us. But we're shielded by the kitchen door, so they can't see a thing as he reaches over my shoulder, forearm brushing against my cheek, and grabs a piece of chocolate from the top fridge.

I freeze, not trusting myself to breathe, my entire body tingling as his skin brushes against mine. It's too, too hot. I feel dizzy.

Finally, he steps back, but I still feel faint, and not in an entirely good way. I do not, of course, but the sentiment is enough to put me on edge until they've left.

After he's gone, I think about him, in the manner of someone who wishes to understand.

Do I love him? Could I? Physical attraction with a handsome man is easy enough, but I want something deeper – something bone-deep. I do not simply want my heart racing from physical contact, but from riveting conversation, from just being in his presence, feeling his gaze on me.

I didn't really feel that excitement when we were sitting together, eating and drinking chai. I just felt ... strange. But maybe it was supposed to be like that, at first? Was I overthinking it?

Rizwan was from a good family, handsome, accomplished, clever ... so why did I feel no anguish at his leaving?

"That Rizwan character was interesting," Papa says, later that evening, though "interesting" is surely meant in a derisive manner. "Can't say I care much for Europeans, though. Something about their manners."

I bite back a laugh. Papa says the most ludicrous things sometimes! Disliking Europeans, I mean, honestly? That is a blatant lie. Whenever we visit, he has an excellent time and no such complaints. Papa will really come up with anything.

It only gets worse. In the middle of the week, it's my birthday. Shanzay bakes me cookies and is in a wonderful mood, which is excellent, for I believe she is truly on the mend, and we spend the morning at the coffee station of the office gossiping about which co-workers must be secretly hooking up.

Things go downhill when I receive a delivery.

"Humaira Mirza?" the delivery boy asks. I cannot see his face because he carries a massive vase of flowers in one arm and a box of chocolates with a teddy bear in the other.

Shanzay and I both squeal. Even Papa is pleased, thinking it was sent by a relative, but he scowls once he finds out it is from Rizwan. Thank god the note is simple:

Happy Birthday! – Rizwan :)

If it was not, Papa would be even more vexed.

"This is a workplace," he grumbles. "Quite inappropriate. It must be because he's European."

"Hey, it's my birthday," I pout. "You cannot lecture me."

Papa sighs, resigned. "Fine, let me call this Rizwan character and lecture *him*."

"No," I say sweetly, kissing his cheek. Mumbling to himself, Papa retreats to his office, leaving Shanzay and I to inspect the flowers. They are beautiful, an arrangement of reds and pinks and whites.

Perhaps it is a bit superfluous, and not what I would have truly wanted, but it is still sweet. I do so love to be spoiled. Maybe I was overthinking my feelings for Rizwan. He is a perfectly adequate suitor. (Right?)

Phuppo and Naadia take me out for afternoon tea, and we have the best time, especially when Phuppo gives me my gift. One part of it is a darling pair of Renee Caovilla heels I've been eyeing, and the second part of it is something soft wrapped in white tissue paper.

"What's this?" I ask, intrigued. Phuppo beams at me, waiting.

"Hurry up! I want to see, too," Naadia says, reaching to take it from my hands. I swat her away and undo the tissue to see it's a cashmere scarf.

"How sweet!" I say, unfolding it. But then I see the end and gasp audibly enough for our waitress to give us an alarmed look. For embroidered across the bottom is one word: *Aapi*, the Urdu word for older sister.

Which can only mean...

"Ohmygod, you're pregnant?!" I cry, before promptly bursting into a puddle of tears.

"What!" Naadia shrieks, grabbing the scarf from my hand. Phuppo nods, laughing and crying as well, as she hands Naadia her own matching scarf with the same embroidery, though hers says *Aapa*, another word for older sister.

"Phuppo, this is the very best gift in the world!" I

blubber, getting up to crush her with a hug. Naadia joins me, and the three of us squeal and shake, bursting with joy.

"I cannot wait to have a little cousin," I say. "Tell us *everything*. How many weeks are you? Do you know the gender yet? Oh, I need to go shopping!"

Phuppo tells us, and we have the best time. I'm still elated when I get home and share the news with Papa, who has already been informed via FaceTime from Phupoo. Papa is just as pleased as I am, and we are both positively buzzing with jubilation.

We spend an entire hour discussing all the fun we'll have when the baby finally comes, until I catch sight of the clock and realize we need to be getting ready for dinner.

Papa is taking me out to a fancy dinner in the city, where Naadia and Phuppo will be joining us with their husbands. We don't usually go crazy for birthdays with gifts or parties, just excellent food.

Papa goes up, but I linger downstairs, searching up stuffed animal toys on my phone. Then, before I go to get ready, I'm distracted by a knock on the front door. Papa is already in the shower, so I put on a scarf and go to answer the door.

It's Fawad.

"Oh, hi!" I say, my heartbeat quickening. Fawad grins when he sees me, holding something in his hands.

"Happy birthday," he says, coming in. I grin, too.

Birthdays really are so fun. I love to have the attention on me, just on me, and be loved and adored all day long. It does make a girl feel special. And there is nothing expected in return.

"Thank you, thank you," I say, taking a few steps back to properly let him in.

Then, the smile fades from his face. Confused, I follow his eyes to where they have flicked over my shoulder: the flowers, teddy bear, and chocolates, sitting on the table.

He opens his mouth as if to ask who they are from, then thinks better of it. He crosses his hands behind his back, but I could have sworn he had something in his hands.

"What is that?" I ask, trying to peek. "A gift for me?"

"Nothing," he says quickly, voice strange. "Just some mail I picked up on my way out."

It was wrapped in brown paper and twine, so it very well could be a package, but I do not know if I believe him.

"Won't you open it?" I ask.

"No, I'll open it later. It's just ... socks." With some difficulty, he gives me a nonchalant smile.

Hm, he is serious.

I want to see what it is, almost sure it is meant for me, but something in his eyes stops me. A pinched quality to them.

He does not look to be in the mood for games. He looks rather ... distressed.

"Oh, okay," I say. He puts the package on the front table, then follows me inside, where I offer to make him tea. He shakes his head.

"I just came to wish you happy birthday and give you

your book back," he says, handing me *The Piper's Son*. I didn't notice he was holding it before.

"Thank you." I take it, holding it to my chest. I hate loaning people my books and always feel much better once they have securely made their way home in one piece. Casually, I inspect the book to check its condition, and Fawad laughs.

"Don't worry," he says. "I haven't harmed it. No dog-eared pages, no stains, no cracked spine."

I let out a laugh. "I appreciate it."

He stands a bit awkwardly, waiting a moment before asking, "Did you ... Did you read *The Secret History*, yet?"

Guilt needles through me.

"No, I haven't," I reply, tone apologetic. "I'm sorry."

I haven't gotten to it. It's been sitting on my side-table, right there, but I just haven't given it my attention.

"No, it's okay, take your time," he says, but disappointment flickers across his face, though he masks it so quickly I wonder if I saw it there at all. "I don't mind waiting."

"Did you like it?" I ask, holding up *The Piper's Son*.

"I did, yes."

"Come, sit, and let's discuss." I love discussing favorite books, analyzing scenes and foreshadowing and symbols and moments. I head toward the living room, so we can sit, but his gaze goes to the flowers on the table again.

"No, I better get going," he says. He runs a hand through his hair, making it a little messy.

"Oh. Okay." I bite my lip. "Well, tell me one thing at least."

"What is it?"

"Did you cry?" I ask enthusiastically. "I always sob through most of it."

"Isn't it one of your favorite books?" he asks, bemused.

"Yes, and that's precisely why," I reply. "I'll do anything to feel something." My tone is light, and it's perhaps only *partly* a joke.

"It did make me cry," he admits. "Which is rare."

"I am glad it made you cry, as strange as that sounds," I respond. If he didn't cry, I might have had to reconsider our friendship. I circle back to what he said. "Is it rare for you to cry because of a book or in general?"

"Both."

"Oh gosh. I'm always crying." I pause. "Though that does not make it mean any less." I feel it fully each time.

"Perhaps I am an emotionless person," he says, tone cavalier, but it does not do well to mask the echoing emptiness beneath the statement. I frown.

"I don't believe that," I say truthfully. "I used to hate crying as well, especially after Mama died. It hurt so much, and it seemed to be all I could do. So for a while, I stopped. But then one day I cried out of happiness, and it changed from this horrible act, only occurring at life's most terrible moments, to something beautiful. It was quite liberating."

"What made you cry out of happiness?"

I consider this. "I'm not sure." I really don't remember what it was exactly. "I think it was an ordinary day, filled with ordinary things, like laughing with my sister, and spending time with Papa, and it was a day filled with happiness, after being sad for so long."

I do not even realize what I am saying until it is said, and then it strikes me just how true the words are. Strange. I didn't know that about myself. Sometimes other people can excavate things buried deep within us we did not even know existed: sentiments, emotions, thoughts.

I look at him as if I have not seen him before. There is a lock of hair curving across his forehead, resting just between his brows, and for some reason I find this quite devastating. I'm enthralled by the curve of it, its silky sheen. I get the impulse to reach out and touch it.

Instead, I fiddle with the end of my scarf.

"Anyways," I say brightly, "since then, I haven't really shied away from crying, though I still don't cry in front of people, as a general rule."

"That's not true," he says. "I've seen you cry."

"That's only because you're always around," I respond. "You don't give me any time at all to put up my pretenses and pretty facades. I can never hide from you."

I am struck by how true this is, too. A peculiar sensation spreads through me. I startle a bit but recover quickly.

"It's very rude," I add, trying to keep the conversation light-hearted. "What if I was an ugly crier? My reputation could be ruined by you witnessing such a sight."

Fawad laughs. "You are an ugly crier."

"I am not!" I smack his arm with the book. "How dare you!" But I'm laughing as well.

Then, something in the air changes. He stops laughing, but the amusement lingers in his half-lidded eyes, in the turn of his smile. His eyelashes flutter as he blinks, looking at me, as if he sees me, truly sees me.

At first, I look away, suddenly shy, but I want to have the courage to seize this moment, whatever it is. I stare back, matching his perceptive gaze.

A jolt of electricity shocks through me as our eyes meet. My breath catches.

"Humaira," he says, voice low as he takes a step closer. A delicious shiver runs through me, urging me toward him.

His lips part, and there is something in his face that tells me whatever he says next will be momentous, will be life-changing, and just as he is about to speak—

"*Humaira!*" Papa calls.

The moment breaks.

I startle back, feeling unsteady.

"I have to go," I blurt. I run up the stairs.

Chapter Sixteen

I decide to throw a tea party.

It's the usual group: Naadia, Asif, Fawad, Shanzay, Rizwan and I, plus Sadaf, though not Haya and Zahra, who are busy with some wedding preparations.

We encounter trouble when Papa ends up mentioning it to Mahum Phuppo, who mentions it to Yasmin—sorry *Jasmine*—who invites herself and Emad over. Dreadful woman.

Though I will not let her ruin my day. The menu is perfect and consists of various sandwiches, shrimp cups, chicken patties, and mushroom tartlets for savory, cardamom buns, mini sponge cakes, orange ricotta pound cake, and coconut cookies for sweet.

Naadia comes over early to help me, but I do mostly everything on my own because I like to be impressive.

I wave her away, thinking I can handle it, but then regret it when everyone has arrived and I am still kneading the coconut cookie dough. At least I got ready first, but everyone is sitting out on the patio, enjoying our backyard – the verdant greenery and lush flowers, the bright sunshine, the beautiful waterfall and our little pond – while I'm stuck inside.

"Naadia!" I call from the window. She is laughing with Sadaf and does not hear. I groan, trying to telepathically communicate with her, and for a moment, I actually think it works when I hear the backdoor opening.

"Finally you hoe, come and help me," I say.

I hear a laugh that is distinctly not Naadia's. *Oopsies.*

"The hoe in question is occupied, but I can help," Fawad says, coming into view. He is wearing a gray suit sans tie, which is quite flattering with his black hair and eyes.

"No, that's okay," I respond quickly, my heartbeat jumping off kilter.

Ordinarily, I would have no qualms about Fawad being my sous chef, but today, I am nervous. I have decided I am too comfortable around Fawad, which is a bad thing. I am afraid of what I will say or do; I do not know how to behave when I am so thoroughly disarmed.

Ignoring me, Fawad enters the kitchen, discarding his blazer and rolling up his sleeves. I stare at the movement, eyes glazing over the veins of his forearms. Oh, it is not looking good for me…

His gaze travels to my face, and he cocks his head to the side. I snap my eyes up, confused as he inspects me.

Pulling something out of his breast pocket, he approaches.

"What are you doing?" I ask, alarmed. I step back.

"Stand still," he scolds, coming closer. He lifts his hand and wipes the soft cotton of his handkerchief across my cheek. I feel the imprint of his fingers through the cloth. Heat spreads through me, pooling in the pit of my stomach.

"Flour," he informs me. He did not even directly touch me, but I feel weak in the knees. Goodness.

"You can assemble the shrimp cups," I say, clearing my throat. "Over there."

I point far away from my counter. The things are already taken out. He nods. As he walks over and begins his work, I press my fingers against the pulse in my throat, willing myself to calm down.

We complete our tasks in comfortable silence until I need the vanilla extract (goddamn the vanilla extract!) which is right in the cabinet in front of him.

"Excuse me," I say softly. He sidesteps, giving me room, and I open the cabinet, then stifle a groan. Naadia put it on the top shelf! I swear this woman is testing me.

I stretch to reach, on my tip-toes, and just as my finger grazes the bottle, a warm body crowds me, a hand coming up just beside mine. I freeze, coming down until my feet flatten.

He stands so close, I feel the breath of his exhale against the fabric of my scarf, fluttering against my neck like the wings of a bird. My heart pounds.

"Thank you," I squeak, turning to take the bottle. He holds it up in the minimal space between us, right between our hearts. I grab it and swallow.

I lean back so not to be in an embrace, gripping the cold countertop, looking up into those impossibly long eyelashes as he looks down at me.

We do not touch, and it's as if that is worse. He is close enough to kiss; it would be so easy, really. I imagine myself grabbing a fistful of his immaculate shirt and pulling his face down to mine.

The idea of it sends a jolt of electricity through me, and I bite my lower lip.

"You're welcome," he says pleasantly, then steps away. I release a breath as he returns to his work. Trying to get a grip, I shake my head.

What! Has gotten! Into me!

I return to my task, assembling the dough, then pouring it onto the clean counter to knead. Before I work the dough, I go to wash my hands, and as I do, I walk past Fawad's back.

For a moment, I have the strange impulse to rest my cheek between his shoulder blades. Just for a moment. Just to rest. I would fit so perfectly. I even slow just behind him as I walk past.

Then I shake my head again, fanning myself with my hands as I look up, entreating the Good Lord to have some mercy on my feeble heart. The heat must be getting to me.

I need to focus. I return to my counter and start kneading the cookie dough. It is enough to divert me. The steady back and forth centers me, and my heartbeat regulates as the dough forms.

Until my blouse sleeve unrolls, getting in my way. With

an aggravated sound, I try to push it up with my cheek, seeing as my hands are buried in sticky cookie dough. It does not work. I try again, meeting the same result.

"Fawad," I say, calling his name as if by instinct.

Too late I realize I need him to stay far away from me before I do something untoward.

"I got it," he says, seeing my struggle.

"Actually, it's okay," I say, as he comes close. I squirm away, but he tsks.

"Hold still," he orders. Standing just beside me, he reaches and takes hold of the edge of my sleeve. He drags it past the delicate skin of my wrist, then up my smooth forearm. The fabric glides across my skin like a caress, stopping above my elbow as he folds it in place.

As he does, his finger brushes against my bare skin. My entire arm tingles.

My breath hitches violently, and I snap my mouth shut.

But not quick enough.

He hears and turns to look at me, still holding my sleeve, fingertips hovering just above my skin.

Feeling brave, I look up at him. He stands close enough that he must turn his chin downwards, but I cannot tell if it is my eyes or my lips that have ensnared his sight.

His eyes are molten as he looks at me, and there is his gaze, flicking once more to my mouth. I am sure he can hear my heart, it is beating so fast.

We are both frozen in place, holding our breaths.

Then the door opens and I hear a sigh; I am not sure if it is his or mine. He steps back, and I automatically shiver from the cold air enveloping the space his body has left behind.

"What's taking so long?" Naadia asks, entering the kitchen. "I'm starving."

I consider throwing a ball of cookie dough at my sister's face, but I can barely stand.

"Is there anything else you need?" Fawad asks, clearing his throat. His hands are behind his back, his biceps flexing as if he is holding his hands together very tightly.

"No, you go," I say, clearing my throat. I offer a bright smile. "Keep Rizwan company; tell him I'll be out soon."

I don't know why I say it, but the effect is immediate. Fawad's face shutters, and all the warmth from earlier is truly gone.

"Got it," he says. He leaves, his back stiff. Naadia turns to me, eyebrows raised.

"Don't look at me," I say, avoiding her gaze. "Make the chai."

"Okie dokie," she sing-songs, hip-checking me as she passes. I hip-check her back.

I have no idea what is going on, but it would help if my heart would stop beating so fast. I feel like my ribs might actually break. I quickly scoop the cookie dough out into balls and roll them in coconut flakes, setting them to bake as Naadia cooks the chai.

I can feel her watching me.

"No lasan?" she asks hopefully. I make a face. What sane person puts ginger in their tea?

"I am not nearly as depraved as you are."

"Boo, you suck."

When the chai is done, Naadia helps me bring all the food out, since the weather is so lovely. Shanzay and Sadaf help, too, and we set everything up on the outdoor dining table, the food under the shade of the umbrella.

Everything is a massive hit. I receive many compliments, much to Fawad's chagrin, I am sure, as Rizwan fawns over me.

After we eat, I avoid the boys, feeling a little unhinged, and instead sit with Naadia and Sadaf. We lounge on the outdoor sofas, taking off our sandals and pulling our feet up.

Shanzay is with us, as well, but she is frighteningly quiet, probably due to Jasmine and Emad feeding each other and being generally disgusting.

I'm glad Sadaf is here to regale us with stories from work. She's a speech therapist.

"My boss slept with the secretary, isn't that awful?" she tells us.

"Of course it is!" Naadia balks. "If my husband were to have an affair, I'd hope he'd be more original than sleeping with the *secretary*."

Asif makes the mistake of walking by just then.

"Asif!" Naadia calls him over. I try to motion for him to flee, but he does not see.

"Yes, angel?" he asks.

"If you were to hypothetically have an affair, you wouldn't sleep with your secretary, would you?" she asks, tone innocuous. "I'd hate to think you were a cliche."

"It would actually be the worst blow," Sadaf added, biting into a cookie, "to find you married a cliche."

"Exactly," Naadia agrees. "You get me."

Asif looks between us girls, panic in his eyes. "I'm ... sensing this is a trick question," he says.

I discreetly call his phone, and he holds it up when it rings. "Gotta answer this." He bolts.

We all laugh.

"I like to keep him on his toes," Naadia confides.

"Men are always best kept on their toes," Sadaf agrees, all bravado.

"Bari ai," Naadia says, smacking her. She snorts. "You've had a crush on the same boy for years and have accomplished approximately nothing."

Sadaf chokes on her lemonade. "My God, don't attack me." She presses a hand to her heart. "I admire from afar. Besides, what can I do if he lives in California?"

"He does visit often to see his sister," Naadia sing-songs. They're talking about Ahsen Paracha, Zahra's older brother, and the second half of Sadaf's long-time *will they, won't they?*

"Didn't he stay here for an entire month that one time, after you graduated?" I ask. "Did anything substantial happen then?"

"And isn't he coming for Haya's wedding, too?" Naadia asks.

"I literally have no idea what you guys are talking about," Sadaf says, fanning herself with a napkin. "Besides, all men are trash, you know this." She waves a hand nonchalantly, but Naadia and I aren't convinced and still giggle at her flustered state. Sometimes, love takes its time. "And Mama has me talking to this rishta, who might even be a little promising..."

She trails off, going into details, but I am distracted as Rizwan comes over, sitting beside me. I turn to face him, smiling politely as a good hostess should.

He asks me what television I've been watching and while we discuss various shows, my attention strays to Shanzay, to ensure she is alright. Rather than being alone and quiet, as she was before, she has moved to now be sitting with Fawad, who is listening tentatively as she launches into a story, words tripping over one another.

I furrow my brows. That's strange.

Something sharp pierces in me as Fawad laughs. Surely Shanzay is not saying anything *that* funny...

"Do you agree?" Rizwan asks. I realize I haven't heard a word he's said but smile brilliantly in reply, anyway.

"Yes, completely," I say, turning my attention to him. "I think it's a very interesting concept, in general, and liked how they explored it."

"Exactly!" he says. "We're so similar. I find it fascinating how the director..."

He goes on, and I listen carefully, not exactly to the words he is saying, but to *him*: the way his eyes light up as he speaks, the way his voice sounds, the feel of him sitting close to me.

It's easy and comfortable to be with him. But I don't think I Love him, and I don't know if I ever will.

Shouldn't this be more exciting? Why do I feel vaguely … bored?

It feels like I'm waiting for something to kick in, and every time I see him, I get this little jolt of excitement, in case *this* is the moment, this is it, but then – nothing.

Perhaps I put too much pressure on True Love. And there is no such thing? Fawad would be the first to tell me so.

But the worse fear that comes creeping in from time to time is that love *is* real, and the problem is within me and my malfunctioning heart.

As if I'm incapable of love.

Chapter Seventeen

The week closes out with Sadaf's sister, Haya's, wedding, which everyone is invited to, and those who aren't (namely Jasmine and Emad) somehow manage to invite themselves. Sadaf invites Rizwan, for my benefit, since he's still here, but I don't feel particularly enthused by the prospect.

Even so, the main event, the baraat, is wonderful; Haya looks stunning in a red and gold outfit, and Carlos, her husband, looks handsome in a white sherwani. He's Chilean but looks just as comfortable as a Pakistani in it, and from what I hear, he's even learned a bit of Urdu to impress Haya's parents.

We meet Sadaf's cousins from Pakistan, Mina and Hamza, who are here for the wedding. Mina is vibrant and fun, while Hamza seems more shy. He's a total cutie and engaged to a girl back home – his bachpan ki mohabbat and neighbor, which I love for him.

Such classic Pakistani drama tropes! I think there is something so romantic about knowing someone before really *knowing* them, something so fateful and divine. An invisible string.

"How are you feeling?" I ask Phuppo, sitting down beside her with a plate full of samosas for her to eat. She's beginning to show a little now and wears her dupatta draped across her stomach, the universal Pakistani way of pregnant women.

"Not too bad," she says, instinctively placing a hand on her stomach. I lean my head on her shoulder a moment. I know she is worried about the pregnancy because of her age, but my best friend Areeba is a genetic counselor and taking good care of her, so there should be nothing to fret about.

Even so, Zeeshan Uncle is not letting her do anything herself, and so she spends most of the event sitting down rather than walking around commenting on people's outfits with me.

Dancing, I am sure, will be out of the question, which is just no fun.

The night is not very eventful, though I love to dress up for weddings and witness the general splendor, and I am of course pleased to see Haya so happy. I'm wearing this gorgeous long kurta and culottes by Dr. Haroon and am told by a few people that I am easily the most beautiful girl in the room – besides the bride, of course, they add in quickly.

I am not too moved by these compliments, even when

one comes from Rizwan. I believe I am getting over him, which is disappointing, for I'll have to find someone else to fixate on.

There is nothing wrong with him, but I need to be enthused about the man I am with – it must be someone who makes me awake, because I'm afraid I'll spend my whole life in gray, asleep.

"Oh no," Shanzay gasps, clutching my arm while we grab drinks from the bar.

"What is it?" I ask, looking to where her gaze is. Someone is entering, a tall, athletic looking girl, and it takes me a moment to register who it is: Madiha Raja – Huzaifa's sister.

Shanzay ducks behind me. "Should I go over and say hello? Or is it best to avoid her entirely?" she chatters. "She must hate me!" She gasps. "Do you think her brother will be here, as well? I must go say salaam, it would be rude not to?" She nibbles on her bottom lip. "Or is it rude *to* say salaam? Like rubbing salt in the wound?"

"Deep breaths," I instruct, breathing in and out with her. "There's nothing wrong with saying salaam."

"Yes, you're right." She nods. "I ought to go."

I watch as she approaches Madiha hesitantly. Madiha's face lights up when she sees Shanzay, then a bit of a reserved expression covers her initial excitement. Shanzay and she speak to one another, and I can tell Madiha is a bit withdrawn at first, and Shanzay a bit nervous, but as they begin speaking further, both girls warm up.

I'm pleased to see Shanzay opening up, back to her

overexcited, rambling self. Madiha is really nice – I've met her a few times at the Chaudrys's house.

Was I too hasty in judging the Rajas? Perhaps I was a bit harsh on Huzaifa. I think about what Emad said, how Shanzay wasn't good enough for him, and how awful I'd thought him for it.

But had I not been equally snobbish in regarding Huzaifa?

Unease settles through me.

But there's nothing to be done, not now at least. Anyway, I've given up matchmaking.

I join Naadia and the rest of the evening carries on. After we eat appetizers and the speeches are given, Naadia and I go to say salaam to Haya up on the stage.

"Thank you so much for coming!" Haya exclaims, grinning. She's positively glowing, and my heart warms at the sight. I reach out and take her hand, squeezing.

Her gold bangles jingle, a little melody adding to the symphony of the wedding around us: the loud music, the droves of family members and friends chatting and laughing, the children running around screaming with glee.

"You look beautiful!" Naadia tells her.

"I'm so happy for you!" I say.

Haya introduces us to Carlos, who is grinning just as wide as she is. He is a real sweetheart, with golden curls and the deepest dimples. His attention is barely diverted from Haya; he is staring at her with open adoration, his hand entwined with hers in his lap.

I feel overjoyed for them, but something in my chest

nudges with a twinge of jealousy, and once it comes, I make dua for her happiness.

There is enough love in this world for all of us, I remind myself. She has gotten hers, and I will get mine. I will. What is mine will be mine. I must believe it.

As we head back to our table, I pass by Papa, who is speaking to Haya's father. My mouth drops at what he is saying, and I politely pull him away.

"Papa!" I scold, squeezing his arm. "You cannot give the bride's father *condolences* on his daughter's wedding day! She is not *dead*!"

"This is a sad day," Papa says solemnly. "I was merely wishing to comfort him."

"Papa," I tsk. "How would you feel if people gave you condolences on *my* wedding? Would that not worry you?"

He looks at me as if I am absurd. "Of course not. I would appreciate their solidarity in my time of grief." He pauses. "Besides, you're not getting married, anyways, so what a silly thing to say." He shakes his head. "Honestly, Humaira."

No, I am not, I think to myself sullenly, as I flit away.

Zahra's brother, Ahsen, is here as well, so perhaps the night is not entirely uneventful, for Sadaf and he have *history* and might one day have a future.

From what I've heard from Naadia, they've been in emotional politics for years, only exacerbated by the fact that he lives a coast away in California and is probably afraid of commitment like most men.

"I wish I had some popcorn," Naadia whispers to me

when I join her. She's watching Sadaf and Ahsen interact, and I follow her gaze. He's a good-looking guy and tall; there's a cool and confident air about him, but I catch the way his fingers drum restlessly against his leg. Not so cool then.

He and Sadaf are standing off to the side, nearly eye level in Sadaf's massive heels. Sadaf is talking, and even from here, I can tell she is speaking a million-words-a-minute, mouth moving fast. Ahsen is listening intently, head cocked, amusement in his eyes and something deeper, too.

Sadaf lifts a hand to adjust her hijab.

"On no," I say. Sadaf's eyes widen when her bangle gets caught in the fabric of her scarf. Ahsen laughs – there is the endearing way his eyes close Sadaf has mentioned – then reaches over to untangle the bangle and scarf.

Sadaf looks like she is going to faint. Or simply drop dead.

"Hai Allah, let me go rescue her," Naadia says, handing me her piña colada. I sip it, watching the scene unravel. It is unnerving to see Sadaf so flustered because she is ordinarily so easy-breezy with boys, putting them in their place and not dealing with their bullshit.

When Naadia reaches them, Ahsen steps back, and Sadaf clutches Naadia's arm, before being whisked away.

Later, when dinner is served, there's a bit of a mix-up with the seating. It is not a sit-down dinner, but a buffet, and everyone is moving around their assigned table, being chaotic.

Rizwan has saved my seat beside him, but when I sit down, I realize some chairs are missing from our table. Shanzay approaches and realizes the same. She waves a hand at me, as if to say, "It's okay!", then goes to find a place to sit at the table adjoining ours.

There is an open seat next to a suited gentleman, and Shanzay approaches him. But just as she nears, the gentleman turns, and it's Emad.

Oh no. Shanzay freezes.

"You cannot sit here," Emad says, putting Jasmine's purse onto the seat, though I can see her coat on the seat on the other side of him. Shanzay looks to the other seat as well. "This seat is for her purse. It's Louis Vuitton—a very expensive designer bag." He laughs shortly. "Though I would not expect you to know anything of it."

Anger cuts through me. What a dickhead! Everyone at the table notices the interaction, looking away in shame, and a few people even snicker. I can imagine what they are thinking: *poor girl!*

I get up, ready to put Emad in his place, wanting to do something, anything – but someone is already to the rescue.

"Come, sit here," Fawad says, taking Shanzay's plate. He sits her down at my table, where he was previously seated. I silently sit back down as Shanzay takes a seat quietly, her eyes brimming with tears, which she hastily wipes away. Fawad returns a moment later with a chair, setting it beside her.

I want to go to her, but Fawad beats me to it. He's

talking to her, and she smiles and starts laughing. They both laugh, and I feel a strange nudge in my chest.

I try to focus as Rizwan chats with me, but I don't really hear a word he says and instead watch Fawad from the corner of my eye, the peculiar feeling never leaving me.

After the cake is cut, Phuppo and Zeeshan Uncle make their rounds of goodbye, since "the baby needs rest," according to Zeeshan Uncle.

"What do you think the baby is doing in there?" Phuppo asks, laughing as she holds onto his arm. "An Olympic routine?"

Since they are leaving, Rizwan must, too.

"I should pack, besides," he says. "My flight is tomorrow."

"Yes," I say. "Well, it was good seeing you."

"Allah hafiz, then," Rizwan says to me, lingering a moment. He opens his mouth as if to say something more, then stops.

With a final wave, he's off, and I'm relieved when he's gone and I don't have to put up with niceties. Many others take their leave at this time, as well, the formalities of the night over. Papa left even before Zeeshan Uncle, along with many of the other older couples.

Naadia and I look at one another and grin.

"Showtime, baby," she says, wiggling her brows. We get up, and I grab Shanzay, and we head to the dance floor. Since it is not a family wedding, we do not have to worry about our phuppos tsk-ing and judging.

"I don't really dance," Shanzay says nervously, standing stiffly.

"Come on!" I cry. "It's Imran Khan! Everyone dances to Imran Khan."

"This is the trash Punjabi music we love," Sadaf says, joining us.

"Don't worry," Naadia says to Shanzay. "We'll cover you."

The girls create a group, Sadaf and Madiha and the other masjid girls joining us. Zahra brings Haya out and we all cheer, crowding around her. The steady beat of the dhol moves us, and we dance and dance, outdoing one another and laughing.

I love to dance, and I lose myself in the music, lose myself entirely.

After a little while, I go to grab a drink, my throat dry.

Fawad is sitting alone at our table, lights dancing off of his face. When I approach, he smiles, holding up his glass of soda in a toast.

"You don't dance?" I ask, sitting down next to him, catching my breath. My feet are aching. I take a long sip of water. He says something, but I cannot hear him over the music. I lean close, and he shouts directly into my ear.

"Not if I can help it!"

I pull back to smile at him. We are nearly in an embrace, but we do not touch. My skin is warm from dancing, and something else, my heart beating exhilaratingly fast.

I lean back and shake my head, before motioning him

forward. "What a terrible bore!" I shout in his ear. He laughs, shaking his head.

"You look like you were having fun, though," he says, not quite screaming anymore. I lean back, looking at his face, looking at his smile. His dark eyes gleam with amusement and fondness.

"Were you watching me very closely, then?" I ask. The smile vanishes, replaced by a nervous knit of his brows.

"N-No, I wasn't." He looks away.

I frown. "I find it vexing when people cannot meet my eyes," I tell him, furrowing my brows. "Am I so intimidating? Or just too beautiful?" The latter is said with mock arrogance.

It isn't that I consider shyness to be a fault, but it is the looking away that I find entirely annoying.

He fixes me with the full heat of his gaze, and for a moment, it is I who wishes to look away. But I stand my ground, a chill running through me. I swallow.

A slow smile spreads across his face.

"It is not that, though surely you know you are excessively beautiful," he says, and a thrill runs through me. "It is your soul. You are brimming to the surface with it." My breath catches at the compliment, the words scoring on my heart. "Of course, people are free to admire you when you do not notice, but the moment you fix your gaze on them, it is frightening, and the intensity of your gaze is what forces their eyes away like a sudden burst of sunshine, painful and bright."

Very purposefully, he does not look away as he speaks. He clenches his jaw; I can tell he is nervous – but he is brave, too.

He looks at me with open wonder, eyes wide with awe, unflinching and mesmerized.

My heartbeat matches the fast pace of the music beating through the wedding hall.

"I am beautiful," I agree, not knowing what else to say. I suddenly stand, clearing my throat. "And ready for more dancing. Do not stare unless you wish to join me."

I join Naadia and Sadaf back on the dance floor, dancing to Bollywood music, doing some steps from the dances Sadaf and I learned for Naadia's wedding, then some from the dances for Phuppo's wedding. We've forgotten half of it, but we dance until my legs hurt and my cheeks hurt from laughing.

We teach Carlos's Chilean family some desi steps, and when the music shifts from Lollywood to Latin music, his family returns the favor and teaches us how to sway our hips and turn.

Naadia genuinely cannot move for the life of her, which makes me and Sadaf absolutely lose it laughing. We double over, clutching our stomachs, but Naadia is unabashed, continuing on. I take her hands and we twirl and twirl, the world a beautiful blur.

From the corner of my eye, I can feel Fawad watching. I risk a glance his way as I turn, and he smiles at me, unashamed.

An electric jolt runs through me. I feel at once over energized and faint.

Maybe it's time to go. I'm not particularly interested in staying too late. Naadia will stay until the end with Sadaf, and Shanzay seems to be enjoying her time with Madiha.

So I say goodbye to everyone, hugging and kissing goodbye.

"You're leaving already?" Sadaf asks, holding onto my hands.

"Cinderella must go!" I tell her with a laugh. She blows me a final kiss as I walk off the dance floor, smiling to myself. Fawad watches me, and when I near him, he stands.

"I'm heading out, too," Fawad says, setting his drink down. "We can walk out together."

I nod, and after the last goodbyes, we grab our coats and make our way out of the hall, away from the noise. Outside, I hand my card to the valet, waiting for my car to be brought around. Fawad stands with me, waiting his turn.

After the loud wedding, the silence is intoxicating. I tip my head back to drink in the night sky, staring at the luminous stars, twinkling down at me like glittering specks of snow.

My jacket hangs loosely on my shoulders, and a chill runs through me from the cold night air. Fawad looks as if he is about to comment, but I point to the sky before he can.

"Orion's Belt," I say, drawing out the constellation with my forefinger. "Big Dipper ... Cassiopeia." I sigh. "That's all I know."

I turn, waiting for him to point out more, but he's

looking at me with an awed and amused look on his face. He holds up his hands.

"I don't know any constellations," he admits. I am positively shocked.

My jaw drops open as I gasp dramatically. He laughs.

"For such a know-it-all, I would expect you to know some," I tease. Then I spot another familiar shape.

"There's the Little Dipper!" I point, drawing the shape, but as I do, my jacket slips from my shoulder. I go to grab it before it falls, just as Fawad does.

His fingers close over mine on the fabric. An electric jolt runs through my arm.

"Would it kill you to wear this properly?" he asks, voice low as he adjusts the coat on my shoulders. Inadvertently, I step closer, looking up into his eyes, the curve of his lashes.

His hands linger on my shoulders, a sure and steady weight. In my heels, we are almost eye level, though I miss looking up at him. His gaze is warm enough to melt any ice in the air, his expression soft.

He looks at me closely, staring into my eyes.

"You have the most beautiful ocean eyes," he says.

"But my eyes are black," I reply stupidly. He's the only one who ever gets away with making me stupid.

"Exactly. It's like the ocean at night, dark and glittering with moonlight."

My breath catches. I shiver.

Clearing his throat, he sputters back, and the air is immediately cold once more.

"Now wear your jacket properly," he orders. "You're going to get sick."

"No I won't," I reply, tone indignant.

"Must you argue with everything?" he asks crossly. "You will get sick."

Why must he always scold!

"What are you, Papa?" I respond just as tartly. "So what if I get sick? Let me get sick!"

He lets out a groan of frustration. "All you do is stress me out."

I let out a sound of disbelief. "Rude!" I smack him with my purse. "I am a goddamn delight!"

"You're goddamn frustrating, is what you are," he says, shaking his head, but there's a smile playing on his lips, and I laugh. The bickering is light-hearted, as if he does not seem to mind.

I don't mind it, either, in truth.

This alarms me.

He steps closer, unraveling his neck-scarf.

"What are you doing?" I ask, brows furrowed. I lean away from him as he approaches.

"Hold still," he orders. I do, and he wraps his scarf around my neck, covering my mouth so I can't speak. He smiles. "There, much better."

I open my mouth to protest, but when I do, I catch the scent of his scarf, his cologne embedded in the fabric, and it disarms me entirely. (I am convinced they put drugs in mens' cologne; it is the only logical explanation.)

"Yes, much better," he says, grinning now. His hands

linger on the scarf ends, pulling me closer as if by instinct. His eyes are as bright as the stars in the night sky, just as magical, just as wonderful.

Something sharp turns in my stomach.

And I don't understand.

Chapter Eighteen

The next morning, I feel unaligned.

After Fajr, I can't fall asleep despite having only slept a few hours. I got home late last night, after the wedding celebrations, but I'm not tired. I'm wide awake.

I lounge on the chaise in my bedroom, one of Mama's shawls wrapped around my shoulders. I am turned backwards to look out the window to my backyard, to see the line of full green trees, the steady trickle of the waterfall into the pond. I watch the sun inch across the sky, dawn spreading its wings to paint the sky pink.

I am ... thinking.

Of him, though I do not wish to admit it. I hope he is mine, for I fear I am already his. And the thought unnerves me. Can it be true? Is that what this is?

It is wholly unexpected. I am ill-prepared, and thus do not know what to do, what to think.

Is he thinking of me? I wish I could see him, though at the same time, I wish to never see him again.

I am pulled from my thoughts at the sound of the doorbell ringing. I sit up, the shawl slipping from my shoulders. I wait, and there it is again.

Who could it be, this early on a Sunday morning?

I put a scarf on and go to answer, bare feet on the cool morning floors, and gasp at who it is.

"Shanzay!" I cry. Her leg is wrapped in a cast. But that isn't all. She is with —"Rizwan! What on earth happened?"

"Humaira, I've had such a night," Shanzay says, limping inside with her crutches. Rizwan is carrying her coat and purse. I motion them to the living room, where I help Shanzay lay down. I turn to grab a blanket for her, but Rizwan has beaten me to it.

After I've gotten her water, and she looks comfortable enough, and I am positively bursting to know the details, she continues the story.

"After the wedding, I got into an accident," she says. "It was literally crazy. Rizwan was driving by—"

"Ohmygod!"

"I left something at the hall, and I thought I recognized the car and the person on the stretcher," Rizwan adds.

"I didn't have anybody to call – I thought of calling you," she says, before I ask.

"But I said not to bother you," Rizwan says.

"So he went with me to the hospital," Shanzay continues, looking at Rizwan, eyes wide with gratitude. "It was so awful, but Rizwan stayed the whole time. Thank you, again. Really."

"It was nothing," Rizwan says.

"It was not nothing," Shanzay insists to me, then turns to him. "I seriously owe you. I don't know what I would have done if I had to deal with all of that alone. I've never been in an accident before."

"Shanzay's right," I say to Rizwan. "That was really sweet of you. Truly commendable. And thank you for bringing her here."

"I didn't want her to be alone," Rizwan says.

"Aw, Rizwan," I say, overcome with gratitude, as well. "You're so kind. A real knight in shining armor."

Distracted by the commotion and emotions, I did not notice someone else slipping through the open, unlocked door. Shanzay's gaze focuses on a figure behind me.

"Fawad, you're here, too!" Shanzay exclaims.

I startle, whirling around. My heart kickstarts as if I've run a mile.

What is he doing here? So early?

He looks as if he has slept even less than I, and is still in his clothes from last night. His tie is still pinned straight, his blazer and slacks not the least bit slovenly. The only part of him disheveled is his hair, sticking in all directions, as if he's run his hands through them dozens of times.

"What are you doing here?" I ask, feeling unsteady.

When he turns his gaze to me, my breath catches. He takes a step toward me, and my heartbeat scatters. His lips part, as if he is about to speak.

Rizwan clears his throat. Fawad blinks and stops suddenly, eyes going from me to Rizwan.

A strange look passes between him and Rizwan, something so quick I cannot decipher it.

"Yes, I—" Fawad begins. He cuts off, as if he's muddled in the head. He takes his glasses off and rubs his eyes, trying to collect his bearings.

"Did you hear what happened?" Shanzay asks. He clenches his jaw.

"Yes, I heard a bit." He does not look at me. Instead, he approaches Shanzay, eyes warm with concern. "Are you alright?"

"I am, now," she says, smiling.

"Good." He nods. "You ought to rest. I better get going, then."

"Me, as well," Rizwan says, standing beside him.

Why did Fawad come? I wonder, as I go to fluff Shanzay's pillow. As the boys exchange some commentary about the accident, Shanzay pulls me close.

"I think I am in love, once more," she whispers into my ear. I can barely suppress my gasp.

"Are you quite sure?" I whisper, pulling back to look into her wide eyes. Her gaze shifts to where the boys are standing in the entryway of the living room and nods just as they exit our sight.

"He was so kind tonight," Shanzay whispers. "I don't think I'll ever forget the service he rendered me."

I get excited, then force myself to calm down. "Shanzay, I have promised to give up matchmaking and never meddle again, so do not say his name. I don't want to know."

"I won't," she says, biting her lip. "But surely you can guess?"

I nod, and we both giggle. "I approve immensely."

"You don't think he's out of my league?" she asks, eyebrows creasing.

"You deserve the world! No one is out of your league," I say. She covers her face with her blanket, smiling.

"You don't mind, do you?" she asks, nervous again. I shake my head.

"No, not at all!"

I must say, I'm actually relieved. Rizwan and Shanzay will be happy together, I am sure of it. He was so attentive to her just now! I haven't been enthusiastic toward him for a little while now, and once he sees how fond Shanzay is, he'll surely forget about me and fall for her immediately!

Perhaps I'm so in love with the idea of love that I put my expectations way too high when there is even the slightest glimmer of hope, which I believe is what happened with Rizwan and I.

No matter! He and Shanzay pair well. And I know I said I am done with meddling, but...

"Wait!" I cry, leaving Shanzay's side. Both boys come rushing back.

"What is it?" Fawad asks, worried.

"What can I do?" Rizwan asks at the same time.

They glance at one another. Fawad's eyebrows furrow ever so slightly in irritation.

"Will you stay?" I ask sweetly. I look at Rizwan, batting my eyelashes. "For breakfast, at least. As thanks for helping Shanzay."

"Of course," Rizwan replies, smiling warmly. "Of course."

I am about to tell Fawad to stay as well, but he is already gone, his shoulders a stiff line as he exits the door and slams it shut behind him.

My stomach sinks with disappointment. And that still does not answer the question: what *was* he doing here?

It seemed like he wanted to say something, but he left without saying it. I feel as if I have missed something vital, like that night I fell asleep and he left without saying goodbye.

But I will deal with it later. For now, I must attend to Shanzay and her budding romance.

I go to the kitchen and make breakfast, whipping up some scrambled eggs, French toast, and chai for my guests. We sit together, eating and crowding Shanzay, my little damsel in distress, as she lies on the couch.

She keeps laughing nervously. Then, when the last dregs of our coffee are done, Rizwan stands.

"Time to go, I think," he says.

"Thank you again," Shanzay says sweetly. He smiles, then I walk him out, saying goodbye and expressing my own gratitude to him.

After he is gone, Shanzay naps, and I cannot exactly leave her to go see Fawad, so I stay, helping her to and fro. She has injured her left ankle, so she can still drive, but there is the matter of getting her car back, if it is salvageable.

I resolve to help her figure it out tomorrow, and drop her home today.

"You don't want to watch a movie or anything?" she asks, when I have settled her back in her room and made sure everything she needs is within reaching distance on her side table.

"No, I think you should rest," I say, handing her a glass of water. I am impatient to return home. "Besides, I have some ... business to attend to."

Shanzay nods, waving goodbye, and I hurry home.

On the drive back, my phone rings. It's Asif.

Alarmed, I immediately pick up. Asif never calls me.

"Hey, salaam," I say, hands tightening on the wheel. "Is everything okay?"

"Uhh," he replies, drawing the word out. He seems lost. "What did you do to Fawad?"

Relief flows through me for a moment – Naadia is fine – then is quickly replaced by concern.

"What do you mean?" I ask. "What's happened to Fawad?"'

"I popped by the house to pick something up and I found him on the living room floor, his clothes strewn about him, his hand over his face, looking depressed."

Blood pounds in my ears.

"I don't see how that's my fault!" I reply, voice high.

"He didn't even notice I came in until I kicked him with my foot, and then he just said, 'She—' and cut off," Asif continues. "And I figured you were the only *she* who could get put him into such a state."

A thrill shoots through me. Silly little me? Reducing Fawad – immaculately dressed, always put together, perfectly composed Fawad – to a disheveled mess?

But wait, no – it can't have been me he was referring to. I haven't done anything to warrant such despair in him. We hardly exchanged two words this morning, and we were getting along so well last night.

Alarm bells ring in my head. Could it be *another* "she"? Some other girl in his life? I frown, brows furrowed.

"Well?" Asif asks.

"I don't know," I reply crossly. "But I didn't do anything. I'll talk to you later, okay?"

We hang up, and I continue the drive home in angry silence. *Who* was this other girl? And how *dare* she bring Fawad to such a state?!

I need to get to the bottom of this.

I arrive home shortly after, and by the time I manage to leave the house again to walk to Fawad's, the evening is fast approaching. The weather is lovely, but even with the longer days spring brings, the sun will be setting soon.

When I arrive at his house, my heart is beating quickly, much too quickly, and I tell myself it is due to my brisk pace.

"Hellooo," I call, opening the unlocked door and entering. The house feels empty; I cannot hear him anywhere. I do catch a slight breeze, coming from the back of the house, and when I go to investigate, the door is opened a crack, and I hear the crunch of a trowel hitting soil.

I know where he is.

Smiling to myself, I head out back, then step down the steps until I find him. There's a chill in the air that makes me shiver, but when I step into the sun, it's heaven, and I tilt my head back to soak in the sun.

Then, I see him.

Fawad is gardening. He sits sowing seeds, gloved hands sure and steady, and I watch the tendons in his arm move as he does, brown skin bare from where he has rolled up his sleeves. His dark hair is curling at the nape of his neck from sweat.

"Salaam," I say. Fawad turns and looks up at me with sunburnt cheeks and smiles as bright as the sun, just as warm, just as lovely. I feel the heat all over me.

"Salaam," he replies, smiling.

I don't know why I've come, or what to say exactly. What is the plan? I don't know. For a moment, this stops me in my tracks. I am always in control – except when I am with him, apparently. It's disarming, and my chest twists with the dangerous concoction of exhilaration and fear.

We just look at one another. It seems he does not know what to say either.

Then, it seems as if something turns in his mind, and he stands. Taking his gloves off, he walks towards me, stopping when he is right before me. There's dirt on his cheekbone.

Instinctively, I lift a hand to brush it aside, then stop

midway. Both of our eyes snag on my hand midair, and I drop it to my side.

"Dirt," I say, rubbing my own cheek. He wipes it away, then smiles, shaking his head.

"Come on, then," he says softly. He heads inside, and I follow. "Sit," he instructs, pointing to the living room. I obey, watching as he disappears.

The moment he is gone, it's as if something in me jolts, and I feel a little ill, my head pounding.

What was I doing here? I must be terribly tired; all that lack of sleep is catching up to me. I can't get my footing. I feel dizzy.

This was a bad idea. I head towards the foyer and front door, ready to bolt.

Fawad comes down the stairs and sees me. He has something in his clean hands. It is a package, wrapped in brown paper and twine.

"A belated birthday gift," he says, handing it to me.

"Oh!" I smile. I love receiving gifts! Without preamble, I undo the twine, then rip the paper off and hand it to his waiting hands.

It's *The Piper's Son*. I lift it, puzzled.

"I already have my own copy of this," I say, amused, "as you might recall, since you borrowed it."

"Open it," he says. Puzzled, I do as he's asked, and then I understand. I flip through the pages; it is filled with blue ink in the margins—his thoughts. "I didn't want to desecrate your own copy, in case you wanted a version without my intrusions."

"Good thinking," I say, voice breathless as I touch the pages. It was excellent thinking, really. I would have had to buy another copy if he had left the notes in mine.

"You said you love discussing your favorite books," he says, waiting to see my reaction. "This is a bit of a permanent discussion you can access whenever you please." He hesitates, eyes hopeful. "Do you like it?"

There are notes on nearly every page, underlined portions and clear sticky notes and arrows and exclamation points.

It must have taken him *hours*.

My eyes well up with tears, and I hastily blink them away. Goodness, what is wrong with me?

"I ... I love it," I say, meaning every word. It is subtle and sweet and exactly what I would have wanted, yet I never would have been able to voice that want. He excavated it from within me.

"Really?" he says, grinning. "Good." He nods. "I was going to give it to you on your birthday but—" He breaks off, scratching his neck. "Anyway. I'm glad you like it."

"I do," I say, but my head is still pounding. It really is the perfect gift.

What does that mean?! I can't think straight.

I feel feverish, both physically and metaphorically. Life can be so symbolic sometimes. It must be the weather changing.

As if on cue, I sneeze. Fawad frowns, taking a step toward me. "I hope you didn't get sick because you refused to wear your jacket properly," he says, inspecting my face with concern. I avoid his perceptive gaze.

"Oh, pish posh," I wave a hand nonchalantly.

He shakes his head, laughing to himself. "Pish posh."

I sneeze again, and he furrows his brows. "Okay, I'm leaving," I say quickly, turning around. "Thank you for this!"

I hold up the book, then dash out before he can stop me.

Outside, I hold the book to my chest tight, as if that can calm my heart's beating, but it cannot.

When I get home, I eat a quick dinner then nestle into bed with the book he's given me, wanting to read his thoughts.

But when I open the first page, it feels too intimate, and I'm afraid of what I'll feel if I do read it.

I put it aside and instead grab my copy of *The Secret History*, which I haven't begun yet, but has been sitting on my bedside table all this time. I start reading. I owe Fawad that much, to read the book he recommended to me.

And, my God, I love it.

I feel a little thrill reading through it, as if he is just beside me, reading over my shoulders. It is as if I can hear his thoughts on certain passages, and it summons something soft in me, like he is in my head, like he is nestled in my heart, and I don't want him to leave.

I read until late, despite how sleepy I am. I read until I am exhausted and cannot keep my eyes open a moment longer.

Reading it feels like going out to the sea from the sands:

at first, the waves are gentle and shy against my feet on the shoreline, lukewarm and sweet; but as I go farther and farther into the waters, the waves crash over me, cold and unrelenting, submerging me, leaving me gasping for breath, until finally, I am drowning in the story.

It's a bit like falling in love.

Chapter Nineteen

I dream about Fawad.

When I wake up, I cannot recall what the dream was about, but it tastes like memories, like something sure and real, like something I have done and will do again, a thousand times.

I blink the last vestiges of sleep away, my chest tight. Nausea comes over me, and I feel wholly disoriented.

I do not know what is going on. It is like with each beat of my heart, the truth runs further from me, and I cannot catch up to my thoughts, my feelings, any of it.

"Humaira, have you made my coffee yet?" Papa calls from downstairs. I groan, shifting in bed.

"No," I try to call back, but my voice comes out as a croak. My throat is dry, but even after drinking water from my bedside table, it does not get much better. I press my palm against my neck; my skin is burning.

Oh dear. I may actually be sick.

I close my eyes, feeling drowsy.

"Humaira, where is the Hoffman file?" Papa calls from downstairs, a moment or ten moments later. I hear him rummaging about in his office, things falling to the floor.

I drift back to sleep before I can respond.

"Humaira, my keys?" Papa calls. "Humaira! Humaira!"

The sound grates on my nerves, even as I sleep. I twist in my sheets, agitated.

"Humaira, why aren't you replying?" Papa asks, tone cross and growing closer. "*Humaira.*"

He opens the door, standing in the doorframe.

"*What?*" I cry, eyes flying open. "What, Papa, what?"

He blinks, seeing me still in bed, the wretched expression that must be twisting my face.

"What's wrong?" he asks, stepping into the room.

"I'm not going to work, I don't feel well," I grumble, burying my cheek deeper into my pillow. "It's fine. You can go."

I just want him to leave, but he comes closer, pressing the back of his hand against my forehead. His hands feel like ice.

"You have a fever!" he exclaims. His eyes widen, and he pulls out his phone. "Should I call the doctor?" He asks me. "What is the doctor's name again?" He waves a hand. "It's no matter. I'll stay home with you. Do you want something to eat? I can go pick something up. Or—"

There are too many words coming out of his mouth, and I cannot bear his panic.

"Papa, I'm fine."

"You're not fine!" he says. "Bedridden! With a fever! I am sure you caught a cold ... did you bring a neck-scarf yesterday? I thought I saw you leave the house without one—"

"*Papa!*" I snap. "I take care of you every day, surely I can take care of myself."

He blinks, taken aback by my tone.

"Oh." He nods. "I can still stay," he says. "I'll take off of work."

"I am twenty-four!" I cry. "Please leave!"

I want to be alone right now so I can process my thoughts and emotions and figure out what the hell is going on.

I am panicking, too, but for entirely other reasons, and I do not need Papa's panic on top of mine.

"But—"

I groan. "You're suffocating me! Go!"

"You don't mean that," he says, even though he looks hurt. He stands perfectly still.

"I do," I say. "It's just a little cold. I do not need you to fuss over me now." I know I should stop there, but I cannot. The words spill out. "What would actually help is if you took care of yourself and did not depend on me. *That* would be more helpful to me than this drama right now!"

Papa is stunned, but he recovers quickly. With a nod, he says, "Okay."

He leaves, closing the bedroom door behind him. I am left alone, just like I wanted, but the silence is deafening. I hear my own shuddering breath as I try to calm the guilt in me, as I try to relax.

Downstairs, the front door closes and locks. My eyes well with tears, my head pounding ferociously.

I force myself to breathe in and breathe out. This will not do.

I get out of bed and freshen up, changing out of my pajamas into loungewear, which is basically pajamas, just more stylish. Then, I go down to make myself coffee and toast and take some medicine.

Feeling more in control, I head back to bed, burying into a pile of pillows with *The Secret History*. I spend the rest of the morning reading, and when I've finished the book, I am stunned to find it's only been a few hours.

It feels like I've traveled thousands of miles yet all the while I've been in the same spot.

There was a bit of romance, like Fawad said, between the protagonist and one of his friends, and those were some of my favorite parts. I liked the way he saw her. Even if they don't end up together, he really *sees* her.

When I finish I want to read it again already. I loved it, even though it was not what I expected or would have chosen for myself, I *loved* it, and I wonder what it means that Fawad was able to choose this for me, I wonder what any of it means.

And it's driving me crazy. Is he thinking of me, too? What was all of this, and all of that, and everything that has happened, and everything that could happen?

I don't know. So I do the only reasonable thing: I go back to sleep.

I do not wake up until well past midday, when it sounds like the front door is opening and closing gently. It must be Papa. I am glad he's come; I should not have been angry with him earlier.

It's different when Naadia snaps at him because he is used to her moodiness and comes equipped to deal with it. From me, however, such crossness is a harsh blow indeed.

I wait for him to come upstairs, watching from my bed. My door is closed, but any second now, the handle will turn, and Papa will enter, and all will be right as rain.

But the handle does not turn.

Papa does not come.

Perhaps Papa has forgotten a file. Or he is simply ignoring me.

So be it. I do not particularly want to get out of bed as it is.

Though I am starving. The toast I ate this morning is not doing much for me, despite the handsome helping of jam I had lathered across it. I want to eat comfort food, but I'm too lazy to get up and go make any. I feel wretched, truly, and it is twice fold because I can recognize it and do nothing about it.

So I nestle back under the covers, determined to sleep the day away.

But just as I am drifting off, I hear a light knocking on my bedroom door.

"It's me," a voice says gently.

My heart stops.

I jump up, then out of bed and head to the door. Maybe I'm delusional and imagining things. Even so, my heartbeat pounds as I lean a hot cheek against the cool door, listening.

"Uncle told me to check on you," he says. I gasp, leaning closer. I can hear him breathing on the other side. He knocks again. "Humaira," he says, voice soft. I shiver, hearing him say my name.

"Just a second!" I manage to say, going to tie my hair up and put a scarf on. I sneak a look at my appearance in the mirror: my eyes are a little puffy and my nose is red. Fantastic. But I do not worry about it; instead, my hand goes to the doorknob.

Then, I stop.

He has never been in my room. This is certainly dangerous.

"I'll meet you downstairs," I say.

"Okay." I listen to the sound of footsteps receding, my pulse racing.

When I head down, he is sitting at the countertop in the kitchen, drinking a mug of coffee. He's wearing a button up shirt without a tie, the top button undone.

"Hey," I say. He stands as I enter, then pulls out a chair for me. I sit down, and he pushes a bowl of cut up fruit my way.

"Yuck," I say, making a face, reaching for his coffee instead.

"You need nutrients," he says, deftly moving his coffee out of reach before I can steal a sip.

I frown. "No fair."

"What's not fair is you getting sick because of your own silliness," he says with a frown. He is annoyed, but I can tell it is more out of concern than anything.

"I'm fine," I say, leaning back against my chair. I wave a hand nonchalantly, then point an accusatory finger. "Though I should have expected you would say I told you so."

"I did not exactly say, *I told you so*," he says, a small smile playing on his lips. "But, I *did* tell you so."

"And there you have gone and said it."

I lean forward to put my arms on the table, then rest my head on my arm and look over at him. With a pitiful pout, I reach for his coffee again. "Please."

I bat my eyelashes for full effect, but he is either immune to my charms or truly cares too much about my health to succumb to my infamous pout. Tragic.

"Have you eaten anything?" Fawad asks. I shake my head. "Would you like some tomato soup? Grilled cheese?"

My mouth juts open, and I lift my head to give him an astonished look. How did he know? That's exactly what I want right now.

He flashes me a brilliant smile. "Give me some credit."

He gets up, then does something with the kettle and a bag of leaves he pulls from his pocket. A few minutes later, he hands me a cup of tea, which smells like jasmine and mint.

"The mint is from my garden," he says. "Drink that, while I make your food."

I obey, sipping the sweet tea in silence as I watch him cook. He rolls his sleeves up, showcasing his forearms, then washes and sets tomatoes, onions, red peppers, and garlic on a tray. While that roasts in the oven, he shreds blocks of cheese, making the sandwiches.

When the vegetables are roasted, he transfers them to a pot and purees them, then adds in heavy cream and basil leaves from the fridge, telling me how he is growing basil in his garden, and how I must stop buying it from the store.

I do not respond, really, I simply watch him. The sunlight washing over his brown skin, the glint of light on his glasses. The way he dips a spoon into the soup, blowing on it gently before bringing the liquid to his lips to taste.

The furrow of his brows as he thinks for a moment before sprinkling some more salt in. The movement of his long, lean body. The shift of the muscles of his back, his arms. The ring on the slender third finger of his right hand. How another ring might look mirrored on the other.

Watching him arouses something ancient in me, a feeling I have never felt yet recognize all the same – something irrefutable and bone-deep. It does not leave me even as we eat together, nor after, when we shift to the family room and I lie down on the sofa. He buries me beneath a fortress of blankets and pillows.

"Feel better?" he asks.

It is strange to be looked after like this. I am usually not fond of such fuss, but with Fawad, I do not mind giving him some of the control. I look at him, his watchful dark eyes, the angle of his jaw, the purse of his soft lips.

He sits down beside my legs, which are covered in blankets, but still; if I stretched, my feet could be in his lap. A little voice dares me to do it.

"I do feel better."

"Have you taken medicine?"

"It's just a little cold," I say flippantly. "Nothing to worry over."

"Is that it?" he asks.

"Really, I'm just sad," I say before I can stop myself.

His eyes are so warm and genuine, I can't help myself from telling him the truth. I stop once the words have left my mouth, regretting them at once. I've never spoken thus with any man; I rarely speak thus with Naadia or Phuppo.

Around him, I am uninhibited: no facades, no pretenses, it is all truth, and that frightens me. Perhaps I am a coward, and the only reason I am so well-liked is because I am careful about what I show people. Beloved because I make myself lovable. But what about the truth?

If he sees who I really am, will he stay?

I shift uncomfortably, closing my eyes. "Will you go, please?"

"Why?" he asks, voice gentle.

"I don't want you to see me like this," I say, voice soft. He doesn't respond, and I open my eyes again, to see if he's heard.

His eyes are steady. He has heard me. "Why don't you want me to see you like this?"

"I don't have the energy to be good-natured."

He gives me a puzzled glance. "Surely I have seen you in a worse state."

He is right. I rub my nose against a blanket, covering half my face in the fabric. My pulse beats erratically, uneven.

"You do not need to pretend," he says, voice soft. "Not with me."

I turn to look at him, really look at him, and I feel something sharp in my chest, something blazing, like a shooting star, magical and bright – or a shooting arrow, sharp and painful. I cannot tell which.

I don't know how I could have missed it, how I could have seen him thousands of times before and never felt this: this pain, sudden and swift, piercing through me.

Everyone has always thought him handsome, and I always found him perfectly tolerable, but now – now I cannot fathom him as anything but beautiful.

It is his soul that I see, and my own that comes roaring to the surface in response.

Something changes in the air between us. His eyelids lower, and he leans forward.

With a gasp, I jolt back, and so does he.

He shakes his head.

Was he about to kiss me? Is that what that was? *Well, that was new.*

He should go. This was certainly against the rules.

But I don't tell him to. Perhaps we only make rules to see who we are willing to break them for.

He gets up and leaves, and I release a breath, trying to

steady myself. He returns a few moments later, and when he does, there's a thermometer in his hands. He sits back down, leaning over my legs toward my mouth.

"Open up," he orders. I do as instructed, and his gaze falls to my mouth. His lips part as I lift my tongue, and for a moment, he doesn't do anything but stare at my lips. My cheeks heat.

Then, with a shake of his head, he sticks the thermometer in, shifting his focus to it.

Surely, my temperature will increase now.

"How do you feel?" he asks, taking the thermometer out to check. "Your fever has gone down."

It surely doesn't feel that way.

"It's nothing," I say, waving a hand. "Just a little cold."

"Good." He pauses, then looks at me. Something in his expression makes me stop breathing entirely. "I believe I am ill as well, though my affliction is of a different sort."

His eyes burn into mine. I suddenly feel feverish once more.

Instinctively, I press my cold fingers against the pulse in my throat. The act centers me when my emotions are spilling out of hand.

With my fingers curled around my throat, it feels like I am holding my heart, the quick and steady pulse just beneath my fingertips.

And if I can hold it, I can contain it.

But this cannot be contained.

Chapter Twenty

Rizwan comes again in June, which isn't at all relevant to me, seeing as I'm over him entirely. He calls me, and I consider not picking up, but then I remember what Shanzay said the morning after Haya's wedding, and I answer immediately.

"I'd like to go on a picnic," he eventually says, after we've exchanged niceties.

"Excellent idea!" I say. "I'll invite everyone."

"Everyone?" he repeats. "Yes – sure."

I know my meddling days are behind me, but surely this does not count? In the two months that have passed since the wedding, Shanzay's ankle healed, and it seems her heart has as well.

She has been in much higher spirits, and I am sure her feelings for Rizwan are to be credited for it.

Nothing like a new crush to help you get over

heartbreak! Not that we have spoken of it. I am resolved not to interfere and cause trouble, and I have not.

Planning a picnic is not meddling! If I was meddling I would invite Shanzay only, then conveniently forget to go myself.

Instead, I invite Naadia and Asif. When I call Fawad to invite him as well – I must confess, I have been avoiding him, and he is the last one I call – he tells me he's already aware. Shanzay called him. I find this strange, but do not dwell on it.

The day of, we all head to a local park, everyone bringing along one dish (except for me, I bring three). The middle of June means the weather is warm but not hot, and I was hoping for today to be one of those blissful afternoons, with shining sun and serene breezes, but we are out of luck in that department.

The sun is harsh, the humidity worse. The asphalt only increases the heat, but the park is filled with huge trees, which will provide ample shade once we settle in.

"Whose idea was this again?" Naadia asks, swatting a bee away in the parking lot. She and Asif arrived at the same time I did, in Asif's BMW truck, which is now parked beside me.

"Hush," I say, standing next to her and checking my reflection in her car window. Massive sunglasses cover half of my face, making me look like a celebrity. I smile. "Anyway, we have to be supportive."

"To who?" Naadia asks. I press my lips together. Oopsies. I shouldn't have said that.

"You might find out soon enough," I sing-song. She shakes my arm. "Ow!"

"Tell me!" she says. "You know I can't stand not knowing juicy secrets."

I wiggle my brows at her. "Just pay attention."

Asif, dear that he is, carries our picnic baskets, putting his muscular arms to good use. I nod approvingly, while Naadia wolf-whistles.

"Don't objectify me in front of your sister," Asif pleads. She ignores him.

"He's been working out," Naadia informs me.

"I love that for him and for you."

"Right."

Asif looks away, cheeks pink. We walk out of the parking lot to the edge of the park, standing in the shade, just as another car pulls up, and out comes Rizwan, skin bronzed and hazel eyes bright. Then, Shanzay arrives, and shortly after, Fawad.

"Here, let me take that," Rizwan offers to Shanzay, taking her basket. Shanzay smiles warmly, and I resist the urge to nudge Naadia to see. They join us in the shade. "Shall we find a spot to sit?" Rizwan asks.

"This way," Asif says, leading the way. "Let's go further in."

Rizwan follows him, and I see Naadia interrogate Shanzay as to who we might be needing to support. Shanzay, bless her, is as clueless as Naadia, even though she must know I have arranged all this for her.

Not that I am meddling! I am simply here for the outing. And perhaps something – *someone* – else...

"Shall we?" Fawad asks, falling into step with me. We round out the back. I nod, and we walk further into the park.

Tall trees spread up around us, shading us with their leaves. It is immediately cooler the farther in we go. Glimmers of sunshine peak between the trees, and as we walk forward, the world is a blend of gold and green, the sweet sound of birdsong background music.

I risk a glance at the man walking beside me. I have not seen much of Fawad in the past two months – or I have seen him the same amount, it just *seems* like I have not seen him much.

As if every time he leaves, it is too soon.

He turns to me, and my heartbeat quickens.

"I thought I said this was casual," I say, when he catches me staring.

"This is casual," he replies, looking at his attire. He is wearing a light brown linen suit with a white shirt and looks quite handsome in it.

"That is not—"

"Because you are dressed so casually?" he asks, amused as he looks me up and down. My cheeks heat under his gaze. I am wearing this gorgeous floral full-sleeved maxi dress and chiffon hijab.

"That's different," I say.

"Why?" he asks. "Because you're a girl."

"No," I say, even though he is right. Flustered, I smack

him with my fan (yes, I have a fan that I brought from Spain).

"Hey!" He clutches his arm, then bends down to pick up a twig, and hits my leg. I gasp.

"Rude!" I go to smack him again, but he deftly avoids me. In the commotion, I trip on my heeled wedges, but if I'm going down, so is he.

I grab onto his arm, and we both go tumbling to the ground.

"Oof!"

"Ow!"

We lie side by side on the grass, recovering from the fall. The sun gleams in my eyes and I turn to the side, where Fawad's chest is shaking with laughter.

"Stop laughing," I scold, trying to be vexed and failing. "Look what you did!"

On the grass, his knuckles brush against mine, and I forget all about being cross to focus on the feel of it, the tingling sensation it sends shooting up my arm. I bite my lip.

A moment later, my palm turns up as his turns down. His hand slips into mine.

Something sharp turns in my stomach. I know I should pull away, but his hand is so lovely on mine, it robs me of my breath. I cannot move. Do not want to.

He strokes my palm with his thumb, and my breath hitches violently, returning to me.

With a jolt, I sit up, removing my hand. I feel very hot. Much too hot.

After a moment, he sits up too, brushing off his jacket. I gasp.

"Hold still!" I say, as I spot something in his dark hair. It distracts me from the too-quick rush of blood pounding in my ears.

"Goodness, what is it?" he asks, concerned.

"A bug, I think." I get up onto my knees so I can see better, but the little caterpillar has disappeared into his thick hair.

Then, I catch a flash of green in the sea of black. "One moment."

I go to grab it, but it wiggles out of reach. His hair is much softer than I imagined, and I would be lying if I said my fingers did not linger in the silk of his locks.

I retrieve the caterpillar, but do not remove my hand from his hair just yet. I revel in being this close to him, my heart beating deliciously fast.

He is eye-level with my heart, and I hope he cannot see just how fast it is beating. But he is looking up, for once, looking up at me, exposing the long column of his throat. His eyes are half-lidded, face solemn, as if he is praying.

"You're at my mercy," I tease.

"Aren't I always?" he responds.

I bite back a smile, then pluck the little creature out of his hair and remove my hand. I sit down so we are eye level again, the grass tickling my ankles and calves under my dress. I lift my hand between us, holding the caterpillar up to show him.

"How cute," he says, picking it off my palm. His dark eyes glitter with amusement. "I shall name her Humaira."

"Rude!" I cry, but I can't help the laugh that escapes me.

He laughs, too, and we both watch as the caterpillar crawls across his index finger. I hold up my hand again, bringing it close to his, until my index finger creates a bridge with him. We do not touch, and it takes all my strength to keep the tremor from my hand.

Slowly, the caterpillar passes onto my finger, and as it does, his finger brushes mine, ever so slightly. His touch is softer than the breeze against my hot cheeks, just as caressing, just as sweet.

My breathing stalls, but I do not withdraw.

Instead, I lift my eyes to his. His mouth parts—

"*There* you are!" a shrill voice calls.

Dread curdles my stomach. *It can't be.* A bright teal dress enters my peripheral vision. Fawad and I both sigh, disappointed.

"Salaams!" Jasmine calls, Emad just behind her.

"What a lovely surprise!" I manage to say, voice saccharine. "How did you—"

"You must have forgotten to mention it," Jasmine says, eyes masked behind massive sunglasses. "Luckily, Mamoo mentioned it to Ammi."

Drat Papa for mentioning it to Mahum Phuppo! Leave it to Emad's wretched fiancée to invite herself yet again. Honestly, does she have nothing better to do?

I glare at Emad, and he does wither slightly.

"There—oh." Rizwan appears as well, hands empty of

the picnic baskets. He looks from me to Fawad on the ground, then to Jasmine and Emad. He looks confused. "We're all set up over there," he finally says.

I stand up, brushing off my dress, and walk ahead with him, wanting to reach Shanzay first to warn her. Behind me, Fawad sighs.

The picnic baskets have been laid out on a large table in the park, beneath the shade of a tree, while a picnic blanket has been set up a little to the side. Asif is feeding Naadia grapes while Shanzay drinks some lemonade. I hurry toward her.

"Shan—" I start, but she looks over my shoulder, spotting Jasmine before I can say another word.

"Don't worry," Shanzay says to me, her smile genuine. "I'm perfectly okay. I've moved on, remember?"

I smile with relief, squeezing her hand.

As the picnic continues, I see she is truly not bothered by Emad and Jasmine's appearance in the slightest. Her new crush really must be a balm! Oh, I am so happy for her.

Rizwan sits beside me, just across from her, and we munch on cold turkey sandwiches. Fawad and Asif throw around a football, while Jasmine and Emad harass Naadia, who sends me SOS signals with her eyes.

I consider leaving Shanzay alone with Rizwan, but then he starts regaling us with stories of his old rugby days, and it feels rude to get up just then.

"What is that?" Shanzay asks.

"You don't know what rugby is?" Rizwan asks,

dumbfounded. He proceeds to explain it to her in detail, and Shanzay listens attentively.

"That does sound fun!"

I smile, listening as well. Then, Shanzay gets up to soak in some sun – she must be nervous! – leaving Rizwan and I alone.

"I have visited the States thrice now, so next time, it is you who must visit me," Rizwan says, giving me a sweet smile. "I can show you around London, and we can go see all the pretty libraries at Oxford."

"That does sound lovely," I say, trying to signal to Shanzay to come join us again, but she isn't paying attention. "But I cannot travel alone."

Not to mention I scarcely think Papa will approve of such a trip, nor would he accompany me.

"Why not?" he asks, eating his cheese and crackers.

"Papa wouldn't like it."

"What do you mean? You are a working adult, surely your father lets you take trips on your own or with friends."

I laugh. "It isn't that he stops me, per se, it's just that he does not wish for me to go."

Technically, I *can* go – I have my own money, I know the way the world works, but Papa is positively frightened by the idea of me traveling alone or with friends. It isn't that he wishes to limit me; he does not see the point in it, since he always obliges whenever Naadia and I wish to go on vacation.

In truth, he is afraid for me to travel alone. I have only ever traveled with him. To a certain extent, I understand:

the world is cruel, and I am a sheltered young lady. Of course, he wishes to keep me safe.

"So you *can* go," Rizwan replies, a little confused.

"Yes, but I don't wish to do anything that would make him unhappy," I explain. I live under his roof; why would I disrespect him so? I show I am grateful by being obedient.

Everything that I am, that I have, is because of him, so I do everything that I can to make him happy, so long as it is not at the expense of my own happiness, of course.

He does make it difficult, as of late. Since the day I was sick and snapped at him, he's been distant. No matter how I try to coax a good mood out of him, offering ice cream or to go for a walk together, he's withdrawn. Not angry, just quiet.

He has even taken to making his own coffee in the mornings and leaving before I come down. I miss our little routine.

I should ask Fawad about it. It seems he sees more of Papa these days than I do. My gaze inadvertently finds him, standing beside Shanzay, the two chatting. Shanzay laughs at something Fawad says, and my eyebrows furrow ever so slightly.

Fawad is not so funny, I think to myself, something strange nudging in my chest.

"You make unlikely friends," Rizwan says, following my gaze.

"Sorry?" I ask, shifting my focus to him.

"You and Shanzay," he says. "I would not expect it."

I consider this. "I did not expect it, at first, either," I

agree. I had befriended her at first because I was bored and lonely and thought I could be helpful to her, but now she's become a true friend.

"She's a bit of a frazzled girl," he says. "Not as refined as you are, or as poised."

"Yes, she rather is," I agree, a smile engulfing my face, for therein lies her charm, which I suspect Rizwan is subtly alluding to as well. She is so innocent and sweet, not constantly trying to be anything other than what she is. She has the courage to be true.

"She's either awfully quiet or chattering on and on," Rizwan adds. I smile at him brightly.

"Isn't she just?" I say. It is yet another reason I like her, her chattering is a comfort to me, bringing vibrant colors to my life when things are fading to gray.

Oh, I am so glad he sees her!

I stifle a laugh, as I see Rizwan and I are the only ones talking. The others are gathered around, mostly quiet, particularly Jasmine, who is whimpering due to the heat, and Emad, who keeps swatting mosquitoes on his arm.

"Let's play cards!" I suggest. Everyone is being so boring. I usher everyone over to the picnic blanket we have laid out on the grass, and we all assemble around in a circle. I sit next to Shanzay, and Rizwan comes to sit next to me, probably wanting to be close to her. I bite back a smile.

We play a round of cards, but it isn't very fun.

"This isn't very diverting," Rizwan whispers to me. I pout in agreement. He wiggles his eyebrows at me, before addressing everyone with lively impudence. "Let's play another game!" he says. "Humaira tells me she wants to know what everyone's thinking."

I smile; oh, that could be fun! Shanzay chatters on in response, saying a great deal, and it only makes Rizwan and I laugh more. She is so sweet!

"Is Humaira sure she wants to hear what we're all thinking?" Fawad asks, voice distinct as he looks from Rizwan to me. His dark eyes are cold.

"No, no," I say, laughing carelessly. "Don't tell me what you're thinking – just say anything good."

"It seems like such an obnoxious thing to say," Jasmine murmurs to Emad. "Some girls are so attention-seeking, don't you agree?"

"Yes, I agree completely," Emad whispers to her. "No one can be as elegant as you, babe."

Rizwan gives me a look, hearing this as well, and I bite back another grin. "No, no, you're right, Fawad, Humaira doesn't want to know what you're thinking," he announces. "Instead, she wants to know one thing very clever, two things moderately clever, or three things boring."

"Oh, I can start then, that should be easy," Shanzay says, smiling. "I probably say three boring things just by opening my mouth, since I am always babbling on."

"Only three?" Rizwan says beneath his breath.

"Surely, Shan, you'll think of more than just three," I say, laughing before I realize what I've said.

I still, heart stopping entirely as the smile freezes on my face.

That came out much harsher than I intended. I laugh

quickly, trying to push the comment away, but Shanzay is clearly hurt. She is no longer smiling at all.

Fawad fixes me with a scalding glance. I look away.

"Yes," Shanzay stutters. "You're right."

She fiddles with the end of her scarf, her gaze trained on her hands. I cannot see her eyes, but I am sure they are filled with tears.

Oh no. I didn't mean it, not like that! Regret lodges in my throat. She did not deserve that. Her bottom lip quivers, and there is a tremor in her hands now.

I look to the others, who are sitting in silence. They avoid my eyes, except for Fawad, who still glares. I look away from him, unable to bear the reproach in his eyes.

"Shan—" I begin, my voice light. She suddenly gets up.

"It's so hot," she says cheerily, forcing a smile on her face. "I think I'll go take a walk."

Before I can respond or say I will join her, she hurries off. Fawad follows her.

"I don't want to play," Jasmine says, flipping her hair. "This game is stupid."

"Agreed," Emad says.

"Come, let's walk, too," Jasmine says. "I'm tired of just sitting in one spot."

So it is Rizwan and I, once more, for Asif and Naadia have not been paying attention to anything but themselves this entire while, the pair giggling and talking in their own little world.

"What bores," Rizwan says, assessing the situation.

My mouth feels dry – guilt riddles through me. I stand up, trying to catch my breath.

It was just a small comment, and Shanzay will know I didn't mean any harm. She'll be fine, as she always is.

Rizwan stands as well, coming in front of me. I brush away my thoughts and fix him with a bright smile, putting up a perfectly fine pretense.

"Shall we walk?" he asks. I nod, and we fall into step together, walking away from the others to some rose bushes. I brush my hands over the petals, trying to calm the unease in my heart.

"I'm glad we are alone," Rizwan says, pulling my gaze toward him. I blink, confused.

"Oh?"

He smiles. "I want to tell you that I really like you," he says. "I have never met a more perfect girl and believe you and I are well-suited. Would you like to be with me? It can be arranged quite easily for us to court and eventually marry."

"W-What?" I sputter, thinking for a moment I am having a stroke due to the heat and emotion. But Rizwan is being perfectly serious.

"You cannot be so surprised," he says, looking at me indulgently. "I knew it at the wedding two months ago, and as I was driving back to tell you, that incident with Shanzay occurred, and afterwards, I lost my courage." He takes a deep breath. "But I won't lose it now. Humaira, you're beautiful, good natured, kind, and sweet. I have never met a more flawless woman, and I truly have deep feelings for you."

"I am not so perfect," I say quietly, shaking my head. Fawad would confirm as much.

"You're too modest," he replies. "Another admirable quality." Perhaps he says something more, continuing to sing my praises, but I do not hear him.

Oh, how could this happen? *Again*?

"I—I don't know what to say," I manage, laughing a little. He smiles.

"You need time, of course," he says. "Think nothing of it. Give me your response whenever you are ready."

I nod, and we walk back to join the others. Polite conversation picks up once more.

The picnic is cleared shortly after, everyone making their way back to their cars in silence. I try to get a moment alone with Shanzay, but she disappears before I can speak with her, which makes me frown.

Surely this is being blown out of proportion?

But things only get worse. I hear someone approach me, as I am putting the picnic basket in my car's trunk, and I do not need to turn to know who it is beside me.

"Time to go, I think," I say, meeting Fawad's face with a smile on my own.

"Humaira, I can't let you go without speaking my mind," he says, clearly angry. He blocks my path, the both of us shielded from everyone else's view by my car's trunk.

I still, taking quick, short breaths.

"Badly done, Humaira," he says, voice disappointed. *"Badly done."*

"Surely—" I begin, but he cuts me off.

"How could you be so cruel?" he asks, astonished. "Shanzay is a supposedly dear friend of yours. Yet you treated her so callously! You go on and on about how important she is to you, yet your behavior is completely opposite to what you say!"

"Oh, it wasn't so bad," I say offhandedly, trying to minimize the situation. "I don't think she was very hurt by it, either."

"She was," he says, eyes blazing. "She spoke of nothing else for the rest of the afternoon! And wondered what she could have done to earn such harshness from you. She thought it was her fault!"

My eyes well with tears as he lectures and scolds. *I am sorry!* I wish to say, but the words do not come. When he is finished, Fawad shakes his head, severely let down.

"This was badly done, Humaira," he says again, voice low, and then he leaves, going to his car. I slam the trunk shut and see everyone else has left, too. When Fawad's car pulls out of the parking lot, I am the only one who remains.

What is left, in the end, but my wretched, wretched heart?

And with nothing to be done, to make matters worse.

Chapter Twenty-One

Rizwan returns to England without an answer.

I don't know what to say to him. Shanzay likes him, though I am sure she would not mind if I truly wanted to be with Rizwan, seeing as I saw him first.

I wish to discuss it with her at work, but she is distant and quiet, even when I bring her donuts from her favorite donut shop. With a stab of guilt, I realize she must have taken my comment from the picnic to heart, when truly I didn't mean it as such.

I will have to visit her to make amends; I make a mental note of it, but to be honest, my mind is a bit jumbled, as it is. The Rizwan situation has certainly stumped me.

I did not *think* I loved him, but now that he's proposed, perhaps I could grow to? Just as everyone said happens after marriage sometimes?

I cannot keep refusing offers forever; maybe this is as

good as it was going to get. Rizwan is handsome, rich, clever, and likes me a great deal.

What else did I need?

I think about what he said, how I am sweet and good-natured, and yes, I am all of those things, but not *only* those things. He said I am perfect, but in a truth I rarely let on, I am not perfect.

Do I really wish to be with someone who sees me simply as a perfect doll?

Is that not setting myself up for disaster? I cannot bear to be put on a pedestal, cursed to be a performer forever.

Does that mean if I am not perfect, he will not love me? I would hope for someone to love me in spite of my flaws, not because they believe I have none.

People love me because of how they perceive me: amiable, sweet, good-natured, lively, and other such silly notions. They love me because of who I am to them: a kind face, a listening ear, a reassuring hand, a warm hug.

They love me because they do not truly know me. They see what they want to see, which is exactly what I show them.

I do not mind, it does not usually bother me, but sometimes it just makes me sad. As if no one will ever truly *know* me, will never truly *see* me.

Perhaps all I am is a glossy veneer, shiny and polished, to cover the coarser truths hidden just beneath the surface.

Perhaps we are all veneers – is that why I cannot seem to fall in love? Because I crave something that cuts deep, right to the bone, and no one can give it to me?

Or can someone? a voice in my mind teases.

The day passes in a wretched blur, and the weather fits my mood: cold and gray. I listen to sad music to further cement my miserable mood as I go to the dry cleaner's to pick up Papa's clothes after work.

"I'm sorry, we don't have anything for Mahmud Mirza," the girl tells me. I frown. That's strange. I always pick up Papa's clothes on the last Monday of the month.

"Did he not drop anything off?" I ask. The girl shrugs.

I head back to the car, driving quite slowly on my way home, something unsettling within me.

Did Papa change his routine without telling me? I do not see why he would. Unless he wishes to keep me even further from him.

He has been terribly distant since I caught a cold after the wedding, which is not what I wanted at all. It isn't that he is angry with me, but it's like he no longer has use of me, and so I scarcely see him. In the morning, he makes his own coffee, and I feel like he's abandoning me.

But I am too worried about Rizwan to focus on Papa, just yet.

Am I being ungrateful if I refuse Rizwan? Do I think too highly of myself in imagining that I deserve true love?

Or perhaps I am just plain stupid, and what I seek does not exist.

What can be done? In matters of the heart, you cannot push, and I cannot accept defeat.

If I am hopeless, what is left? A life of gray.

I will not give up on love. I would rather be miserable than hopeless.

Mist rolls across the horizon, as haunting as I feel, as I pull into a coffee shop parking lot. More, I always want more; I am insatiable, never satisfied, never content.

Does it have to do with those encounters and memories and feelings with a certain someone that I have locked away? There is something in the back of my mind, a hidden box that I dare not open for fear of what will come out if I do – for fear of *who* will come out, to be more precise. Here is something – someone – that perhaps could not be mine.

I head into the cafe to grab a scone and tea, cold raindrops wetting my cheeks and eyes. I sit inside, sipping my tea, watching the rain fall. The sky is parchment white, the trees a subdued green and brown.

People pass by, students and parents and toddlers and lovers and old couples. I watch them, smiling warmly on instinct if our eyes meet. It unnerves me to see how well I can play pretend. I am afraid I will spend my whole life in pretense.

What is to be done?

Rizwan is great, there is no doubting that, but am I a fool for wanting *more*? Am I a fool to wait?

I am afraid if I refuse him, I will lose this chance. He is so close to all I desire – perhaps time together will bring the rest. Will I regret refusing him if I do? I know marriage is a choice you make every day – that once you choose someone to marry, you must keep choosing to love them every day, despite difficulties that might arise - but the first time you choose someone should surely be the easiest, not the hardest, right?

I cannot come to a decision, so I drive home.

Perhaps a hot shower will help.

When I return home, Papa's car is already there. I unlock the front door, and as I enter, I hear the sound of laughter – his and another's – coming from the office. Heading to the door, I say, "Salaam."

It's Fawad in there with Papa. He looks at me quickly, returning my greeting, then looks back to Papa, who is not being exactly warm, either.

Something in me unravels, but I haphazardly push it back in place. I stay in the doorframe, not entering.

"I went to pick up your dry-cleaning," I say. "There wasn't any. Did you forget to drop it off?" My tone is gentle, bright.

"I switched places, did I not tell you?" Papa says, not looking up from his papers. "Fawad brought it for me."

This startles me. I blink, looking at Fawad.

"It was no trouble," he says easily. "I was picking up my own anyway, and we are neighbors."

"Oh." I stand stupidly for a moment, not knowing what to say. "Have you eaten anything, Papa?" I ask, voice sweet. "There's nihari and naan."

"No, that's alright," Papa says, looking at Fawad. "We were just going to get some sushi."

My brows knit together.

"Will you join us?" Fawad asks me. I open my mouth to say yes, but Papa interjects.

"No, I am sure Humaira would like the evening to herself," he says, voice even. "You and I will go."

Tears fill my eyes, and I set my jaw, pushing them away. I can bear it no longer.

"Well, there is the son you have always wanted," I say, voice hard. "I am glad for you, Papa."

I leave before either of them can react, tears spilling onto my cheeks. I hastily wipe them away, letting out a wavering breath as I go to the kitchen for a glass of water. I drink it in slow sips, looking out the window at the rain, trying to relax, to stay calm.

It was an unfair thing for me to say, but I am feeling unstable, and cruel.

What is *really* unfair is how Papa is treating me. I was cross with him once – *once!* – and he has replaced me so easily! As if he has no need of me unless I am amiable and doting.

Naadia is always irritable, and Papa has never been so cold to her for such a long period of time.

At the sound of footsteps approaching, I clutch the edge of the countertop, trying to steady my features.

"What was that?" Fawad asks. I do not turn, unable to hide my trembling lip. "Uncle has never made you – or Naadia for that matter – feel he has lacked in his life from the want of a son. You know that."

Suddenly, I am angry with him, too. I do not need him to be right, just now.

I whirl around to face him.

"Just because your father is not around does not mean you get to steal mine," I snap.

His face shutters.

"I thank you for the reminder," he says quietly. Without another word, he turns and leaves. For once, he does not fight, does not bicker – he just leaves.

And that hurts more.

Fawad and Papa leave soon after for food, and I am left alone in the mess I've made. I have been unkind and cruel and now I have hurt the people I love – Shanzay, Papa, Fawad.

They have seen the truth of me – how wretched I really am – and they have taken their leave. They love me for my perfection, and now that I have shown them my flaws, they have left me.

I am alone, soaked to my skin in grief.

Chapter Twenty-Two

When Shanzay continues to be quiet at work the next day, I decide a personal visit is in order. Aided with Thai food takeout, I go to Shanzay's apartment in the evening to make amends.

"Oh! Humaira, hello," Shanzay says, when she opens her door.

"Hi!" I say, smiling brightly. She lets me into her apartment, which is small and quiet. I set the food down on the table, unpacking it. "I've brought all your favorites," I say, hoping to win her over.

"Thank you," she says, "but I don't..."

She trails off. I release a long breath, gathering my wits about me.

"I want to apologize for my comment at the picnic," I say, hoping she can see how sincere I am. "I – I don't know what got into me. It was terribly rude."

Shanzay shrugs. "It's okay, really..."

"No, it wasn't," I say, reaching out to take her hand. "You are a dear friend, and I shouldn't have been so mean."

"Thank you for the apology." Shanzay squeezes my hand, smiling. "You can be a bit bitchy sometimes, you know that, right?"

She laughs, and I laugh, too, covering my face with a hand.

"Yes, I know. I'm sorry again."

"Don't worry about it. Besides, I think you were goaded on a bit by Rizwan."

"Yes, a bit," I admit, gauging her reaction. But she does not seem too upset by this. *Hm.* She opens the boxes of food, inhaling the smell.

"Ooh, yummy," she says, going to the kitchen to get us plates and forks.

"Are you ... alright?" I ask her, inspecting her carefully as she comes back. She hands me a plate, then starts piling food onto her own.

"Why wouldn't I be?" she asks, sitting down. I sit down beside her.

"About Rizwan, I mean," I say gently.

"Oh." She shrugs. "Well, he doesn't really know me, so it's alright if he finds me boring."

"But I thought..." I trail off, confused. "You don't ... like him?"

"He's perfectly okay, I guess," she says, eating her basil fried rice. "Why? Do *you* like him again? I thought you were over all that."

"*I* am," I say, dumbfounded. "But I thought ... well, not too long ago, you said *you* had feelings for him."

Shanzay sets her fork down, confused. "Me?" She laughs, shaking her head. "What gave you that idea?"

"You – You said! After the wedding," I say, trying to refresh her memory. "The service he rendered you? His kindness?"

Shanzay does not recall what I speak of. I can see her trying very hard to remember the conversation we had.

"After you got in the car accident? And he brought you to my house?" I prompt.

Realization dawns on her. "Ooh, you thought—" She laughs. "No, oh, how silly of us! No, I didn't mean Rizwan, and I can't believe you thought it was him I spoke of! Of course, I was speaking of Fawad."

Fawad? Dread grips me. Surely she cannot mean that. Fawad is—

"B—But the service Rizwan rendered you?" I sputter, feeling unaligned. "You said..."

"No, I meant the service Fawad rendered me, at the wedding?" Now it is her turn to speak slowly, so that I remember. "He was so kind to me, in finding me a seat, when Emad and his dreadful fiancée were laughing at me? I know we said we wouldn't speak of it, but there it is. I like Fawad!"

No. My heart drops. She giggles.

"Yes, but—" I begin, but I do not know where I am going. But what? "Do you – Do you believe he feels the same?" I ask, clearing my throat. She nods excitely.

"I think it'll take some time to truly grow," she says, "but I see potential there."

"Oh." I blink, a lump growing in my throat. I do not cry, but the grief lingers, clawing at my eyes, pulling at my heart.

Maybe Fawad was right: I do go on about Shanzay being such a dear friend, yet my behavior has suggested otherwise.

How could I not have seen it was Fawad who has occupied her interest all these months, not Rizwan?

Is our friendship really so surface-level? Or have I been so self-absorbed as to not notice?

Suddenly, I am exhausted. And a million emotions more. But Shanzay is waiting for my response.

"Fawad is the last man to lead a girl on," I manage to say, forcing myself to keep my voice steady. "So if you feel there's something there, I'm sure there is."

"Thank you," Shanzay says, sighing contentedly. "Won't you eat?"

"Yes," I say quietly. "Yes..."

Shanzay, sweetheart that she is, makes me a plate, being sure not to include broccoli, for she knows I don't like it, and how can I say anything, now? And what to say, to begin with?

That if Fawad should marry anyone, it should be me?

I love him. The thought enters my mind suddenly, and I know it to be true.

Fuck!

How inopportune that I should realize just now! When everything is a mess. And he might hate me, anyway.

But I love him!

No—no, I cannot think such things! Not now! Not when it is too late!

Oh, why did I not realize sooner? Love is not at all how I imagined it to be. I did not recognize him, not when he was standing in front of me all this time.

I drove myself crazy searching and searching for the great love of my life, when all along he was right there. He has always been there.

But there is nothing to be done. Shanzay likes him, and I won't hurt her.

Yes, it is best not to say anything. I sit and eat, listening as Shanzay explains her summer course to me, nodding and smiling at her.

But no matter how hard I try, the voice does not leave my mind, the words repeating themselves over and over:

I love him.

Chapter Twenty-Three

No matter how I try, I cannot stop thinking of him. It terrifies me, which only makes the feeling twice fold. I am *never* terrified. It's a point of great pride for me that I am not easily fazed or frightened, but what I feel for him ... it scares me straight to tears. All this love I have for him – if I cannot give it to him, where do I put it? Who do I give it to? *Another*?

No, this love is tailored specifically for him, I cannot re-gift it to another, nor do I wish to.

I am afraid to see him, for what if Shanzay is right, and he does love her? I have never liked a man who did not first like me; this is new territory. What if I make a fool of myself? I so hate being a fool. And I cannot ruin things, for he is family!

At the very least, I eventually decide, I should go apologize. That seems like a good start. I was terribly rude the other day.

I walk to his house, and it is not too hot for the exercise to wind me, but I do feel breathless all the same when I knock on the door, waiting for him to open it.

"Salaam," he says, stepping aside so I can come in. That must be a good sign.

"Salaam," I respond. He's wearing a loose, linen shirt with the sleeves rolled up over his forearms. I nibble my bottom lip, unsure of how to proceed.

"Tea?" he asks, walking toward the kitchen. I follow, sitting down at the island.

"Yes, please."

He takes out Earl Gray for me and breakfast blend for himself, turning the kettle on. The roar of water boiling crescendos, steam pouring out of the kettle until it finally quiets with a steady bubble of water.

"I wanted to apologize," I say, as he pours the water into teacups over the bags. He sets them under a tea cozy to brew.

"For what?" he asks, taking out milk, sugar, and honey.

"What I said the other day."

He blinks, then his lips part as he remembers.

"It's alright," he says. "Don't worry about it."

He really seems unbothered by what I said, when I thought he might hate me. I watch as he makes our teas, taking the teabags out, adding milk to both, then sugar to mine and honey to his. He hands me my mug, giving me a small smile.

Relief warms my chest, and I take a sip of my tea, which

is perfect. He sips his as well, leaning back against the kitchen counter, facing me.

"It was still ... rude," I say tentatively. A smile tugs at his lips, and he shakes his head. "What?" I ask, confused.

"I—" He breaks off. "Nothing."

He steps forward, leaning against the island. His face is somber, and he takes his glasses off to run a hand over his eyes, then slips the glasses back on. "I have been greedy with your father, and it's true, what you said, that my own is never around."

He swallows, struggling with the words as a muscle tics in his jaw.

"The harsher truth," he continues, "is that my father has never loved me the way your papa loves you, or even how Mahmud Uncle loves me."

His eyes are open with sadness. My heart splinters for him.

"It is why I am always in such a mood when they visit," he says. "My parents have been separated for years, but even before then, it was always a loveless marriage."

My mouth drops. "I didn't know," I say, dumbfounded. "I never—"

"Good," Fawad says. "I've always tried to protect Asif from it. I'm sure if he knew, Naadia would, too, and you would, as well."

"You did a good job," I say, quietly. To not only endure witnessing his parents in a loveless marriage, but to protect his younger brother from it. It hurts to look at him, but I do not look away. "Fawad, I'm so sorry."

"Thank you," he says. "It's why they stay in Pakistan: they both have their own social circles, and it is easier to avoid one another." His focus shifts to his teacup. "Actually, I was the one who told them to go, after I graduated college. Things were getting worse, and I couldn't bear it any longer."

I want to reach out and hold his hand, but I do not. Instead, my grip on my teacup tightens.

"It's why Asif and I are so close," he says, smiling at me now, "and why I am always over at your house. Your papa has always treated me with kindness. He has reminded me that there is love in this world." He pauses, his hand fidgeting. "At times, I must confess I thought myself incapable of love, just like my father. We are so alike, you know."

You are not incapable, I want to say, but I do not interrupt.

"Asif is different because he never knew how cruel my parents were to one another, so he grew up with hope," he says. "But from a young age, I saw there was no love between my parents, so I never believed in it." He laughs, looking at me. "It is blasphemy, to you, I know, but I always thought love to be one of those cosmic things, happening to a few, never to happen to me. I've discussed it at length with my therapist, and I think I'm starting to realize that that isn't true."

He pauses, as if contemplating exactly what to say next, and if he should say it or not. I look at him expectantly, taking in the sight of his dark hair, falling over his forehead, the slant of his nose, the curve of his lips. He is so beautiful; I could spend all day staring at him.

"I never used to believe," he says. Something in his expression changes. He leans closer, voice soft. "But you made me believe, Humaira. You *make* me believe."

Time slows, then stops entirely.

My breath catches. I abruptly stand, teacup clinking on the table as I release it.

"I must go," I whisper. I cannot hear this, whatever it is he's going to say.

He'll tell me he is in love—with Shanzay—and I cannot bear to hear it.

Tears flood my eyes. I quickly blink them away as I rush to the front door. I step outside just as he reaches me.

"I'm sorry," he says, face downcast but concerned. "Subjects of love must be difficult. Are you upset by Rizwan's behavior at the picnic? He was unkind to Shanzay." He looks at me carefully. "Is she alright?"

He would ask after her; he really does love her. My heart twists painfully.

"Yes, we made amends," I say, blinking rapidly. "She's alright."

"And—And you?" he asks, voice catching. "Were you ... disappointed?"

I blink, trying to understand what he is saying.

Disappointed? Oh, he must think I am heartbroken by Rizwan's behavior.

Perhaps I would have seen his rude behavior to my

friend as a harsher crime had I been in love with him, but in truth, I have not been interested in him for months.

And the reason stands before me.

But I cannot think that. Not when he is Shanzay's. I turn away from him and start walking down the driveway, the sun warm on my back. He follows me.

"You don't have to worry," I say over my shoulder. "No, really," I repeat, when he begins to protest. I stop and face him. "I did think I liked him, but I've been examining the workings of my heart, and I can truthfully say ... he hasn't injured me. Or Shanzay, for that matter. We're both fine."

Fawad shakes his head. "Rizwan is a fortunate man, for how readily you both forgave him."

There is an edge to his tone.

"You speak as if you envy him," I say, confused. He looks at me, stepping closer.

"I do envy him, Humaira," he says, eyelashes fluttering. "I envy him one thing."

I don't understand.

I say nothing.

"You won't ask?" When I don't reply, he nods to himself. "You're wise." He sighs, then takes a step toward me. "But I cannot be. I have to tell you what you won't ask, even if I might regret it the moment it is said."

He must want to discuss Shanzay with me.

"Don't!" I cry, eyes wide. We are both startled by this outburst. I level my tone. "Don't say it, if you'll regret it."

He nods, stepping back. "As you wish."

He turns, going back into the house, leaving me alone on

the driveway. I watch as he enters the house. He does not close the front door.

I stand still for a moment, heart pounding.

I cannot let him go.

I walk up and into the house, where he is sitting on the staircase. When he sees me, he stands abruptly. I'm shocked to see his eyes are wet.

"I'm sorry," I say, swallowing the lump in my throat. "We're friends. If you want to speak to me – as a friend – I'll listen to what you have to say, about whoever, and give you my honest thoughts." I swallow. "As a friend."

He scoffs. "As a *friend*? I don't—" He breaks off, shaking his head, then bridges the space between us until he stands directly in front of me. A muscle ticks in his jaw, and he lets out a deep breath.

His strong hands fall to my shoulders, making my knees weak, but I am utterly rooted in place, looking up at him, inhaling the rich scent of his cologne, looking into those dark, beautiful eyes.

"Tell me, Humaira," he says, voice soft. "Is there no chance for me?"

I don't understand. He forges on, eyes blazing and brilliant.

"I cannot make speeches," he says. "If I loved you less, I might be able to talk about it more. You know what I am – I have lectured you and scolded you ... but you understand? You understand my feelings?"

He asks the questions with fear and hope, drawing

closer, until we are breathing the same air, his fingers firm on my shoulders.

"Humaira," he says. "I love you."

My heart soars – then sinks. I step back, shaking my head.

"You can't," I whisper, covering my mouth with my hand. *Shanzay*. I cannot break her heart again.

"What?" he asks, not hearing me. I cannot tell him, for I know he will convince me, and I cannot do that to Shanzay. I will not hurt her.

"You don't love me," I say quietly, avoiding his gaze. "You love the idea of me, not the truth. No one could love the truth."

"Look at me," he says. I do, and see that his brows are furrowed with anger. "What are you talking about?"

"People only love me because they believe I am good and kind and perfect," I say quickly. "They only love me for what I am to them, because they need me."

"That's not true," he says, voice sure. "Humaira, that is not *true*. I have seen you be wretched and cruel and petulant and arrogant and spoiled and silly. I have also seen you be kind and attentive and clever and warm and sweet. I have seen – *I see you*, all of you." He pauses. "The people who truly love you love all of you. As I do."

"You can't," I say, voice small.

"Why?" he asks.

My voice breaks. "I can't tell you."

He shakes his head. "Do you enjoy making fools out of perfectly reasonable men?" he asks, frustrated.

"I do, yes!" I snap, just as irritated, but not by him, by myself.

As if sensing this, his anger melts, and he gives me a small smile.

"I don't mind, Humaira," he says, coming close. "Beloved Humaira, I will be a fool for you a thousand times over."

Oh, why must he say these things! I cannot bear it.

"I don't – I don't know what you're saying," I respond, flustered. He waits patiently, while I collect my thoughts, but there is nothing to be said to change the circumstance, so I stand in silence, fumbling.

"You're afraid," he says. "I understand. Take all the time you need. There is no pressure from me. I wished to tell you that I love you, and I have. I do not expect anything in return."

I blink at him in response, then finally manage to nod.

With that, it is truly time for me to go, but I do not want to.

Even though we say nothing, I wish to stay here, to stay with him, just to be in his presence, to be with him. I do not want to go, but I must, which only makes the feeling worse.

"I can't think of anything clever to say," I admit. He smiles.

"You don't have to say anything clever," he tells me. "You don't—"

"I must go."

Silently, we both walk towards the door. As I go to open it, he puts his hand on the door to stop me.

"You don't have to leave," he says, voice low with misery.

Don't I? I want to say.

"You can stay as long as you'd like," he adds quietly.

But that's just it: I want to stay forever. And I cannot.

I must go. So I do.

———————

When I return home, my eyes are puffy, my nose running. Papa unlocks the door for me, and as I step inside, I can see him assessing the situation, taking in the fact that I have clearly been crying.

He opens his mouth, as if to say something, then stops. Silently, he retreats back to his office.

Another sob rises within me, and I rush up to my room, closing the door before collapsing on my bed. I curl into a ball, letting my tears soak the pillows, pressing my hands against my heart as if I can contain this.

After some time, I hear soft knocking on my door. Papa slowly opens the door, coming in. I sit up, facing him.

"I won't bother you," he says, setting a plate of cut up fruit on my side table. He moves to leave, reaching the doorway.

"Papa, won't you sit with me?" I ask quietly. He stops, then nods.

He sits down at the edge of my bed, looking around. I do not know what to say, but I want him here with me. I listen to the sound of his breathing, watching the wrinkles in his hands fold as he taps his fingers together.

"Shall I read to you?" Papa finally says. I nod. It is precisely what I want.

When I was a little girl, I loved when Papa read to me. It was his duty to take Naadia and I to the library, as well. He was never fond of reading – he thinks literature is nonsensical and lies – but he took us every other week without fail.

"What's this?" Papa asks, picking up the book on my side table. It's *The Secret History*. Clearing his throat, Papa begins reading, tripping over some of the words. He stops, catching his breath.

"This is not *Bears in the Night* now is it?" he asks, smiling. I giggle. "You would beg me to read it to you every night." I recall the memories, lying under my ballerina quilt with Papa beside me, listening to his voice.

"It was my favorite," I say, rubbing my nose.

"You know, I rather think I still have that book memorized," Papa says, setting *The Secret History* down and clearing his throat. "In bed, out of bed ... to the window, out the window..." he recites from memory, managing to recall most of it, then making up the parts he does not.

I laugh.

Papa smiles, then stands. "Try to eat some fruit," he says. "Your vitamin levels are shockingly low."

"It runs in the family," I say. "You ought to eat some, too."

He snags a strawberry, then leaves. A weight is lifted off my chest.

Papa and I will be alright. But as Papa reaches the door, he pauses, then looks at me. "You must know you are irreplaceable to me," he says, face sincere.

My lower lip trembles, tears threatening to overcome me once more. "You have been so distant," I say quietly. "It felt like you didn't need me anymore, and thus did not love me any longer."

"Silly girl. I will *always* love you, even when I do not need you," Papa says, voice steady. "I didn't mean to be distant. I realized that I do depend on you too much and wanted to change that."

"I don't mind doing things for you, Papa," I tell him. Those are the moments we get to spend together; we are not big on expressing emotions, but making him coffee or listening to his stories is how I show Papa I love him.

"I was trying to give you space," Papa says.

"Well, I do not need that much space," I tell him with a slight roll of my eyes.

"Good," Papa says, a smile spreading across his face. "For I was getting tired of making my own coffee anyway."

I laugh. "Doubly good, for my car needs an oil change."

We do not apologize; we just act nice to each other until things are normal again. And this is normal.

After Papa is gone, I read *The Piper's Son*, the one with all of Fawad's thoughts, and it makes me laugh and cry because so many of his notes are precisely what I was thinking.

He and I are so alike, we're *so* alike, and he loves me, and I love him – and we cannot be together for the mess I have made of things with my meddling, the very mess he warned me about.

I hold the book to my heart, as if the ink can transfuse his touch onto my skin.

Chapter Twenty-Four

At least one thing is abundantly and obviously clear: I cannot marry Rizwan.

I call him to say as much, and he is a good sport about it, for which I am glad. I am fond of him, in a way, but he is not the Great Love of My Life, and he deserves better than someone who is settling for him. He deserves someone who loves him just as much as he loves her.

And he does not love me, not really. He does not know me or see me, not the *true* me. Not the way Fawad does.

"I won't easily forget you," Rizwan tells me, as we say goodbye. "You were my first love."

And that's it! I feel a literal lightbulb going off over my head. I think I know a way to fix all of this without everyone being miserable for the rest of their lives.

(Cannot do much for Rizwan, unfortunately, but he's handsome, clever, rich, and has a British accent, so I am sure he will be fine, in the end.)

When the workday is over, I stop by the grocery store for a basket, and various delicious things to fill it with, then text Sadaf for the address. I rush home to assemble the basket and wrap it prettily, hoping it will get my foot in the door.

After that, I am on my own.

"Humaira?!" Madiha Raja says, as I stand in front of her house carrying a basket half the size of me. "H-Hi. Salaam. What—"

"Salaam!" I say, voice overly bright to mask how nervous I feel. "Can I come in?"

"Yeah—Yes, of course," she says, stepping aside to let me in. Her small house is cozy and smells like ghee in a very homey way. Setting the basket down on the table, I risk a quick glance around.

"No one's home," Madiha says. "Except my Dhadi, who's napping upstairs." She looks at the basket, eyes wide as she takes all of it in. "What is this for?"

"For your brother," I say, trying to keep my voice even despite my embarrassment. "It's an apology. I was hoping to speak with him, actually."

"He's out," Madiha says, "but he'll be back soon." She pauses, looking at me carefully. "Is this about ... Shanzay?" she asks hopefully. I swallow the lump in my throat.

"I've made a terrible mistake."

For a moment, I'm not sure if Madiha will lash out at me, be angry or upset, as she has every right to be, after I have jeopardized her brother's happiness, but instead, she surprises me by smiling.

"I was hoping you would say that."

Just then, we turn at the sound of the front door opening.

A handsome young man enters, then stops when he sees me. I take a deep breath and smile nervously.

"Huzaifa, I'd like to speak to you…"

After it is done, there is the waiting, the dreadful waiting.

I wonder if Huzaifa will speak to Shanzay tonight, or if he will wait, or if he will speak with her at all. I want to call Shanzay and tell her of all that has happened, but I hold back, waiting, waiting and praying to see how things will fall into place, if they even will at all.

Then, two days later, at work, Shanzay pulls me aside, and we huddle at the coffee station. Her face is serious.

"Huzaifa called me last night," she says. I cannot decipher what she is feeling. Oh dear. I am afraid my meddling will have made things worse… "He proposed to me," she says, hiding her smile. "And I have accepted."

"Thank God," I breathe, then I scream and hug her. "I'm so happy for you!"

And I am, truly. Even though he is still studying and perhaps isn't in a financial position to take care of her, he loves her, and she loves him, so everything else will fall into place.

She screams as well, clutching me tightly, and we

bounce up and down. My heart is so full, I think I will burst. We pull apart, though our hands remain clasped.

"Shanzay, I'm so glad we're friends," I say, squeezing her hand. "I know I haven't been the best friend to you. I've been a bit self-centered and delusional, which is why things got a little messy there for a second, but I promise I'll do better."

"Aw, Humaira, thank you. You can be a bit self-centered, yes, but I'm so glad to have you as a friend," she says. "And it all worked out in the end, didn't it?"

I squeal, overjoyed. "I'm so happy it did! You'll be married! We have to go shopping!"

She laughs. I hug her again, and she squeezes back.

"Now let's compose ourselves before Uncle scolds us," Shanzay says, giggling. I nod.

"I have something to tell you as well," I say, taking a deep breath. "I think ... I am also in love." I brace for her reaction, and she grins.

"With Fawad?" she asks. I gasp, looking around nervously as if he will appear.

"Shh!" I order her. She giggles. "How did you know?"

"You looked so heartbroken when I said I liked him," she tells me. "I began piecing two and two together and realized just how silly my crush was when you both are clearly in love with each other."

I gasp, shocked by this information.

"Who is it clear to?" I ask. Shanzay laughs.

"We are all fools in love."

"You're not angry with me?" I ask. "Be honest."

Shanzay shakes her head. "Don't fret over me. I truly love Huzaifa – I think I have loved him since the very beginning. I was hoping he would call, oh, I was *praying* he would call. Every day." She breaks off, emotional. "And he did! I am so happy."

My eyes well with tears, seeing her so content. "Me, too," I cry.

A coworker walks in to get coffee, then promptly turns around when he sees both of us nearly sobbing and laughing. A short while later, someone else enters, releasing an alarmed noise.

"Goodness," Papa says, seeing the sight of us. "What on earth is happening?" He comes to stand in front of me, putting his hands on my shoulders. "Is everything alright?"

I nod, enveloping him in a tight hug. For a moment, he doesn't react, but then his arms come around me.

"I am not suffocating you, am I?" he whispers, voice unsure.

"No, Papa, you aren't," I reply, tears wetting his blazer. "I love to have you just this close." His body relaxes, tension leaving him, and he hugs me tighter.

When I pull back, I can see his eyes are misty.

"Why on earth are the both of you crying?" he asks.

"Shanzay is getting married!"

He shakes his head, pulling away from me to go to pour himself some coffee. "You girls are so emotional," he says. Then, he looks at me. "You won't leave me, will you?"

Shanzay and I exchange a glance.

"I don't know if I will marry soon, Papa," I say. "But I promise, I will never leave you."

I kiss his cheek, and when I pull back, I see his eyes are filled with tears, which makes me lose it once more, and Shanzay starts crying again, as well.

"Good God!" Papa says, voice stern. "This is a workplace! Get it together!" He shakes his head. "Take the rest of the day off, the both of you!"

He does not need to tell me twice. I quickly drive home, wiping my tears, grinning, laughing, smiling as I do. Without stopping to check my appearance or do anything else, I rush over and knock on Fawad's door, hoping he is home.

Luckily, he is. The door opens, and he stands in front of me, eyes worried when he takes in my disheveled state.

"What is it?" he asks, stepping outside.

"Ask me!" I say, grinning. He furrows his brows, confused.

"What?"

"Ask me!" I scold, growing impatient, already.

"Ask you what?" He repeats, growing impatient, too.

I lift up my left hand, fingers splayed, prompting him, and the anger melts away. His eyes well with tears, and my mouth drops open.

"No, don't cry!" I say, heart constricting. "Don't cry!"

He lets out a little laugh, then says, "Marry me, Humaira, marry me, won't you please?"

"Yes!" I cry. "Yes!"

Oh, how I wish I could be kissed now! But we do not touch, for fear of things getting carried away.

We simply look at one another, and even that is enough to make my heartbeat flutter and my cheeks heat.

Then I start to cry, realizing something, and blurt out, "But we can never marry!"

I turn and run. He immediately follows.

"Humaira!" he calls. "Humaira!" he cries, catching up to me at the end of his driveway. "Good God, woman, will you not rest until you've killed me?" he asks, holding a hand over his heart.

I start crying harder, and his voice softens.

"Beloved, why can we not marry?" he asks, drawing near. His hands fall to my shoulders, holding me steady.

"Papa," I sniffle. "I cannot leave him."

"Ah," Fawad says, understanding. "Yes, I have given it some thought, and I believe I have found a solution."

"There is no solution! I cannot leave him alone in that great big house."

Fawad shakes his head.

"My heart is here, with you," he says, face tender, "so what does it matter where I live, if my heart is with me?" He smiles. "I will move in with you – for however long is required."

I gasp, looking at him. "You—You would do that? For me?"

"I will walk back to my own house a few times a day for my sanity, but yes." His face is bright. "Yes, and I would do

335

far more than that without a second thought." I take in a shuddering breath. "Please stop crying now," he says, giving me his handkerchief. "I cannot bear to see you upset."

"I am sorry," I say, wiping my tears. "I know you think I'm an ugly crier."

He laughs out loud. "No—No you are beautiful, you are always beautiful." He taps my nose. "It is your heart, etched onto your face." He looks at me with open adoration. "I will love you until the end of my days."

"And I will love you until the end of mine," I swear.

Smiling, he leads me inside, where he makes me lemonade, then we go out and sit on the grass in the front, beneath the sun, eating strawberries from his garden.

It is only when Papa's car drives by that we jolt back to reality.

"Let's go tell him," Fawad says, standing.

"Now?" I ask, alarmed. He grins.

"Yes."

Together, we walk back to my house, where Papa is just coming out of his car in the driveway. He looks at the both of us, and it is as if he knows.

He sighs, looking up at the heavens.

"Papa—" I start, batting my eyelashes at him very sweetly. If we ease him into it gently, I am sure he'll be fine.

"I love your daughter," Fawad says, completely lacking tact. "I would very much like to marry her."

Papa looks at us, and I brace for a dramatic reaction. He opens his mouth and ... smiles?

That cannot be right. I blink, taking a step toward him

and inspecting his face. But yes, he is smiling! His eyes are mischievous.

"It's about time," he finally says.

"What?" I say, positively shocked. "After all the fuss you made about not wanting me to get married!"

"Well, I realized you must be married eventually," Papa says casually, "so I thought it may as well be someone of my choosing."

"*Your* choosing?"

"Yes," he says, quite pleased with himself. "You chose each other, just as I had planned."

"The matchmaker has been outmatched," Fawad says, laughing. "Oh, well done, Mahmud Uncle." He is just as pleased.

"I cannot believe this!" I exclaim. "Papa, you are so devious!"

"Where do you suppose you get it from?" He grins devilishly.

"But how did you accomplish such a thing?" I ask. "And how could I have not noticed?"

"You are not so clever, after all," Papa says. "Did you not find it peculiar it was always Fawad I called upon to check on you? When you were sick or scared from watching horror movies? Did you not notice I often left you two to your own devices and retreated to my office so you could better mingle?"

If I think about it now, I can see it clear as day.

Oh, how silly I have been! Maybe I am truly not so clever, after all.

"Well, it's good he's so acquainted with our house. Papa, you'll be happy to learn Fawad is also willing to move in with us," I say.

This pushes Papa over the edge of happiness into absolute glee. He lets out a laugh.

"Is he? How splendid!" he asks, clapping his hands. "Oh, what an excellent match I made. I knew Fawad would not disappoint me!" He chatters excitedly. "Now, do not worry, for I won't infringe on your privacy at all. Won't this be such fun? The three of us, together! We must..."

Papa walks ahead, Fawad and I behind him. I look at the face of my future husband. He smiles, just for me, his hand brushing against mine as we walk forward, into the beginning of the rest of forever.

Acknowledgments

Alhamdulillah! I am so grateful and overjoyed to publish this book, and I wouldn't have made it here without all the wonderful people in my life who support me.

Firstly, thank you to my superstar agent, Emily Keyes, who is my constant champion and support; I appreciate you so, so much. Thank you for your tireless effort. Thank you to my editor, Charlotte Ledger, who's enthusiasm for this book was a saving grace for me after a particularly painful period of my career. Thank you for loving this book and allowing me to fall in love with it all over again as we worked together.

Thank you to the entire team at One More Chapter, for being such a lovely home for this beloved book of mine. Thank you to Lucy Bennett for the beautiful cover design. Thank you to Katrice Williams-Dredden for the gorgeous cover illustration; I am obsessed! Thank you to my wonderful copyeditor, Sarah Khan, and amazing proofreader, Caroline Scott-Bowden. Thank you to Emma Petfield and Chloe Cummings in Marketing and Publicity for your phenomenal work promoting my book. Thank you to Bethan Morgan, for recommending I submit to OMC and starting this entire journey!

Thank you to my family: Mama, Baba, Sameer, Zaineb, and Ibraheem. Baba gets a special shoutout for inspiring so much of Humaira's father with his absurdly hilarious conversations and personality. Thank you to Papa, Mimi, Khala, and all the kids.

Thank you to my best-friend-cousins, Hamnah, Umaymah, Noor, and Mahum, and again to my sister, Zaineb; the relationship between the girls in my books is always inspired by you ladies and all the time we spend together laughing at inane things and going insane over generally just about everything. It's always a good time with you gals. My life would fall to gray without all the constant color you provide, so thank you.

Thank you to the best friends in the whole world. Arusa, the cynic to my hopeless romantic, who has suffered through years of my silly crushes. Isra, for being delusional with me. Sara, for being my baking buddy. Justine, for being obnoxious with me. You are all infused into this story! Thank you also to Sadaf, Uroosa, Fatima, and Ifrah. And thank you to Silke, Famke, and Narjis. I love you all!!!

Thank you to my early readers: Meha, Narjis, Amani, Razan, and Humnah. Thanks for showing enthusiasm and support for this book long before it was ever anything official.

Thank you to the authors who blurbed this book. Thank you to everyone on social media who showed excitement for my writing. Thank you to everyone who's spread the word about my books. Thank you to everyone who's bought a copy, or requested it at their library, or made their friends buy a copy. Thank you to everyone who's left a review. The love and support of perfect strangers is always such a beautiful wonder to me.

Reading has always been a source of joy for me – particularly romance novels – and I hope this book is a fun story for all who read it. I hope it makes you feel less lonely, makes you believe in love, makes you laugh, and makes the world a little less awful, even if only for a little while.

And for everyone out there waiting to meet the Great Love of Their Life – just wait a little longer! They are coming, I promise. Don't give up. Always have faith.

As always, please pray for me. I love you.

Q&A

What does your writing day look like?

I always start my day with some stretching and yoga! Since I'm at my desk for the majority of my day, it's always nice to be a little active before sitting down. After I've done that, I always make myself breakfast (I don't know how people survive without breakfast!), then finally sit down with a cup of tea or coffee and get writing. While I'm doing that, I'll either throw open the window and listen to the wind and leaves, or listen to music, or listen to those ten-hour-long rain videos as background noise. Once I've sat down, I try to write for a few hours before breaking for lunch, then write a bit more afterwards before stopping for the day. I'll usually go out for a walk at that time because by then my eyes and head hurt from staring at a screen for most of the day, so it's nice to look out at the trees and get some sunshine and feel the breeze. Then, after my walk, I'll have a cup of tea and do some work around the house (cook/clean/etc.). If I'm on a tight deadline or just really excited about a project, then after dinner, I'll sit down to get a few more hours of writing in before sleeping.

That is, of course, the plan! But my days rarely go as planned...

What was the inspiration for *If I Loved You Less*?

Of course, I love Jane Austen's novel, *Emma*, and I also absolutely adored Autumn de Wilde's 2020 adaptation; it was such a riot. When I was watching it, I thought of how well such a story would fit into a modern-day Pakistani, Muslim community. It was an idea I was keen to explore, and once I began writing, I just couldn't stop. It was so much fun! This manuscript was probably the quickest one I've ever written, and it was—still is!—an immense joy.

Other than the hilarious nature of the story, the obnoxious yet lovable heroine, and the deliciously tense romance, I was also mainly inspired by Emma's relationship with her father, which Anya Taylor Joy and Bill Nighy both did a fantastic job of portraying in the 2020 film. Mr. Woodhouse is absolutely ridiculous in the very best way and reminds me so much of my own father (I say this with love!); a few of my friends who watched the film actually told me as much, which made me laugh so hard. Many of Mr. Mirza's lines in *If I Loved You Less* are pulled directly from things my father has said, and I'm so happy I can immortalise a bit of his spirit in my book.

How much do you draw from your community and experiences when writing?

An immense amount! Especially when it comes to secondary characters, such as sisters or friends, I draw hugely from the characters that make my own life so vibrant. For example, I was editing this book shortly after my sister got married and moved out, so the ache Humaira feels in missing her sister came directly from me missing mine. Things like that! I won't go into excessive detail for fear of outing myself, but part of why writing this book was so easy was because of how much I was pulling from my own experiences. Writing can be a bit of a time capsule for authors, capturing specific memories or moments in time we don't want to forget into the pages of our novels. I always love how there are bits of me in all my books—though perhaps the most in this specific one, which is why it holds such a special place in my heart.

Why is Jane Austen so relevant to the Pakistani community and what insights can we glean from Austen's novels?

I once read this review of Pride and Prejudice that stated it was "just a bunch of people, going to a bunch of other people's houses" which is really very true for Pakistanis!

Whether it's tea parties or dinners or wedding events, the social calendar is always packed, much like the London season. Many of the rules or norms that existed in Austen's novels funnily enough still apply (to some extent) in Pakistani communities as well: the absurdly over-involved family members, the tight-knit and sometimes nosy community, the arrangement of suitable marriages, the affectionate bickering, the distance and consequent yearning between burgeoning lovers ... It is why so many Pakistanis —and South Asians at large—find Austen's works so comforting. Austen does a wonderful job showcasing how even characters or communities with faults can still be lovable; that actually it is the very mistakes they make that help characters grow and eventually brings the characters closer together. That is timeless.

What makes a good love story?

To me, as both a reader and a writer, it's really important to be able to root for characters as individuals, as well as together as a couple. I firmly believe that both romantic leads should be fully developed and compelling on their own, but then even better when they are together. They should challenge and push one another to become the very best versions of themselves. I think, also, that they should be equals, that they should be a match, and enrich one another's lives.

The road to love is often messy and full of trials because love must be tested, then tested again, before one can see if it is true, if it is real. All good things require a bit of hard work (as Humaira would remind you!), and the same applies for a good romance. And then the reward is so delightfully delicious!

He went to take or other place and put these to gain
to do what he had done to her as easy as he was out
... with the world. And ... giving ... a gift of the
work, and I ... watch ... good ... into the ...
at ... for a good job, see. And then the people is so
... him? Or course.

Playlist

I Was Made For Loving You - Tori Kelly, Ed Sheeran 🤍

Say You Won't Let Go - James Arthur 🤍

this is how you fall in love - Jeremy Zucker, Chelsea Cutler 🤍

Truly Madly Deeply - Yoke Lore 🤍

Somebody To You (Acoustic) - The Vamps 🤍

Like Real People Do - Hozier 🤍

We'll Never Have Sex - Leith Ross 🤍

Bless The Broken Road - Rascal Flatts 🤍

Love of My Life - Avery Lynch 🤍

Brooklyn - Emily James 🤍

The blue - Gracie Abrams 🤍

Be - Garrett Kato 🤍

Come to Me - The Goo Goo Dolls 🤍

Favorite Place to Go - Layup 🤍

You & Me - James TW 🤍

Ho Hey - The Lumineers 🤍

Pointless - Lewis Capaldi 🤍

Beige - Yoke Lore 🤍

Peach New Am - Emily James 🤍

Crazier - Taylor Swift 🤍

Seeds - Yoke Lore ♥

Blossom - Dermot Kennedy ♥

Francesca - Hozier ♥

Grow Old with Me - Tom Odell ♥

Iris - The Goo Goo Dolls ♥

Stay Stay Stay (Taylor's Version) - Taylor ♥
Swift

I Love You Always Forever - Betty Who ♥

Love Love Love - Avalanche City ♥

Heavenly Kind of State Of Mind - Lewis ♥
Capaldi

Kiss Me - Dermot Kennedy ♥

Absolute Must-Watch Period Dramas: A Definitive List by Humaira Mirza

1. Emma (2020)
2. BBC North and South
3. Little Women (2019)
4. Sanditon
5. Pride and Prejudice (2005)
6. Miss Scarlet and the Duke
7. BBC's War and Peace
8. The Last Letter to Your Lover
9. Bridgerton Season 2
10. The Guernsey Literary and Potato Peel Pie Society

The Very Best Rom-Coms by the Mirza Sisters

1. Letters to Juliet
2. Love, Rosie
3. Just Like Heaven
4. About Time
5. Leap Year
6. Confessions of a Shopaholic
7. Just Like Heaven
8. The Holiday
9. While You Were Sleeping
10. To All the Boys I've Loved Before

Fawad's Reading List

1. *The Piper's Son* by Melina Marchetta (as recommended by Humaira)
2. *The Secret History* by Donna Tartt
3. *White Nights* by Fyodor Dostoevsky
4. *Beautiful World Where Are You* by Sally Rooney
5. *Letters to Milena* by Franz Kafka
6. *A Place for Us* by Fatima Farheen Mirza
7. *The Odyssey* by Homer, translated by Emily Wilson
8. *On Earth We're Briefly Gorgeous* by Ocean Vuong
9. *War and Peace* by Leo Tolstoy
10. *A Victorian Flower Dictionary* by Mandy Kirkby

Humaira's Reading List

1. *The Secret History* by Donna Tartt (as recommended by Fawad)
2. *The Piper's Son* by Melina Marchetta
3. *Bringing Down the Duke* by Evie Dunmore
4. *You Deserve Each Other* by Sarah Hogle
5. *North and South* by Elizabeth Gaskell
6. *Seven Days in June* by Tia Williams
7. *Much Ado About Nada* by Uzma Jalaluddin
8. *To Love and to Loathe* by Martha Waters
9. *Book Lovers* by Emily Henry
10. *The Wisteria Society of Lady Scoundrels* by India Holton

Brownie Recipe by Naadia Mirza

1. Buy a box of Betty Crocker Fudge Brownie Mix
2. Follow instructions on the box
3. Add in a heaping tablespoon (or two) of Nutella
4. Pour into a glass tray
5. Bake for 3-4 minutes less than directed
6. Let cool for 5 minutes
7. Serve!

Grilled Cheese and Tomato Soup by Fawad Sheikh

(SPECIFICALLY FOR HUMAIRA MIRZA WHEN SHE IS IN NEED OF COMFORT FOOD)

1. Preheat oven to 400 degrees.
2. Half 10-12 fresh tomatoes from your garden and put on a sheet pan along with 8-10 peeled garlic cloves, 1 red bell pepper, and 1 yellow onion. Drizzle with the very best olive oil and season generously with salt and pepper. Roast for 40-45 minutes.
3. After the vegetables are done roasting, empty into a large pot. Use a handheld immersion blender to blend until smooth.
4. Turn heat to medium low and season soup with fresh basil leaves from the garden, oregano, more salt and pepper to taste, as well as 1 Knorr chicken cube and a cup of water.
5. To finish the soup, add in a touch of heavy cream.
6. Once the soup is ready, make your grilled cheese.

7. Slather both sides of bread with mayonnaise, then butter.
8. On one slice of bread, add a healthy amount of sharp cheddar cheese, a touch of parmesan, a bit of mozzarella, and a small amount of gruyere, ending with more sharp cheddar. Top with the second piece of bread.
9. Add butter to the pan, then add your sandwich. Cover and cook on low heat.
10. Flip and cook both sides until adequately golden and the cheese is completely melted.
11. Serve with the soup and enjoy!

Papa's Rules for Life in No Specific Order

- ALWAYS wear a sweater. You do not want to catch a chill.
- NEVER wear high heels. You will fall and break your ankles.
- ALWAYS have a scarf and gloves on hand. This is self-explanatory.
- DO NOT make jokes about impressing boys.
- ALWAYS remember no boys are good enough.
- ANYTHING can be fixed with a good bagel.
- ALWAYS dress smartly. For men, this means suits. For ladies, this means…I don't know, actually. Consult Humaira.
- DO NOT drive anywhere more than thirty minutes away. There are crazy people on the roads.
- This one is for fathers and brothers specifically: ALWAYS give the darling girls' husbands a tough

time. Someone must keep them on their toes, after all.

- And the most important one: ALWAYS get your daughter married to your neighbor, so she's never far away. Even better if said neighbor loves her so much he is willing to move into your house with her, so she never leaves you!

ONE MORE CHAPTER

YOUR NUMBER ONE STOP
FOR PAGETURNING BOOKS

The author and One More Chapter would like to thank everyone who contributed to the publication of this story...

Analytics
Emma Harvey
Maria Osa

Audio
Fionnuala Barrett
Ciara Briggs

Contracts
Georgina Hoffman
Florence Shepherd

Design
Lucy Bennett
Fiona Greenway
Holly Macdonald
Liane Payne
Dean Russell

Digital Sales
Laura Daley
Lydia Grainge
Georgina Ugen

Editorial
Arsalan Isa
Sarah Khan
Charlotte Ledger
Jennie Rothwell
Caroline Scott-Bowden
Kimberley Young

International Sales
Bethan Moore

Marketing & Publicity
Chloe Cummings
Emma Petfield

Operations
Melissa Okusanya
Hannah Stamp

Production
Emily Chan
Denis Manson
Francesca Tuzzeo

Rights
Lana Beckwith
Rachel McCarron
Agnes Rigou
Hany Sheikh
Mohamed
Zoe Shine
Aisling Smyth

The HarperCollins Distribution Team

The HarperCollins Finance & Royalties Team

The HarperCollins Legal Team

The HarperCollins Technology Team

Trade Marketing
Ben Hurd

UK Sales
Yazmeen Akhtar
Laura Carpenter
Isabel Coburn
Jay Cochrane
Tom Dunstan
Gemma Rayner
Erin White
Harriet Williams
Leah Woods

And every other essential link in the chain from delivery drivers to booksellers to librarians and beyond!